Nina Balatka

Anthony Trollope

IAP © 2010

Trollope, Anthony

　　Nina Balatka - Anthony Trollope – 1st ed.

　　1.　Literature / Classics

Introduction

Anthony Trollope was an established novelist of great renown when *Nina Balatka* was published in 1866, twenty years after his first novel. Except for *La Vendee*, his third novel, set in France during the Revolution, all his previous works were set in England or Ireland and dealt with the upper levels of society: the nobility and the landed gentry (wealthy or impoverished), and a few well-to-do merchants--people several strata above the social levels of the characters popularized by his contemporary Dickens. Most of Trollope's early novels were set in the countryside or in provincial towns, with occasional forays into London. The first of his political novels, *Can You Forgive Her*, dealing with the Pallisers was published in 1864, two years before *Nina*. By the time he began writing *Nina*, shortly after a tour of Europe, Trollope was a master at chronicling the habits, foibles, customs, and ways of life of his chosen subjects.

Nina Balatka is, on the surface, a love story--not an unusual theme for Trollope. Romance and courtship were woven throughout all his previous works, often with two, three, or even more pairs of lovers per novel. Most of his heroes and heroines, after facing numerous hurdles, often of their own making, were eventually happily united by the next-to-last chapter. A few were doomed to disappointment (Johnny Eames never won the heart of Lily Dale through two of the "Barsetshire" novels), but marital bliss--or at least the prospect of bliss--was the usual outcome. Even so, the reader of Trollope soon notices his analytical description of Victorian courtship and marriage. In the circles of Trollope's characters, only the wealthy could afford to marry for love; those without wealth had to marry for money, sometimes with disastrous consequences. By the time of *Nina*, Trollope's best exploration of this subject was the marriage between Plantagenet Palliser and Lady Glencora M'Cluskie, the former a cold fish and the latter a hot-blooded heiress in love with a penniless scoundrel (*Can You Forgive Her?* 1865). Yet to come was the disastrous marriage of intelligent Lady Laura Standish to the wealthy but old-maidish Robert Kennedy in *Phineas Finn* and its sequel.

But *Nina Balatka* is different from Trollope's previous novels in four respects. First, Trollope was accustomed to include in his novels his own witty editorial comments about various subjects, often paragraphs or even several pages long. No such comments are found in *Nina*. Second, the story is set in Prague instead of the British isles. Third, the hero and heroine are already in love and engaged to one another at the opening; we are not told any details about their falling in love. The hero, Anton Trendellsohn is a successful businessman in his mid- thirties--not the typical Trollopian hero in his early twenties, still finding himself, and besotted with love. Anton is rather cold as lovers go, seldom whispering words of endearment to Nina. But it is the fourth difference which really sets this novel apart and makes it both a masterpiece and an enigma. That fourth--and most important--difference is clearly stated in the remarkable opening sentence of the novel:

Nina Balatka was a maiden of Prague, born of Christian parents, and herself a Christian--but she loved a Jew; and this is her story.

Marriage--even worse, love--between a Christian and a Jew would have been unacceptable to Victorian British readers. Blatant anti-semitism was prevalent--perhaps ubiquitous--among the upper classes.

Let us consider the origins of this anti-semitism. Jews were first allowed into England by William the Conqueror. For a while they prospered, largely through money-lending, an occupation to which they were restricted. In the 13th century a series of increasingly oppressive laws and taxes reduced the Jewish community to poverty, and the Jews were expelled from England in 1290. They were not allowed to return until 1656, when Oliver Cromwell authorized their entry over the objections of British merchants. Legal protection for the Jews increased gradually; even the "Act for the More Effectual Suppressing of Blasphemy and Profaneness" (1698) recognized the practice of Judaism as legal, but there were probably only a few hundred Jews in the entire country. The British Jewish community grew gradually, and efforts to emancipate the Jews were included in various "Reform Acts" in the first half of the 19th century, although many failed to become law. Gradually Jews were admitted to the bar and other professions. Full citizenship and rights, including the right to sit in Parliament, were granted in 1858--only seven years before Trollope began writing *Nina Balatka*. By this time wealthy Jewish families were growing in number. This upward mobility and increasing economic and political power no doubt made the British upper classes envious and resentful, fuelling anti-semitism.

Trollope chose to have *Nina* published anonymously in *Blackwood's Magazine* for reasons which he described in his autobiography:

From the commencement of my success as a writer . . . I had always felt an injustice in literary affairs which had never afflicted me or even suggested itself to me while I was unsuccessful. It seemed to me that a name once earned carried with it too much favor . . . The injustice which struck me did not consist in that which was withheld from me, but in that which was given to me. I felt that aspirants coming up below me might do work as good as mine, and probably much better work, and yet fail to have it appreciated. In order to test this, I determined to be such an aspirant myself, and to begin a course of novels anonymously, in order that I might see whether I could succeed in obtaining a second identity,--whether as I had made one mark by such literary ability as I possessed, I might succeed in doing so again.

Why did Trollope start his "new" career with a novel whose central theme was a subject of distaste at best--more likely revulsion--to the vast majority of the reading public? Perhaps the nature of the novel itself led him to consider publishing it anonymously, although we know he was not averse to controversial subjects. In his first book, *The Macdermots of Ballycloran*, which he thought had the best plot of all his novels, the principal female character is seduced by a scoundrel and dies giving birth to an illegitimate child.

Certainly *Nina* was well-suited for the experiment because of it's different setting and subject matter. Perhaps further to disguise his authorship, Trollope wrote *Nina* in a style of prose that reads almost like a translation from a foreign language.

The experiment did not last long enough to test Trollope's hypothesis. Mr. Hutton, critic for the *Spectator*, recognized Trollope as the author and so stated in his review. Trollope did not deny the accusation.

One cannot discuss *Nina Balatka* without addressing the question, was Trollope himself anti-semitic? A careful reading of his works does not provide a clear answer. Jews appear in some of his books and are referred to in others, often as disreputable characters or money-lenders. They are seldom mentioned by his Christian characters with respect, probably realistically reflecting the sentiments of the classes he wrote about. Some of his greatest villains in his later novels--Melmotte in *The Way We Live Now (1875)* and *Lopez in The Prime Minister* (1876)--are rumored to be Jewish, but Trollope never unequivocally identifies them as Jewish. Perhaps his Christian characters expect them to be Jewish because they are foreigners and villains.

However, if one ignores the dialogue of his characters, even the descriptive and editorial comments by Trollope himself at first seem anti-semitic. He consistently uses "Jew" as a pejorative adjective instead of "Jewish." His descriptions of the appearance of Jewish characters are usually unflattering and stereotypical. Even Anton Trendellsohn, the hero of *Nina Balatka*, is described as follows:

To those who know the outward types of his race there could be no doubt that Anton Trendellsohn was a very Jew among Jews. He was certainly a handsome man, not now very young, having reached some year certainly in advance of thirty, and his face was full of intellect. He was slightly made, below the middle height, but was well made in every limb, with small feet and hands, and small ears, and a well-turned neck. He was very dark--dark as a man can be, and yet show no sign of color in his blood. No white man could be more dark and swarthy than Anton Trendellsohn. His eyes, however, which were quite black, were very bright. His jet-black hair, as it clustered round his ears, had in it something of a curl. Had it been allowed to grow, it would almost have hung in ringlets; but it was worn very short, as though its owner were jealous even of the curl. Anton Trendellsohn was decidedly a handsome man; but his eyes were somewhat too close together in his face, and the bridge of his aquiline nose was not sharply cut, as is mostly the case with such a nose on a Christian face. The olive oval face was without doubt the face of a Jew, and the mouth was greedy, and the teeth were perfect and bright, and the movement of the man's body was the movement of a Jew.

This is not the typical description of the romantic hero of a Victorian novel. Even so, Trollope's description of Anton is less derogatory than his description of Ezekiel Brehgert, a character in a later novel, *The Way We Live Now*:

He was a fat, greasy man, good-looking in a certain degree, about fifty, with hair dyed black, and beard and moustache dyed a dark purple color. The charm of his face consisted in a pair of very bright black eyes, which were, however, set too near together in his face for the general delight of Christians. He was stout fat all over rather than corpulent and had that look of command in his face which has become common to master-butchers, probably by long intercourse with sheep and oxen.

The case for Trollope being anti-semitic is harder to support, however, when one considers the behavior of his Jewish characters. Brehgert, whose physical description above is stereotypic, is one of the few characters in *The Way We Live Now* whose actions are completely honorable. Trollope wrote 16 novels before *Nina Balatka*; only two of those contain Jewish characters. The first, who plays a minor role in *Orley Farm* (1862), is Soloman Aram, an attorney--a Victorian Rumpole --known for defending the accused at the Old Bailey. His skill is needed to defend Lady Mason against a charge of perjury, much to the distaste of her Christian advisors. He acts with dignity and shows great consideration for the personal comfort of Lady Mason during her trial. The second Jewish character in Trollope's novels was Mr. Hart, a London tailor who runs for a seat in Parliament in *Rachel Ray* (1863). This served no purpose in the plot; the situation probably was included because legislation to allow Jews to serve in Parliament had been passed only five years before, and the issue was still one of public discussion. Mr. Hart's appearance is brief; he speaks only one or two lines, and the reader is not told enough about him to judge his character. Trollope describes him thus:

. . . and then the Jewish hero, the tailor himself, came among them, and astonished their minds by the ease and volubility of his speeches. He did not pronounce his words with any of those soft slushy Judaic utterances by which they had been taught to believe he would disgrace himself. His nose was not hookey, with any especial hook, nor was it thicker at the bridge than was becoming. He was a dapper little man, with bright eyes, quick motion, ready tongue, and a very new hat. It seemed that he knew well how to canvass. He had a smile and a good word for all--enemies as well as friends.

In that novel, Trollope, himself, comments on prejudice and bigotry:

. . . Mrs. Ray, in her quiet way, expressed much joy that Mr. Comfort's son-in-law should have been successful, and that Baslehurst should not have disgraced itself by any connection with a Jew. To her it had appeared monstrous that such a one should have been even permitted to show himself in the town as a candidate for its representation. To such she would have denied all civil rights, and almost all social rights. For a true spirit of persecution one should always go to a woman; and the milder, the sweeter, the more loving, the more womanly the woman, the stronger will be that spirit within her. Strong love for the thing loved necessitates strong hatred for the thing hated, and thence comes the spirit of persecution. They in England who are now keenest against the Jews, who would again take from them rights that they have lately won, are certainly those who think most of the faith of a Christian. The most deadly enemies of the Roman Catholics are they who love best their religion as Protestants. When we look to individuals we always find it so, though it hardly suits us to admit as much when we discuss these subjects broadly. To Mrs. Ray it was wonderful that a Jew should have been entertained in Baslehurst as a future member for the borough, and that he should have been admitted to speak aloud within a few yards of the church tower!

Nina Balatka presents a sharp contrast between the behaviors of the Jewish and Christian characters. Nina and her father Josef Balatka live on the edge of poverty; he was cheated out of his business by his Christian brother-in-law, who is now wealthy. Josef's only source of money was to sell his house to Anton Trendellsohn's father, who for many years has allowed Josef and Nina to remain in the house without paying any rent. Nina's Christian relatives use every form of deceit in their attempt to turn Anton against Nina. Nina's Aunt Sophie spews invective in every direction. She tells Nina, "Impudent girl!--brazen-faced, impudent, bad girl! Do you not know that you would bring disgrace upon us all?" To Nina's father she says, "Tell me that at once, Josef, that I may know. Has she your sanction for--for--for this accursed abomination?" To her husband she says, "Oh, I hate them! I do hate them! Anything is fair against a Jew." And during a meeting with Anton she exclaims, "How dares he come here to talk of his love? It is filthy--it is worse than filthy--it is profane."

Anton's family also opposes the marriage, but Anton's father's behavior toward Nina is in sharp contrast to that of her aunt:

The old man's heart was softened towards her. He could not bring himself to say a word to her of direct encouragement, but he kissed her before she went, telling her that she was a good girl, and bidding her have no care as to the house in the Kleinseite. As long as he lived, and her father, her father should not be disturbed.

Anton, being more a businessman than a lover, at times behaves insensitively toward Nina. Otherwise, throughout the novel, the Jewish characters act with honesty and kindness. Even the Jewish maiden who wants to marry Anton does not scheme to break up his engagement to Nina but rather befriends Nina and eventually saves her life. One has to wonder whether Trollope intended this contrast to induce his readers to reconsider their prejudices. Consider his perception of his duty as a writer:

. . . And the criticism [of my work offered by Hawthorne], whether just or unjust, describes with wonderful accuracy the purport that I have ever had in view in my writing. I have always desired to 'hew out some lump of the earth', and to make men and women walk upon it just as they do walk here among us,--with not more of excellence, nor with exaggerated baseness,--so that my readers might recognize human beings like to themselves, and not feel themselves to be carried away among gods or demons. If I could do this, then I thought I might succeed in impregnating the mind of the novel-reader with a feeling that honesty is the best policy; that truth prevails while falsehood fails; that a girl will be loved as she is pure, and sweet, and unselfish; that a man will be honored as he is true, and honest, and brave of heart; that things meanly done are ugly and odious, and things nobly done beautiful and gracious. . . There are many who would laugh at the idea of a novelist teaching either virtue or nobility,--those, for instance, who regard the reading of novels as a sin, and those also who think it to be simply an idle pastime. They look upon the tellers of stories as among the tribe of those who pander to the wicked pleasures of a wicked world. I have regarded my art from so different a point of view that I have ever thought of myself as a preacher of sermons, and my pulpit as one which I could make both salutary and agreeable to my audience. I do believe that no girl has risen from the reading of my pages less modest than she was before, and that some may have learned from them that modesty is a charm well worth preserving. I think that no youth has been taught that in falseness and flashness is to be found the road to manliness; but some may perhaps have learned from me that it is to be found in truth and a high but gentle spirit. Such are the lessons I have striven to teach; and I have thought that it might best be done by representing to my readers characters like themselves,--or to which they might liken themselves.[1]

Given Trollope's philosophy, it is reasonable to believe that the actions of his characters should speak louder than their words. If so, Trollope might well have been holding up a mirror to his audience that they might examine their own prejudices. Unfortunately, we shall never know.

---

[1] Anthony Trollope. *An Autobiography*. Oxford University Press, Oxford, 1950.

Volume 1

Chapter 1

Nina Balatka was a maiden of Prague, born of Christian parents, and herself a Christian--but she loved a Jew; and this is her story.

Nina Balatka was the daughter of one Josef Balatka, an old merchant of Prague, who was living at the time of this story; but Nina's mother was dead. Josef, in the course of his business, had become closely connected with a certain Jew named Trendellsohn, who lived in a mean house in the Jews' quarter in Prague--habitation in that one allotted portion of the town having been the enforced custom with the Jews then, as it still is now. In business with Trendellsohn, the father, there was Anton, his son; and Anton Trendellsohn was the Jew whom Nina Balatka loved. Now it had so happened that Josef Balatka, Nina's father, had drifted out of a partnership with Karil Zamenoy, a wealthy Christian merchant of Prague, and had drifted into a partnership with Trendellsohn. How this had come to pass needs not to be told here, as it had all occurred in years when Nina was an infant. But in these shiftings Balatka became a ruined man, and at the time of which I write he and his daughter were almost penniless. The reader must know that Karil Zamenoy and Josef Balatka had married sisters. Josef's wife, Nina's mother, had long been dead, having died--so said Sophie Zamenoy, her sister--of a broken heart; of a heart that had broken itself in grief, because her husband had joined his fortunes with those of a Jew. Whether the disgrace of the alliance or its disastrous result may have broken the lady's heart, or whether she may have died of a pleurisy, as the doctors said, we need not inquire here. Her soul had been long at rest, and her spirit, we may hope, had ceased to fret itself in horror at contact with a Jew. But Sophie Zamenoy was alive and strong, and could still hate a Jew as intensely as Jews ever were hated in those earlier days in which hatred could satisfy itself with persecution. In her time but little power was left to Madame Zamenoy to persecute the Trendellsohns other than that which nature had given to her in the bitterness of her tongue. She could revile them behind their back, or, if opportunity offered, to their faces; and both she had done often, telling the world of Prague that the Trendellsohns had killed her sister, and robbed her foolish brother-in-law. But hitherto the full vial of her wrath had not been emptied, as it came to be emptied afterwards; for she had not yet learned the mad iniquity of her niece. But at the moment of which I now speak, Nina herself knew her own iniquity, hardly knowing, however, whether her love did or did not disgrace her. But she did know that any thought as to that was too late. She loved the man, and had told him so; and were he gipsy as well as Jew, it would be required of her that she should go out with him into the wilderness. And Nina Balatka was prepared to go out into the wilderness. Karil Zamenoy and his wife were prosperous people, and lived in a comfortable modern house in the New Town. It stood in a straight street, and at the back of the house there ran another straight street. This part of the city is very little like that old Prague, which may not be so comfortable, but which, of all cities on the earth, is surely the most picturesque. Here lived Sophie

Zamenoy; and so far up in the world had she mounted, that she had a coach of her own in which to be drawn about the thoroughfares of Prague and its suburbs, and a stout little pair of Bohemian horses--ponies they were called by those who wished to detract somewhat from Madame Zamenoy's position. Madame Zamenoy had been at Paris, and took much delight in telling her friends that the carriage also was Parisian; but, in truth, it had come no further than from Dresden. Josef Balatka and his daughter were very, very poor; but, poor as they were, they lived in a large house, which, at least nominally, belonged to old Balatka himself, and which had been his residence in the days of his better fortunes. It was in the Kleinseite, that narrow portion of the town, which lies on the other side of the river Moldau--the further side, that is, from the so-called Old and New Town, on the western side of the river, immediately under the great hill of the Hradschin. The Old Town and the New Town are thus on one side of the river, and the Kleinseite and the Hradschin on the other. To those who know Prague, it need not here be explained that the streets of the Kleinseite are wonderful in their picturesque architecture, wonderful in their lights and shades, wonderful in their strange mixture of shops and palaces-- and now, alas! also of Austrian barracks--and wonderful in their intricacy and great steepness of ascent. Balatka's house stood in a small courtyard near to the river, but altogether hidden from it, somewhat to the right of the main street of the Kleinseite as you pass over the bridge. A lane, for it is little more, turning from the main street between the side walls of what were once two palaces, comes suddenly into a small square, and from a corner of this square there is an open stone archway leading into a court. In this court is the door, or doors, as I may say, of the house in which Balatka lived with his daughter Nina. Opposite to these two doors was the blind wall of another residence. Balatka's house occupied two sides of the court, and no other window, therefore, besides his own looked either upon it or upon him. The aspect of the place is such as to strike with wonder a stranger to Prague--that in the heart of so large a city there should be an abode so sequestered, so isolated, so desolate, and yet so close to the thickest throng of life. But there are others such, perhaps many others such, in Prague; and Nina Balatka, who had been born there, thought nothing of the quaintness of her abode. Immediately over the little square stood the palace of the Hradschin, the wide-spreading residence of the old kings of Bohemia, now the habitation of an ex- emperor of the House of Hapsburg, who must surely find the thousand chambers of the royal mansion all too wide a retreat for the use of his old age. So immediately did the imperial hill tower over the spot on which Balatka lived, that it would seem at night, when the moon was shining as it shines only at Prague, that the colonnades of the palace were the upper stories of some enormous edifice, of which the broken merchant's small courtyard formed a lower portion. The long rows of windows would glimmer in the sheen of the night, and Nina would stand in the gloom of the archway counting them till they would seem to be uncountable, and wondering what might be the thoughts of those who abode there. But those who abode there were few in number, and their thoughts were hardly worthy of Nina's speculation. The windows of kings' palaces look out from many chambers. The windows of the Hradschin look out, as we are told, from a thousand. But the rooms within have seldom many tenants, nor the tenants, perhaps, many thoughts. Chamber after chamber, you shall pass through them by the score, and know by signs unconsciously recognized that there is not, and never has been, true habitation within them. Windows almost innumerable are there, that they may be seen from the outside--and such is the use of palaces. But Nina, as she would look, would people the rooms with throngs of bright inhabitants, and would think of the joys of happy girls who were loved by Christian youths, and who could dare to tell their friends of their love. But Nina Balatka was no coward, and she had already determined that she would at once tell her love to those who had a right to know in what way she intended to dispose of herself. As to her father, if only he could have been alone in the matter, she would have had some hope of a compromise which would have made it not absolutely necessary that she should separate herself from him for ever in giving herself to Anton Trendellsohn. Josef Balatka would doubtless express horror, and would feel shame that his daughter should love a Jew--though he had not scrupled to allow Nina to go frequently among these people, and to use her services with them for staving off the ill consequences of his own idleness and ill-fortune; but he was a meek, broken man, and was so accustomed to yield to Nina that at last he might have yielded to her even in this. There was, however, that Madame Zamenoy, her aunt--her aunt with the bitter tongue; and there was Ziska Zamenoy, her cousin--her rich and handsome cousin, who would so soon declare himself willing to become more than cousin, if Nina would but give him one nod of encouragement, or half a smile of welcome. But Nina hated her Christian lover, cousin though he was, as warmly as she loved the Jew. Nina, indeed, loved none of the Zamenoys-- neither her cousin Ziska, nor her very Christian aunt Sophie with the bitter tongue, nor her prosperous, money-loving, acutely mercantile uncle Karil; but, nevertheless, she was in some degree so subject to them, that she knew that she was bound to tell them what path in life she meant to tread. Madame Zamenoy had offered to take her niece to the prosperous house in the Windberg-gasse when the old house in the Kleinseite had become poor and desolate; and though this generous offer had been most fatuously declined--most wickedly declined, as aunt Sophie used to declare--nevertheless other favors had been vouchsafed; and other favors had been accepted, with sore injury to Nina's pride. As she thought of this, standing in the gloom of the evening under the archway, she remembered that the very frock she wore had been sent to her by her aunt. But I in spite of the bitter tongue, and in spite of Ziska's derision, she would tell her tale, and would tell it soon. She knew her own courage, and trusted it; and, dreadful as the hour would be, she would not put it off by one moment. As soon as Anton should desire her to declare her purpose, she would declare it; and as he who stands on a precipice, contemplating the expediency of throwing himself from the rock, will feel himself gradually seized by a mad desire to do the deed out of hand at once, so did Nina feel anxious to walk off to the Windberg-gasse, and dare and endure all that the Zamenoys could say or do. She knew, or thought she knew, that persecution could not go now beyond the work of the tongue. No priest could immure her. No law could touch her because she was minded to marry a Jew. Even the people in these days were mild and forbearing in their usages with the Jews, and she thought that the girls of the Kleinseite would not tear her clothes from her back even when they knew of her love. One thing, however, was certain. Though every rag should be torn from her--though some priest might have special power given him to persecute her--though the Zamenoys in their wrath should be able to crush her--even though her own father should refuse to see her, she would be true to the Jew. Love to her should be so sacred that no other sacredness should be able to touch its sanctity. She had thought much of love, but had never loved before. Now she loved, and, heart and soul, she belonged to him to whom she had devoted herself. Whatever suffering might be before her, though it were suffering unto death, she would endure it if her lover demanded such endurance. Hitherto, there was but one person who suspected her. In her father's house there still remained an old dependant, who, though he was a man, was cook and housemaid, and washer-woman and servant-of-all-work; or perhaps it would be more true to say that he and Nina between them did all that the requirements of the house demanded.

Souchey--for that was his name--was very faithful, but with his fidelity had come a want of reverence towards his master and mistress, and an absence of all respectful demeanor. The enjoyment of this apparent independence by Souchey himself went far, perhaps, in lieu of wages.

"Nina," he said to her one morning, "you are seeing too much of Anton Trendellsohn."

"What do you mean by that, Souchey?" said the girl, sharply.

"You are seeing too much of Anton Trendellsohn," repeated the old man.

"I have to see him on father's account. You know that. You know that, Souchey, and you shouldn't say such things."

"You are seeing too much of Anton Trendellsohn," said Souchey for the third time. "Anton Trendellsohn is a Jew."

Then Nina knew that Souchey had read her secret, and was sure that it would spread from him through Lotta Luxa, her aunt's confidential maid, up to her aunt's ears. Not that Souchey would be untrue to her on behalf of Madame Zamenoy, whom he hated; but that he would think himself bound by his religious duty--he who never went near priest or mass himself--to save his mistress from the perils of the Jew. The story of her love must be told, and Nina preferred to tell it herself to having it told for her by her servant Souchey. She must see Anton. When the evening therefore had come, and there was sufficient dusk upon the bridge to allow of her passing over without observation, she put her old cloak upon her shoulders, with the hood drawn over her head, and, crossing the river, turned to the left and made her way through the narrow crooked streets which led to the Jews' quarter. She knew the path well, and could have found it with blindfolded eyes. In the middle of that close and densely populated region of Prague stands the old Jewish synagogue--the oldest place of worship belonging to the Jews in Europe, as they delight to tell you; and in a pinched-up, high-gabled house immediately behind the synagogue, at the corner of two streets, each so narrow as hardly to admit a vehicle, dwelt the Trendellsohns. On the basement floor there had once been a shop. There was no shop now, for the Trendellsohns were rich, and no longer dealt in retail matters; but there had been no care, or perhaps no ambition, at work, to alter the appearance of their residence, and the old shutters were upon the window, making the house look as though it were deserted. There was a high-pitched sharp roof over the gable, which, as the building stood alone fronting upon the synagogue, made it so remarkable, that all who knew Prague well, knew the house in which the Trendellsohns lived. Nina had often wished, as in latter days she had entered it, that it was less remarkable, so that she might have gone in and out with smaller risk of observation. It was now the beginning of September, and the clocks of the town had just struck eight as Nina put her hand on the lock of the Jew's door. As usual it was not bolted, and she was able to enter without waiting in the street for a servant to come to her. She went at once along the narrow passage and up the gloomy wooden stairs, at the foot of which there hung a small lamp, giving just light enough to expel the actual blackness of night. On the first landing Nina knocked at a door, and was desired to enter by a soft female voice. The only occupant of the room when she entered was a dark-haired child, some twelve years old perhaps, but small in stature and delicate, and, as appeared to the eye, almost wan. "Well, Ruth dear," said Nina, "is Anton at home this evening?"

"He is up-stairs with grandfather, Nina. Shall I tell him?"

"If you will, dear," said Nina, stooping down and kissing her.

"Nice Nina, dear Nina, good Nina," said the girl, rubbing her glossy curls against her friend's cheeks. "Ah, dear, how I wish you lived here!"

"But I have a father, as you have a grandfather, Ruth."

"And he is a Christian."

"And so am I, Ruth."

"But you like us, and are good, and nice, and dear--and oh, Nina, you are so beautiful! I wish you were one of us, and lived here. There is Miriam Harter--her hair is as light as yours, and her eyes are as grey."

"What has that to do with it?"

"Only I am so dark, and most of us are dark here in Prague. Anton says that away in Palestine our girls are as fair as the girls in Saxony."

"And does not Anton like girls to be dark?"

"Anton likes fair hair--such as yours--and bright grey eyes such as you have got. I said they were green, and he pulled my ears. But now I look, Nina, I think they are green. And so bright! I can see my own in them, though it is so dark. That is what they call looking babies."

"Go to your uncle, Ruth, and tell him that I want him--on business."

"I will, and he'll come to you. He won't let me come down again, so kiss me, Nina; good-bye."

Nina kissed the child again, and then was left alone in the room. It was a comfortable chamber, having in it sofas and arm-chairs--much more comfortable, Nina used to think, than her aunt's grand drawing-room in the Windberg-gasse, which was covered all over with a carpet, after the fashion of drawing-rooms in Paris; but the Jew's sitting-room was dark, with walls painted a gloomy green color, and there was but one small lamp of oil upon the table. But yet Nina loved the room, and as she sat there waiting for her lover, she wished that it had been her lot to have been born a Jewess. Only, had that been so, her hair might perhaps have been black, and her eyes dark, and Anton would not have liked her. She put her hand up for a moment to her rich brown tresses, and felt them as she took joy in thinking that Anton Trendellsohn loved to look upon fair beauty.

After a short while Anton Trendellsohn came down. To those who know the outward types of his race there could be no doubt that Anton Trendellsohn was a very Jew among Jews. He was certainly a handsome man, not now very young, having reached some year certainly in advance of thirty, and his face was full of intellect. He was slightly made, below the middle height, but was well made in every limb, with small feet and hands, and small ears, and a well-turned neck. He was very dark--dark as a man can be, and yet show no sign of color in his blood. No white man could be more dark and swarthy than Anton Trendellsohn. His eyes, however, which were quite black, were very bright. His jet-black hair, as it clustered round his ears, had in it something of a curl. Had it been allowed to grow, it would almost have hung in ringlets; but it was worn very short, as though its owner were jealous even of the curl. Anton Trendellsohn was decidedly a handsome man; but his eyes were somewhat too close together in his face, and the bridge of his aquiline nose was not sharply cut, as is mostly the case with such a nose on a Christian face. The olive oval face was without doubt the face of a Jew, and the mouth was greedy, and the teeth were perfect and bright, and the movement of the man's body was the movement of a Jew. But not the less on that account had he behaved with Christian forbearance to his Christian debtor, Josef Balatka, and with Christian chivalry to Balatka's daughter, till that chivalry had turned itself into love.

"Nina," he said, putting out his hand, and holding hers as he spoke, "I hardly expected you this evening; but I am glad to see you--very glad."

"I hope I am not troubling you, Anton?"

"How can you trouble me? The sun does not trouble us when we want light and heat."

"Can I give you light and heat?"

"The light and heat I love best, Nina."

"If I thought that--if I could really think that--I would be happy still, and would mind nothing."

"And what is it you do mind?"

"There are things to trouble us, of course. When aunt Sophie says that all of us have our troubles--even she--I suppose that even she speaks the truth."

"Your aunt Sophie is a fool."

"I should not mind if she were only a fool. But a fool can sometimes be right."

"And she has been scolding you because--you--prefer a Jew to a Christian."

"No--not yet, Anton. She does not know it yet; but she must know it."

"Sit down, Nina." He was still holding her by the hand; and now, as he spoke, he led her to a sofa which stood between the two windows. There he seated her, and sat by her side, still holding her hand in his. "Yes," he said, "she must know it of course--when the time comes; and if she guesses it before, you must put up with her guesses. A few sharp words from a foolish woman will not frighten you, I hope."

"No words will frighten me out of my love, if you mean that--neither words nor anything else."

"I believe you. You are brave, Nina. I know that. Though you will cry if one but frowns at you, yet you are brave."

"Do not you frown at me, Anton."

"I am one of those that do frown at times, I suppose; but I will be true to you, Nina, if you will be true to me."

"I will be true to you--true as the sun."

As she made her promise she turned her sweet face up to his, and he leaned over her, and kissed her.

"And what is it that has disturbed you now, Nina? What has Madame Zamenoy said to you?"

"She has said nothing--as yet. She suspects nothing--as yet."

"Then let her remain as she is."

"But, Anton, Souchey knows, and he will talk."

"Souchey! And do you care for that?"

"I care for nothing--for nothing; for nothing, that is, in the way of preventing me. Do what they will, they cannot tear my love from my heart."

"Nor can they take you away, or lock you up."

"I fear nothing of that sort, Anton. All that I really fear is secrecy. Would it not be best that I should tell father?"

"What!--now, at once?"

"If you will let me. I suppose he must know it soon."

"You can if you please."

"Souchey will tell him."

"Will Souchey dare to speak of you like that?" asked the Jew.

"Oh, yes; Souchey dares to say anything to father now. Besides, it is true. Why should not Souchey say it?"

"But you have not spoken to Souchey; you have not told him?"

"I! No indeed. I have spoken never a word to anyone about that--only to you. How should I speak to another without your bidding? But when they speak to me I must answer them. If father asks me whether there be aught between you and me, shall I not tell him then?"

"It would be better to be silent for a while."

"But shall I lie to him? I should not mind Souchey nor aunt Sophie much; but I never yet told a lie to father."

"I do not tell you to lie."

"Let me tell it all. Anton, and then, whatever they may say, whatever they may do, I shall not mind. I wish that they knew it, and then I could stand up against them. Then I could tell Ziska that which would make him hold his tongue for ever."

"Ziska! Who cares for Ziska?"

"You need not, at any rate."

"The truth is, Nina, that I cannot be married till I have settled all this about the houses in the Kleinseite. The very fact that you would be your father's heir prevents my doing so."

"Do you think that I wish to hurry you? I would rather stay as I am, knowing that you love me."

"Dear Nina! But when your aunt shall once know your secret, she will give you no peace till you are out of her power. She will leave no stone unturned to make you give up your Jew lover."

"She may as well leave the turning of such stones alone."

"But if she heard nothing of it till she heard that we were married--"

"Ah! but that is impossible. I could not do that without telling father, and father would surely tell my aunt."

"You may do as you will, Nina; but it may be, when they shall know it, that therefore there may be new difficulty made about the houses. Karil Zamenoy has the papers, which are in truth mine--or my father's--which should be here in my iron box." And Trendellsohn, as he spoke, put his hand forcibly on the seat beside him, as though the iron box to which he alluded were within his reach.

"I know they are yours," said Nina.

"Yes; and without them, should your father die, I could not claim my property. The Zamenoys might say they held it on your behalf--and you my wife at the time! Do you see, Nina? I could not stand that--I would not stand that."

"I understand it well, Anton."

"The houses are mine--or ours, rather. Your father has long since had the money, and more than the money. He knew that the houses were to be ours."

"He knows it well. You do not think that he is holding back the papers?"

"He should get them for me. He should not drive me to press him for them. I know they are at Karil Zamenoy's counting-house; but your uncle told me, when I spoke to him, that he had no business with me; if I had a claim on him, there was the law. I have no claim on him. But I let your father have the money when he wanted it, on his promise that the deeds should be forthcoming. A Christian would not have been such a fool."

"Oh, Anton, do not speak to me like that."

"But was I not a fool? See how it is now. Were you and I to become man and wife, they would never give them up, though they are my own--my own. No; we must wait; and you--you must demand them from your uncle."

"I will demand them. And as for waiting, I care nothing for that if you love me."

"I do love you."

"Then all shall be well with me; and I will ask for the papers. Father, I know, wishes that you should have all that is your own. He would leave the house tomorrow if you desired it."

"He is welcome to remain there."

"And now, Anton, good-night."

"Good-night, Nina."

"When shall I see you again?"

"When you please, and as often. Have I not said that you are light and heat to me? Can the sun rise too often for those who love it?" Then she held her hand up to be kissed, and kissed his in return, and went silently down the stairs into the street. He had said once in the course of the conversation--nay, twice, as she came to remember in thinking over it--that she might do as she would about telling her friends; and she had been almost craftily careful to say nothing herself, and to draw nothing from him, which could be held as militating against this authority, or as subsequently negativing the permission so given. She would undoubtedly tell her father--and her aunt; and would as certainly demand from her uncle those documents of which Anton Trendellsohn had spoken to her.

Chapter 2

Nina, as she returned home from the Jews' quarter to her father's house in the Kleinseite, paused for a while on the bridge to make some resolution--some resolution that should be fixed--as to her immediate conduct. Should she first tell her story to her father, or first to her aunt Sophie? There were reasons for and against either plan. And if to her father first, then should she tell it tonight? She was nervously anxious to rush at once at her difficulties, and to be known to all who belonged to her as the girl who had given herself to the Jew. It was now late in the evening, and the moon was shining brightly on the palace over against her. The colonnades seemed to be so close to her that there could hardly be room for any portion of the city to cluster itself between them and the river. She stood looking up at the great building, and fell again into her trick of counting the windows, thereby saving herself a while from the difficult task of following out the train of her thoughts. But what were the windows of the palace to her? So she walked on again till she reached a spot on the bridge at which she almost always paused a moment to perform a little act of devotion. There, having a place in the long row of huge statues which adorn the bridge, is the figure of the martyr St John Nepomucene, who at this spot was thrown into the river because he would not betray the secrets of a queen's confession, and was drowned, and who has ever been, from that period downwards, the favorite saint of Prague--and of bridges. On the balustrade, near the figure, there is a small plate inserted in the stone-work and good Catholics, as they pass over the river, put their hands upon the plate, and then kiss their fingers. So shall they be saved from drowning and from all perils of the water--as far, at least, as that special transit of the river may be perilous. Nina, as a child, had always touched the stone, and then touched her lips, and did the act without much thought as to the saving power of St John Nepomucene. But now, as she carried her hand up to her face, she did think of the deed. Had she, who was about to marry a Jew, any right to ask for the assistance of a Christian saint? And would such a deed that she now proposed to herself put her beyond the pale of Christian aid? Would the Madonna herself desert her should she marry a Jew? If she were to become truer than ever to her faith--more diligent, more thoughtful, more constant in all acts of devotion--would the blessed Mary help to save her, even though she should commit this great sin? Would the mild-eyed, sweet Savior, who had forgiven so many women, who had saved from a cruel death the woman taken in adultery, who had been so gracious to the Samaritan woman at the well--would He turn from her the graciousness of His dear eyes, and bid her go out for ever from among the faithful? Madame Zamenoy would tell her so, and so would Sister Teresa, an old nun, who was on most friendly terms with Madame Zamenoy, and whom Nina altogether hated; and so would the priest, to whom, alas! she would be bound to give faith. And if this were so, whither should she turn for comfort? She could not become a Jewess! She might call herself one; but how could she be a Jewess with her strong faith in St Nicholas, who was the saint of her own Church, and in St John of the River, and in the Madonna? No; she must be an outcast from all religions, a Pariah, one devoted absolutely to the everlasting torments which lie beyond Purgatory--unless, indeed, unless that mild- eyed Savior would be content to take her faith and her acts of hidden worship, despite her aunt, despite that odious nun, and despite the very priest himself! She did not know how this might be with her, but she did know that all the teaching of her life was against any such hope.

But what was--what could be the good of such thoughts to her? Had not things gone too far with her for such thoughts to be useful? She loved the Jew, and had told him so; and not all the penalties with which the priests might threaten her could lessen her love, or make her think of her safety here or hereafter, as a thing to be compared with her love. Religion was much to her; the fear of the everlasting wrath of Heaven was much to her; but love was paramount! What if it were her soul? Would she not give even her soul for her love, if, for her love's sake, her soul should be required from her? When she reached the archway, she had made up her mind that she would tell her aunt first, and that she would do so early on the following day. Were she to tell her father first, her father might probably forbid her to speak on the subject to Madame Zamenoy, thinking that his own eloquence and that of the priest might prevail to put an end to so terrible an iniquity, and that so Madame Zamenoy might never learn the tidings. Nina, thinking of all this, and being quite determined that the Zamenoys should know what she intended to tell them, resolved that she would say nothing on that night at home.

"You are very late, Nina," said her father to her, crossly, as soon as she entered the room in which they lived. It was a wide apartment, having in it now but little furniture--two rickety tables, a few chairs, an old bureau in which Balatka kept, under lock and key, all that still belonged to him personally, and a little desk, which was Nina's own repository.

"Yes, father, I am late; but not very late. I have been with Anton Trendellsohn."

"And what have you been there for now?"

"Anton Trendellsohn has been talking to me about the papers which uncle Karil has. He wants to have them himself. He says they are his."

"I suppose he means that we are to be turned out of the old house."

"No, father; he does not mean that. He is not a cruel man. But he says that--that he cannot settle anything about the property without having the papers. I suppose that is true."

"He has the rent of the other houses," said Balatka.

"Yes; but if the papers are his, he ought to have them."

"Did he send for them?"

"No, father; he did not send."

"And what made you go?"

"I am so of often going there. He had spoken to me before about this. He thinks you do not like him to come here, and you never go there yourself."

After this there was a pause for a few minutes, and Nina was settling herself to her work. Then the old man spoke again.

"Nina, I fear you see too much of Anton Trendellsohn." The words were the very words of Souchey; and Nina was sure that her father and the servant had been discussing her conduct. It was no more than she had expected, but her father's words had come very quickly upon Souchey's speech to herself. What did it signify? Everybody would know it all before twenty-four hours had passed by. Nina, however, was determined to defend herself at the present moment, thinking that there was something of injustice in her father's remarks. "As for seeing him often, father, I have done it because your business has required it. When you were ill in April I had to be there almost daily."

"But you need not have gone tonight. He did not send for you."

"But it is needful that something should be done to get for him that which is his own." As she said this there came to her a sting of conscience, a thought that reminded her that, though she was not lying to her father in words, she was in fact deceiving him; and remembering her assertion to her lover that she had never spoken falsely to her father, she blushed with shame as she sat in the darkness of her seat.

"Tomorrow father," she said, "I will talk to you more about this, and you shall not at any rate say that I keep anything from you."

"I have never said so, Nina."

"It is late now, father. Will you not go to bed?"

Old Balatka yielded to this suggestion, and went to his bed; and Nina, after some hour or two, went to hers. But before doing so she opened the little desk that stood in the corner of their sitting-room, of which the key was always in her pocket, and took out everything that it contained. There were many letters there, of which most were on matters of business--letters which in few houses would come into the hands of such a one as Nina Balatka, but which, through the weakness of her father's health, had come into hers. Many of these she now read; some few she tore and burned in the stove, and others she tied in bundles and put back carefully into their place. There was not a paper in the desk which did not pass under her eye, and as to which she did not come to some conclusion, either to keep it or to burn it. There were no love-letters there. Nina Balatka had never yet received such a letter as that. She saw her lover too frequently to feel much the need of written expressions of love; and such scraps of his writing as there were in the bundles, referred altogether to small matters of business. When she had thus arranged her papers, she too went to bed. On the next morning, when she gave her father his breakfast, she was very silent. She made for him a little chocolate, and cut for him a few slips of white bread to dip into it. For herself, she cut a slice from a black loaf made of rye flour, and mixed with water a small quantity of the thin sour wine of the country. Her meal may have been worth perhaps a couple of kreutzers, or something less than a penny, whereas that of her father may have cost twice as much. Nina was a close and sparing housekeeper, but with all her economy she could not feed three people upon nothing. Latterly, from month to month, she had sold one thing out of the house after another, knowing as each article went that provision from such store as that must soon fail her. But anything was better than taking money from her aunt whom she hated--except taking money from the Jew whom she loved. From him she had taken none, though it had been often offered. "You have lost more than enough by father," she had said to him when the offer had been made. "What I give to the wife of my bosom shall never be reckoned as lost," he had answered. She had loved him for the words, and had pressed his hand in hers--but she had not taken his money. From her aunt some small meager supply had been accepted from time to time--a florin or two now, and a florin or two again--given with repeated intimations on aunt Sophie's part, that her husband Karil could not be expected to maintain the house in the Kleinseite. Nina had not felt herself justified in refusing such gifts from her aunt to her father, but as each occasion came she told herself that some speedy end must be put to this state of things. Her aunt's generosity would not sustain her father, and her aunt's generosity nearly killed herself. On this very morning she would do that which should certainly put an end to a state of things so disagreeable. After breakfast, therefore, she started at once for the house in the Windberg-gasse, leaving her father still in his bed. She walked very quick, looking neither to the right nor the left, across the bridge, along the river-side, and then up into the straight ugly streets of the New Town. The distance from her father's house was nearly two miles, and yet the journey was made in half an hour. She had never walked so quickly through the streets of Prague before; and when she reached the end of the Windberg-gasse, she had to pause a moment to collect her thoughts and her breath. But it was only for a moment, and then the bell was rung.

Yes; her aunt was at home. At ten in the morning that was a matter of course. She was shown, not into the grand drawing-room, which was only used on grand occasions, but into a little back parlor which, in spite of the wealth and magnificence of the Zamenoys, was not so clean as the room in the Kleinseite, and certainly not so comfortable as the Jew's apartment. There was no carpet; but that was not much, as carpets in Prague were not in common use. There were two tables crowded with things needed for household purposes, half-a-dozen chairs of different patterns, a box of sawdust close under the wall, placed there that papa Zamenoy might spit into it when it pleased him. There was a crowd of clothes and linen hanging round the stove, which projected far into the room; and spread upon the table, close to which was placed mamma Zamenoy's chair, was an article of papa Zamenoy's dress, on which mamma Zamenoy was about to employ her talents in the art of tailoring. All this, however, was nothing to Nina, nor was the dirt on the floor much to her, though she had often thought that if she were to go and live with aunt Sophie, she would contrive to make some improvement as to the cleanliness of the house.

"Your aunt will be down soon," said Lotta Luxa as they passed through the passage. "She is very angry, Nina, at not seeing you all the last week."

"I don't know why she should be angry, Lotta. I did not say I would come."

Lotta Luxa was a sharp little woman, over forty years of age, with quick green eyes and thin red-tipped nose, looking as though Paris might have been the town of her birth rather than Prague. She wore short petticoats, clean stockings, an old pair of slippers; and in the back of her hair she still carried that Diana's dart which maidens wear in those parts when they are not only maidens unmarried, but maidens also disengaged. No one had yet succeeded in drawing Lotta Luxa's arrow from her head, though Souchey, from the other side of the river, had made repeated attempts to do so. For Lotta Luxa had a little money of her own, and poor Souchey had none. Lotta muttered something about the thoughtless thanklessness of young people, and then took herself down- stairs. Nina opened the door of the back parlor, and found her cousin Ziska sitting alone with his feet propped upon the stove.

"What, Ziska," she said, "you not at work by ten o'clock!"

"I was not well last night, and took physic this morning," said Ziska. "Something had disagreed with me."

"I'm sorry for that, Ziska. You eat too much fruit, I suppose."

"Lotta says it was the sausage, but I don't think it was. I'm very fond of sausage, and everybody must be ill sometimes. She'll be down here again directly;" and Ziska with his head nodded at the chair in which his mother was wont to sit.

Nina, whose mind was quite full of her business, was determined to go to work at once. "I'm glad to have you alone for a moment, Ziska," she said.

"And so am I very glad; only I wish I had not taken physic, it makes one so uncomfortable."

At this moment Nina had in her heart no charity towards her cousin, and did not care for his discomfort. "Ziska," she said, "Anton Trendellsohn wants to have the papers about the houses in the Kleinseite. He says that they are his, and you have them."

Ziska hated Anton Trendellsohn, hardly knowing why he hated him. "If Trendellsohn wants anything of us," said he, "why does he not come to the office? He knows where to find us."

"Yes, Ziska, he knows where to find you; but, as he says, he has no business with you--no business as to which he can make a demand. He thinks, therefore, you would merely bid him begone."

"Very likely. One doesn't want to see more of a Jew than one can help."

"That Jew, Ziska, owns the house in which father lives. That Jew, Ziska, is the best friend that--that--that father has."

"I'm sorry you think so, Nina."

"How can I help thinking it? You can't deny, nor can uncle, that the houses belong to him. The papers got into uncle's hands when he and father were together, and I think they ought to be given up now. Father thinks that the Trendellsohns should have them. Even though they are Jews, they have a right to their own."

"You know nothing about it, Nina. How should you know about such things as that?"

"I am driven to know. Father is ill, and cannot come himself."

"Oh, laws! I am so uncomfortable. I never will take stuff from Lotta Luxa again. She thinks a man is the same as a horse."

This little episode put a stop to the conversation about the title- deeds, and then Madame Zamenoy entered the room. Madame Zamenoy was a woman of a portly demeanor, well fitted to do honor by her personal presence to that carriage and horses with which Providence and an indulgent husband had blessed her. And when she was dressed in her full panoply of French millinery--the materials of which had come from England, and the manufacture of which had taken place in Prague--she looked the carriage and horses well enough. But of a morning she was accustomed to go about the house in a pale-tinted wrapper, which, pale- tinted as it was, should have been in the washing-tub much oftener than was the case with it--if not for cleanliness, then for mere decency of appearance.

And the mode in which she carried her matutinal curls, done up with black pins, very visible to the eye, was not in itself becoming. The handkerchief which she wore in lieu of cap, might have been excused on the score of its ugliness, as Madame Zamenoy was no longer young, had it not been open to such manifest condemnation for other sins. And in this guise she would go about the house from morning to night on days not made sacred by the use of the carriage. Now Lotta Luxa was clean in the midst of her work; and one would have thought that the cleanliness of the maid would have shamed the slatternly ways of the mistress. But Madame Zamenoy and Lotta Luxa had lived together long, and probably knew each other well.

"Well, Nina," she said, "so you've come at last?"

"Yes; I've come, aunt. And as I want to say something very particular to you yourself, perhaps Ziska won't mind going out of the room for a minute." Nina had not sat down since she had been in the room, and was now standing before her aunt with almost militant firmness. She was resolved to rush at once at the terrible subject which she had in hand, but she could not do so in the presence of her cousin Ziska.

Ziska groaned audibly. "Ziska isn't well this morning," said Madame Zamenoy, "and I do not wish to have him disturbed."

"Then perhaps you'll come into the front parlor, aunt."

"What can there be that you cannot say before Ziska?"

"There is something, aunt," said Nina.

If there were a secret, Madame Zamenoy decidedly wished to hear it, and therefore, after pausing to consider the matter for a moment or two, she led the way into the front parlor.

"And now, Nina, what is it? I hope you have not disturbed me in this way for anything that is a trifle."

"It is no trifle to me, aunt. I am going to be married to--Anton Trendellsohn." She said the words slowly, standing bolt-upright, at her greatest height, as she spoke them, and looking her aunt full in the face with something of defiance both in her eyes and in the tone of her voice. She had almost said, "Anton Trendellsohn, the Jew;" and when her speech was finished, and admitted of no addition, she reproached herself with pusillanimity in that she had omitted the word which had always been so odious, and would now be doubly odious--odious to her aunt in a tenfold degree.

Madame Zamenoy stood for a while speechless--struck with horror. The tidings which she heard were so unexpected, so strange, and so abominable, that they seemed at first to crush her. Nina was her niece--her sister's child; and though she might be repudiated, reviled, persecuted, and perhaps punished, still she must retain her relationship to her injured relatives. And it seemed to Madame Zamenoy as though the marriage of which Nina spoke was a thing to be done at once, out of hand--as though the disgusting nuptials were to take place on that day or on the next, and could not now be avoided. It occurred to her that old Balatka himself was a consenting party, and that utter degradation was to fall upon the family instantly. There was that in Nina's air and manner, as she spoke of her own iniquity, which made the elder woman feel for the moment that she was helpless to prevent the evil with which she was threatened.

"Anton Trendellsohn--a Jew," she said, at last.

"Yes, aunt; Anton Trendellsohn, the Jew. I am engaged to him as his wife."

There was a something of doubtful futurity in the word engaged, which gave a slight feeling of relief to Madame Zamenoy, and taught her to entertain a hope that there might be yet room for escape. "Marry a Jew, Nina," she said; "it cannot be possible!"

"It is possible, aunt. Other Jews in Prague have married Christians."

"Yes, I know it. There have been outcasts among us low enough so to degrade themselves--low women who were called Christians. There has been no girl connected with decent people who has ever so degraded herself. Does your father know of this?"

"Not yet."

"Your father knows nothing of it, and you come and tell me that you are engaged--to a Jew!" Madame Zamenoy had so far recovered herself that she was now able to let her anger mount above her misery.

"You wicked girl! Why have you come to me with such a story as this?"

"Because it is well that you should know it. I did not like to deceive you, even by secrecy. You will not be hurt. You need not notice me any longer. I shall be lost to you, and that will be all."

"If you were to do such a thing you would disgrace us. But you will not be allowed to do it."

"But I shall do it."

"Nina!"

"Yes, aunt. I shall do it. Do you think I will be false to my troth?"

"Your troth to a Jew is nothing. Father Jerome will tell you so."

"I shall not ask Father Jerome. Father Jerome, of course, will condemn me; but I shall not ask him whether or not I am to keep my promise--my solemn promise."

"And why not?"

Then Nina paused a moment before she answered. But she did answer, and answered with that bold defiant air which at first had disconcerted her aunt.

"I will ask no one, aunt Sophie, because I love Anton Trendellsohn, and have told him that I love him."

"Pshaw!"

"I have nothing more to say, aunt. I thought it right to tell you, and now I will go."

She had turned to the door, and had her hand upon the lock when her aunt stopped her. "Wait a moment, Nina. You have had your say; now you must hear me."

"I will hear you if you say nothing against him."

"I shall say what I please."

"Then I will not hear you." Nina again made for the door, but her aunt intercepted her retreat. "Of course you can stop me, aunt, in that way if you choose."

"You bold, bad girl!"

"You may say what you please about myself."

"You are a bold, bad girl!"

"Perhaps I am. Father Jerome says we are all bad. And as for boldness, I have to be bold."

"You are bold and brazen. Marry a Jew! It is the worst thing a Christian girl could do."

"No, it is not. There are things ten times worse than that."

"How you could dare to come and tell me!"

"I did dare, you see. If I had not told you, you would have called me sly."

"You are sly."

"I am not sly. You tell me I am bad and bold and brazen."

"So you are."

"Very likely. I do not say I am not. But I am not sly. Now, will you let me go, aunt Sophie?"

"Yes, you may go--you may go; but you may not come here again till this thing has been put an end to. Of course I shall see your father and Father Jerome, and your uncle will see the police. You will be locked up, and Anton Trendellsohn will be sent out of Bohemia. That is how it will end. Now you may go." And Nina went her way.

Her aunt's threat of seeing her father and the priest was nothing to Nina. It was the natural course for her aunt to take, and a course in opposition to which Nina was prepared to stand her ground firmly. But the allusion to the police did frighten her. She had thought of the power which the law might have over her very often, and had spoken of it in awe to her lover. He had reassured her, explaining to her that, as the law now stood in Austria, no one but her father could prevent her marriage with a Jew, and that he could only do so till she was of age. Now Nina would be twenty-one on the first of the coming month, and therefore would be free, as Anton told her, to do with herself as she pleased. But still there came over her a cold feeling of fear when her aunt spoke to her of the police. The law might give the police no power over her; but was there not a power in the hands of those armed men whom she saw around her on every side, and who were seldom countrymen of her own, over and above the law? Were there not still dark dungeons and steel locks and hard hearts? Though the law might justify her, how would that serve her, if men--if men and women, were determined to persecute her? As she walked home, however, she resolved that dark dungeons and steel locks and hard hearts might do their worst against her. She had set her will upon one thing in this world, and from that one thing no persecution should drive her. They might kill her, perhaps. Yes, they might kill her; and then there would be an end of it. But to that end she would force them to come before she would yield. So much she swore to herself as she walked home on that morning to the Kleinseite.

Madame Zamenoy, when Nina left her, sat in solitary consideration for some twenty minutes, and then called for her chief confidant, Lotta Luxa. With many expressions of awe, and with much denunciation of her niece's iniquity, she told to Lotta what she had heard, speaking of Nina as one who was utterly lost and abandoned. Lotta, however, did not express so much indignant surprise as her mistress expected, though she was willing enough to join in abuse against Nina Balatka.

"That comes of letting girls go about just as they please among the men," said Lotta.

"But a Jew!" said Madame Zamenoy. "If it had been any kind of a Christian, I could understand it."

"Trendellsohn has such a hold upon her, and upon her father," said Lotta.

"But a Jew! She has been to confession, has she not?"

"Regularly," said Lotta Luxa.

"Dear, dear! what a false hypocrite! And at mass?"

"Four mornings a-week always."

"And to tell me, after it all, that she means to marry a Jew. Of course, Lotta, we must prevent it."

"But how? Her father will do whatever she bids him."

"Father Jerome would do anything for me."

"Father Jerome can do little or nothing if she has the bit between her teeth," said Lotta. "She is as obstinate as a mule when she pleases. She is not like other girls. You cannot frighten her out of anything."

"I'll try, at least," said Madame Zamenoy.

"Yes, we can try," said Lotta.

"Would not the mayor help us--that is, if we were driven to go to that?"

"I doubt if he could do anything. He would be afraid to use a high hand. He is Bohemian. The head of the police might do something, if we could get at him."

"She might be taken away."

"Where could they take her?" asked Lotta. "No; they could not take her anywhere."

"Not into a convent--out of the way somewhere in Italy?"

"Oh, heaven, no! They are afraid of that sort of thing now. All Prague would know of it, and would talk; and the Jews would be stronger than the priests; and the English people would hear of it, and there would be the very mischief."

"The times have come to be very bad, Lotta."

"That's as may be," said Lotta as though she had her doubts upon the subject. "That's as may be. But it isn't easy to put a young woman away now without her will. Things have changed--partly for the worse, perhaps, and partly for the better. Things are changing every day. My wonder is that he should wish to many her."

"The men think her very pretty. Ziska is mad about her," said Madame Zamenoy.

"But Ziska is a calf to Anton Trendellsohn. Anton Trendellsohn has cut his wise teeth. Like them all, he loves his money; and she has not got a kreutzer."

"But he has promised to marry her. You may be sure of that."

"Very likely. A man always promises that when he wants a girl to be kind to him. But why should he stick to it? What can he get by marrying Nina--a penniless girl, with a pauper for a father? The Trendellsohns have squeezed that sponge dry already."

This was a new light to Madame Zamenoy, and one that was not altogether unpleasant to her eyes. That her niece should have promised herself to a Jew was dreadful, and that her niece should be afterwards jilted by the Jew was a poor remedy. But still it was a remedy, and therefore she listened.

"If nothing else can be done, we could perhaps put him against it," said Lotta Luxa.

Madame Zamenoy on that occasion said but little more, but she agreed with her servant that it would be better to resort to any means than to submit to the degradation of an alliance with the Jew.

Chapter 3

On the third day after Nina's visit to her aunt, Ziska Zamenoy came across to the Kleinseite on a visit to old Balatka. In the mean time Nina had told the story of her love to her father, and the effect on Balatka had simply been that he had not got out of his bed since. For himself he would have cared, perhaps, but little as to the Jewish marriage, had he not known that those belonging to him would have cared so much. He had no strong religious prejudice of his own, nor indeed had he strong feeling of any kind. He loved his daughter, and wished her well; but even for her he had been unable to exert himself in his younger days, and now simply expected from her hands all the comfort which remained to him in this world. The priest he knew would attack him, and to the priest he would be able to make no answer. But to Trendellsohn, Jew as he was, he would trust in worldly matters, rather than to the Zamenoys; and were it not that he feared the Zamenoys, and could not escape from his close connection with them, he would have been half inclined to let the girl marry the Jew. Souchey, indeed, had frightened him on the subject when it had first been mentioned to him; and Nina, coming with her own assurance so quickly after Souchey's suspicion, had upset him; but his feeling in regard to Nina had none of that bitter anger, no touch of that abhorrence which animated the breast of his sister-in-law. When Ziska came to him he was alone in his bedroom. Ziska had heard the news, as had all the household in the Windberg-gasse, and had come over to his uncle's house to see what he could do, by his own diplomacy, to put an end to an engagement which was to him doubly calamitous. "Uncle Josef," he said, sitting by the old man's bed, have you heard what Nina is doing?"

"What she is doing!" said the uncle. "What is she doing?" Balatka feared all the Zamenoys, down to Lotta Luxa; but he feared Ziska less than he feared any other of the household.

"Have you heard of Anton Trendellsohn?"

"What of Anton Trendellsohn? I have been hearing of Anton Trendellsohn for the last thirty years. I have known him since he was born."

"Do you wish to have him for a son-in-law?"

"For a son-in-law?"

"Yes, for a son-in-law--Anton Trendellsohn, the Jew. Would he be a good husband for our Nina? You say nothing, uncle Josef."

"What am I to say?"

"You have heard of it, then? Why can you not answer me, uncle Josef? Have you heard that Trendellsohn has dared to ask Nina to be his wife?"

"There is not so much of daring in it, Ziska. Among you all the poor girl is a beggar. If some one does not take pity on her, she will starve soon."

"Take pity on her! Do not we all take pity on her?"

"No," said Josef Balatka, turning angrily against his nephew; "not a scrap of pity--not a morsel of love. You cannot rid yourself of her quite--of her or me--and that is your pity."

"You are wrong there."

"Very well; then let me be wrong. I can understand what is before my eyes. Look round the house and see what we are coming to. Nina at the present moment has not got a florin in her purse. We are starving, or next to it, and yet you wonder that she should be willing to marry an honest man who has plenty of money."

"But he is a Jew!"

"Yes; he is a Jew. I know that."

"And Nina knows it."

"Of course she does. Do you go home and eat nothing for a week, and then see whether a Jew's bread will poison you."

"But to marry him, uncle Josef!"

"It is very bad. I know it is bad, but what can I do? If she says she will do it, how can I help it? She has been a good child to me--a very good child; and am I to lie here and see her starve? You would not give to your dog the morsel of bread which she ate this morning before she went out."

All this was a new light to Ziska. He knew that his uncle and cousin were very poor, and had halted in his love because he was ashamed of their poverty; but he had never thought of them as people hungry from want of food, or cold from want of clothes. It may be said of him, to his credit, that his love had been too strong for his shame, and that he had made up his mind to marry his cousin Nina in spite of her poverty. When Lotta Luxa had called him a calf she had not inappropriately defined one side of his character. He was a good- looking well-grown young man, not very wise, quickly susceptible to female influences, and gifted with eyes capable of convincing him that Nina Balatka was by far the prettiest woman whom he ever saw. But, in connection with such calf-like propensities, Ziska was endowed with something of his mother's bitterness and of his father's persistency; and the old Zamenoys did not fear but that the fortunes of the family would prosper in the hands of their son. And when it was known to Madame Zamenoy and to her husband Karil that Ziska had set his heart upon having his cousin, they had expressed no displeasure at the prospect, poor as the Balatkas were. "There is no knowing how it may go about the houses in the Kleinseite," Karil Zamenoy had said. "Old Trendellsohn gets the rent and the interest, but he has little or nothing to show for them--merely a written surrender from Josef, which is worth nothing." No hindrance, therefore was placed in the way of Ziska's suit, and Nina might have been already accepted in the Windberg-gasse had Nina chosen to smile upon Ziska. Now Ziska was told that the girl he loved was to marry a Jew because she was starving, and the tidings threw a new light upon him. Why had he not offered assistance to Nina? It was not surprising that Nina should be so hard to him--to him who had as yet offered her nothing in her poverty but a few cold compliments.

"She shall have bread enough, if that is what she wants," said Ziska.

"Bread and kindness," said the old man.

"She shall have kindness too, uncle Josef. I love Nina better than any Jew in Prague can love her."

"Why should not a Jew love? I believe the man loves her well. Why else should he wish to make her his wife?"

"And I love her well--and I would make her my wife."

"You want to marry Nina!"

"Yes, uncle Josef. I wish to marry Nina. I will marry her tomorrow-- or, for that matter, today--if she will have me."

"You! Ziska Zamenoy!"

"I, Ziska Zamenoy."

"And what would your mother say?"

"Both father and mother will consent. There need be no hindrance if Nina will agree. I did not know that you were so badly off. I did not indeed, or I would have come to you myself and seen to it."

Old Balatka did not answer for a while, having turned himself in his bed to think of the proposition which had been made to him. "Would you not like to have me for a son-in-law better than a Jew, uncle Josef?" said Ziska, pleading for himself as best he knew how to plead.

"Have you ever spoken to Nina?" said the old man.

"Well, no; not exactly to say what I have said to you. When one loves a girl as I love her, somehow--I don't know how--But I am ready to do so at once.

"Ah, Ziska, if you had done it sooner!"

"But is it too late? You say she has taken up with this man because you are both so poor. She cannot like a Jew best."

"But she is true--so true!"

"If you mean about her promise to Trendellsohn, Father Jerome would tell her in a minute that she should not keep such a promise to a Jew."

"She would not mind Father Jerome."

"And what does she mind? Will she not mind you?"

"Me; yes--she will mind me, to give me my food."

"Will she not obey you?"

"How am I to bid her obey me? But I will try, Ziska."

"You would not wish her to marry a Jew?"

"No, Ziska; certainly I should not wish it."

"And you will give me your consent?"

"Yes, if it be any good to you."

"It will be good if you will be round with her, telling her that she must not do such a thing as this. Love a Jew! It is impossible. As you have been so very poor, she may be forgiven for having thought of it. Tell her that, uncle Josef; and whatever you do, be firm with her."

"There she is in the next room," said the father, who had heard his daughter's entrance. Ziska's face had assumed something of a defiant look while he was recommending firmness to the old man; but now that the girl of whom he had spoken was so near at hand, there returned to his brow the young calf-like expression with which Lotta Luxa was so well acquainted. "There she is, and you will speak to her yourself now," said Balatka.

Ziska got up to go, but as he did so he fumbled in his pocket and brought forth a little bundle of bank-notes. A bundle of bank-notes in Prague may be not little, and yet represent very little money. When bank-notes are passed for two-pence and become thick with use, a man may have a great mass of paper currency in his pocket without being rich. On this occasion, however, Ziska tendered to his uncle no two- penny notes. There was a note for five florins, and two or three for two florins, and perhaps half-a-dozen for a florin each, so that the total amount offered was sufficient to be of real importance to one so poor as Josef Balatka.

"This will help you awhile," said Ziska, "and if Nina will come round and be a good girl, neither you nor she shall want anything; and she need not be afraid of mother, if she will only do as I say." Balatka had put out his hand and had taken the money, when the bedroom door was opened, and Nina came in.

"What, Ziska," said she, "are you here?"

"Why not? why should I not see my uncle?"

"It is very good of you, certainly; only, as you never came before--"

"I mean it for kindness, now I have come, at any rate," said Ziska.

"Then I will take it for kindness," said Nina.

"Why should there be quarrelling among relatives?" said the old man from among the bed-clothes.

"Why, indeed?" said Ziska.

"Why, indeed," said Nina, "--if it could be helped?"

She knew that the outward serenity of the words spoken was too good to be a fair representation of thoughts below in the mind of any of them. It could not be that Ziska had come there to express even his own consent to her marriage with Anton Trendellsohn; and without such consent there must of necessity be a continuation of quarrelling. "Have you been speaking to father, Ziska, about those papers?" Nina was determined that there should be no glozing of matters, no soft words used effectually to stop her in her projected course. So she rushed at once at the subject which she thought most important in Ziska's presence.

"What papers?" said Ziska.

"The papers which belong to Anton Trendellsohn about this house and the others. They are his, and you would not wish to keep things which belong to another, even though he should be a--Jew."

Then it occurred to Ziska that Trendellsohn might be willing to give up Nina if he got the papers, and that Nina might be willing to be free from the Jew by the same arrangement. It could not be that such a girl as Nina Balatka should prefer the love of a Jew to the love of a Christian. So at least Ziska argued in his own mind. "I do not want to keep anything that belongs to anybody," said Ziska. "If the papers are with us, I am willing that they should be given up--that is, if it be right that they should be given up."

"It is right," said Nina.

"I believe the Trendellsohns should have them--either father or son," said old Balatka.

"Of course they should have them," said Nina; "either father or son--it makes no matter which."

"I will try and see to it," said Ziska.

"Pray do," said Nina; "it will be only just; and one would not wish to rob even a Jew, I suppose." Ziska understood nothing of what was intended by the tone of her voice, and began to think that there might really be ground for hope.

"Nina," he said, "your father is not quite well. I want you to speak to me in the next room."

"Certainly, Ziska, if you wish it. Father, I will come again to you soon. Souchey is making your soup, and I will bring it to you when it is ready." Then she led the way into the sitting-room, and as Ziska came through, she carefully shut the door. The walls dividing the rooms were very thick, and the door stood in a deep recess, so that no sound could be heard from one room to another. Nina did not wish that her father should hear what might now pass between herself and her cousin, and therefore she was careful to shut the door close.

"Ziska," said she, as soon as they were together, "I am very glad that you have come here. My aunt is so angry with me that I cannot speak with her, and uncle Karil only snubs me if I say a word to him about business. He would snub me, no doubt, worse than ever now; and yet who is there here to speak of such matters if I may not do so? You see how it is with father."

"He is not able to do much, I suppose."

"He is able to do nothing, and there is nothing for him to do--nothing that can be of any use. But of course he should see that those who have been good to him are not--are not injured because of their kindness."

"You mean those Jews--the Trendellsohns."

"Yes, those Jews the Trendellsohns! You would not rob a man because he is a Jew," said she, repeating the old words.

"They know how to take care of themselves, Nina."

"Very likely."

"They have managed to get all your father's property between them."

"I don't know how that is. Father says that the business which uncle and you have was once his, and that he made it. In these matters the weakest always goes to the wall. Father has no son to help him, as uncle Karil has--and old Trendellsohn."

"You may help him better than any son."

"I will help him if I can. Will you and uncle give up those papers which you have kept since father left them with uncle Karil, just that they might be safe?"

This question Ziska would not answer at once. The matter was one on which he wished to negotiate, and he was driven to the necessity of considering what might be the best line for his diplomacy. "I am sure, Ziska," continued Nina, "you will understand why I ask this. Father is too weak to make the demand, and uncle would listen to nothing that Anton Trendellsohn would say to him."

"They say that you have betrothed yourself to this Jew, Nina."

"It is true. But that has nothing to do with it."

"He is very anxious to have the deeds?"

"Of course he is anxious. Father is old and poorly; and what would he do if father were to die?"

"Nina, he shall have them--if he will give you up."

Nina turned away from her cousin and looked out from the window into the little court. Ziska could not see her face; but had he done so he would not have been able to read the smile of triumph with which for a moment or two it became brilliant. No; Anton would make no such bargain as that! Anton loved her better than any title-deeds. Had he not told her that she was his sun--the sun that gave to him light and heat? "If they are his own, why should he be asked to make any such bargain?" said Nina.

"Nina," said Ziska, throwing all his passion into his voice, as he best knew how, "it cannot be that you should love this man."

"Why not love him?"

"A Jew!"

"Yes--a Jew! I do love him."

"Nina!"

"What have you to say, Ziska? Whatever you say, do not abuse him. It is my affair, not yours. You may think what you like of me for taking such a husband, but remember that he is to be my husband."

"Nina, let me be your husband."

"No, Ziska; that cannot be."

"I love you. I love you fifty times better than he can do. Is not a Christian's love better than a Jew's?"

"Because I do not love you. Can there be any other reason in such a matter? I do not love you. I do not care if I never see you. But him I love with all my heart. To see him is the only delight of my life. To sit beside him, with his hand in mine, and my head on his shoulder, is heaven to me. To obey him is my duty; to serve him is my pleasure. To be loved by him is the only good thing which God has given me on earth. Now, Ziska, you will know why I cannot be your wife." Still she stood before him, and still she looked up into his face, keeping her gaze upon him even after her words were finished.

"Accursed Jew!" said Ziska.

"That is right, Ziska; curse him; it is so easy."

"And you too will be cursed--here and hereafter. If you marry a Jew you will be accursed to all eternity."

"That, too, is very easy to say."

"It is not I who say it. The priest will tell you the same."

"Let him tell me so; it is his business, but it is not yours. You say it because you cannot have what you want yourself; that is all. When shall I call in the Ross Markt for the papers?" In the Ross Markt was the house of business of Karil Zamenoy, and there, as Nina well knew, were kept the documents which she was so anxious to obtain. But the demand at this moment was made simply with the object of vexing Ziska, and urging him on to further anger.

"Unless you will give up Anton Trendellsohn, you had better not come to the Ross Markt."

"I will never give him up."

"We will see. Perhaps he will give you up after a while. It will be a fine thing to be jilted by a Jew."

"The Jew, at any rate, shall not be jilted by the Christian. And now, if you please, I will ask you to go. I do not choose to be insulted in father's house. It is his house still."

"Nina, I will give you one more chance."

"You can give me no chance that will do you or me any good. If you will go, that is all I want of you now."

For a moment or two Ziska stood in doubt as to what he would next do or say. Then he took up his hat and went away without another word. On that same evening some one rang the bell at the door of the house in the Windberg-gasse in a most humble manner--with that weak, hesitating hand which, by the tone which it produces, seems to insinuate that no one need hurry to answer such an appeal, and that the answer, when made, may be made by the lowest personage in the house. In this instance, however, Lotta Luxa did answer the bell, and not the stout Bohemian girl who acted in the household of Madame Zamenoy as assistant and fag to Lotta. And Lotta found Nina at the door, enveloped in her cloak. "Lotta," she said, "will you kindly give this to my cousin Ziska?" Then, not waiting for a word, she started away so quickly that Lotta had not a chance of speaking to her, no power of uttering an audible word of abuse. When Ziska opened the parcel thus brought to him, he found it to contain all the notes which he had given to Josef Balatka.

Chapter 4

When Nina returned to her father after Ziska's departure, a very few words made everything clear between them. "I would not have him if there was not another man in the world," Nina had said. "He thinks that it is only Anton Trendellsohn that prevents it, but he knows nothing about what a girl feels. He thinks that because we are poor I am to be bought, this way or that way, by a little money. Is that a man, father, that any girl can love?" Then the father had confessed his receipt of the bank-notes from Ziska, and we already know to what result that confession had led.

Till she had delivered her packet into the hands of Lotta Luxa, she maintained her spirits by the excitement of the thing she was doing. Though she should die in the streets of hunger, she would take no money from Ziska Zamenoy. But the question now was not only of her wants, but of her father's. That she, for herself, would be justified in returning Ziska's money there could be no doubt; but was she equally justified in giving back money that had been given to her father? As she walked to the Windberg-gasse, still holding the parcel of notes in her hand, she had no such qualms of conscience; but as she returned, when it was altogether too late for repentance, she made pictures to herself of terrible scenes in which her father suffered all the pangs of want, because she had compelled him to part with this money. If she were to say one word to Anton Trendellsohn, all her trouble on that head would be over. Anton Trendellsohn would at once give her enough to satisfy their immediate wants. In a month or two, when she would be Anton's wife, she would not be ashamed to take everything from his hand; and why should she be ashamed now to take something from him to whom she was prepared to give everything? But she was ashamed to do so. She felt that she could not go to him and ask him for bread. One other resource she had. There remained to her of her mother's property a necklace, which was all that was left to her from her mother. And when this had been given to her at her mother's death, she had been specially enjoined not to part with it. Her father then had been too deeply plunged in grief to say any words on such a subject, and the gift had been put into her hands by her aunt Sophie. Even aunt Sophie had been softened at that moment, and had shown some tenderness to the orphan child. "You are to keep it always for her sake," aunt Sophie had said; and Nina had hitherto kept the trinket, when all other things were gone, in remembrance of her mother. She had hitherto reconciled herself to keeping her little treasure, when all other things were going, by the sacredness of the deposit; and had told herself that even for her father's sake she must not part with the gift which had come to her from her mother. But now she comforted herself by the reflection that the necklace would produce for her enough to repay her father that present from Ziska which she had taken from him. Her father had pleaded sorely to be allowed to keep the notes. In her emotion at the moment she had been imperative with him, and her resolution had prevailed. But she thought of his entreaties as she returned home, and of his poverty and wants, and she determined that the necklace should go. It would produce for her at any rate as much as Ziska had given. She wished that she had brought it with her, as she passed the open door of a certain pawnbroker, which she had entered often during the last six months, and whither she intended to take her treasure, so that she might comfort her father on her return with the sight of the money. But she had it not, and she went home empty-handed. "And now, Nina, I suppose we may starve," said her father, whom she found sitting close to the stove in the kitchen, while Souchey was kneeling before it, putting in at the little open door morsels of fuel which were lamentably insufficient for the poor man's purpose of raising a fire. The weather, indeed, was as yet warm--so warm that in the middle of the day the heat was matter of complaint to Josef Balatka; but in the evening he would become chill; and as there existed some small necessity for cooking, he would beg that he might thus enjoy the warmth of the kitchen.

"Yes, we shall starve now," said Souchey, complacently. "There is not much doubt about our starving."

"Souchey, I wonder you should speak like that before father," said Nina.

"And why shouldn't he speak?" said Balatka. "I think he has as much right as any one."

"He has no right to make things worse than they are."

"I don't know how I could do that, Nina," said the servant. "What made you take that money back to your aunt?"

"I didn't take it back to my aunt."

"Well, to any of the family then? I suppose it came from your aunt?"

"It came from my cousin Ziska, and I thought it better to give it back. Souchey, do not you come in between father and me. There are troubles enough; do not you make them worse."

"If I had been here you should never have taken it back again," said Souchey, obstinately.

"Father," said Nina, appealing to the old man, "how could I have kept it? You knew why it was given."

"Who is to help us if we may not take it from them?"

"Tomorrow," said Nina, "I can get as much as he brought. And I will, and you shall see it."

"Who will give it you, Nina?"

"Never mind, father, I will have it."

"She will beg it from her Jew lover," said Souchey.

"Souchey," said she, with her eyes flashing fire at him, "if you cannot treat your master's daughter better than that, you may as well go."

"Is it not true?" demanded Souchey.

"No, it is not true; it is false. I have never taken money from Anton; nor shall I do so till we are married."

"And that will be never," said Souchey. "It is as well to speak out at once. The priest will not let it be done."

"All the priests in Prague cannot hinder it," said Nina.

"That is true," said Balatka.

"We shall see," said Souchey. "And in the mean time what is the good of fighting with the Zamenoys? They are your only friends, Nina, and therefore you take delight in quarrelling with them. When people have money, they should be allowed to have a little pride." Nina said nothing further on the occasion, though Souchey and her father went on grumbling for an hour. She discovered, however, from various words that her father allowed to fall from him, that his opposition to her marriage had nearly faded away. It seemed to be his opinion that if she were to marry the Jew, the sooner she did it the better.

Now, Nina was determined that she would marry the Jew, though heaven and earth should meet in consequence. She would marry him if he would marry her. They had told her that the Jew would jilt her. She did not put much faith in the threat; but even that was more probable than that she should jilt him.

On the following morning Souchey, in return, as it were, for his cruelty to his young mistress on the preceding day, produced some small store of coin which he declared to be the result of a further sale of the last relics of his master's property; and Nina's journey with the necklace to the pawnbroker was again postponed. That day and the next were passed in the old house without anything to make them memorable except their wearisome misery, and then Nina again went out to visit the Jews' quarter. She told herself that she was taken there by the duties of her position; but in truth she could hardly bear her life without the comfort of seeing the only person who would speak kindly to her. She was engaged to marry this man, but she did not know when she was to be married. She would ask no question of her lover on that matter; but she could tell him--and she felt herself bound to tell him --what was really her own position, and also all that she knew of his affairs. He had given her to understand that he could not marry her till he had obtained possession of certain documents which he believed to be in the possession of her uncle. And for these documents she, with his permission, had made application. She had at any rate discovered that they certainly were at the office in the Ross Markt. So much she had learned from Ziska; and so much, at any rate, she was bound to make known to her lover. And, moreover, since she had seen him she had told all her relatives of her engagement. They all knew now that she loved the Jew, and that she had resolved to marry him; and of this also it was her duty to give him tidings. The result of her communication to her father and her relatives in the Windberg-gasse had been by no means so terrible as she had anticipated. The heavens and the earth had not as yet shown any symptoms of coming together. Her aunt, indeed, had been very angry; and Lotta Luxa and Souchey had told her that such a marriage would not be allowed. Ziska, too, had said some sharp words; and her father, for the first day or two, had expostulated. But the threats had been weak threats, and she did not find herself to be annihilated--indeed, hardly to be oppressed--by the scolding of any of them. What the priest might say she had not yet experienced; but opposition from other quarters had not as yet come upon her in any form that was not endurable. Her aunt had intended to consume her with wrath, but Nina had not found herself to be consumed. All this it was necessary that she should tell to Anton Trendellsohn. It was grievous to her that it should be always her lot to go to her lover, and that he should never--almost never--be able to seek her. It would in truth be never now, unless she could induce her father to receive Anton openly as his acknowledged future son-in-law; and she could hardly hope that her father would yield so far as that. Other girls, she knew, stayed till their lovers came to them, or met them abroad in public places--at the gardens and music-halls, or perhaps at church; but no such joys as these were within reach of Nina. The public gardens, indeed, were open to her and to Anton Trendellsohn as they were to others; but she knew that she would not dare to be seen in public with her Jew lover till the thing was done and she and the Jew had become man and wife. On this occasion, before she left her home, she was careful to tell her father where she was going. "Have you any message to the Trendellsohns?" she asked.

"So you are going there again?" her father said.

"Yes, I must see them. I told you that I had a commission from them to the Zamenoys, which I have performed, and I must let them know what I did. Besides, father, if this man is to be my husband, is it not well that I should see him?" Old Balatka groaned, but said nothing further, and Nina went forth to the Jews' quarter.

On this occasion she found Trendellsohn the elder standing at the door of his own house.

"You want to see Anton," said the Jew. Anton is out. He is away somewhere in the city--on business."

"I shall be glad to see you, father, if you can spare me a minute."

"Certainly, my child--an hour if it will serve you. Hours are not scarce with me now, as they used to be when I was Anton's age, and as they are with him now. Hours, and minutes too, are very scarce with Anton in these days. Then he led the way up the dark stairs to the sitting-room, and Nina followed him. Nina and the elder Trendellsohn had always hitherto been friends. Before her engagement with his son they had been affectionate friends, and since that had been made known to him there had been no quarrel between them. But the old man had hardly approved of his son's purpose, thinking that a Jew should look for the wife of his bosom among his own people, and thinking also, perhaps, that one who had so much of worldly wealth to offer as his son should receive something also of the same in his marriage. Old Trendellsohn had never uttered a word of complaint to Nina--had said nothing to make her suppose that she was not welcome to the house; but he had never spoken to her with happy, joy-giving words, as the future bride of his son. He still called her his daughter, as he had done before; but he did it only in his old fashion, using the affectionate familiarity of an old friend to a young maiden. He was a small, aged man, very thin and meager in aspect--so meager as to conceal in part, by the general tenuity of his aspect, the shortness of his stature. He was not even so tall as Nina, as Nina had discovered, much to her surprise. His hair was grizzled, rather than grey, and the beard on his thin, wiry, wizened face was always close shorn. He was scrupulously clean in his person, and seemed, even at his age, to take a pride in the purity and fineness of his linen. He was much older than Nina's father--more than ten years older, as he would sometimes boast; but he was still strong and active, while Nina's father was worn out with age. Old Trendellsohn was eighty, and yet he would be seen trudging about through the streets of Prague, intent upon his business of money-making; and it was said that his son Anton was not even as yet actually in partnership with him, or fully trusted by him in all his plans.

"Father," Nina said, "I am glad that Anton is out, as now I can speak a word to you."

"My dear, you shall speak fifty words."

"That is very good of you. Of course I know that the house we live in does in truth belong to you and Anton."

"Yes, it belongs to me," said the Jew.

"And we can pay no rent for it."

"Is it of that you have come to speak, Nina? If so, do not trouble yourself. For certain reasons, which Anton can explain, I am willing that your father should live there without rent."

Nina blushed as she found herself compelled to thank the Jew for his charity. "I know how kind you have been to father," she said.

"Nay, my daughter, there has been no great kindness in it. Your father has been unfortunate, and, Jew as I am, I would not turn him into the street. Do not trouble yourself to think of it."

"But it was not altogether about that, father. Anton spoke to me the other day about some deeds which should belong to you."

"They do belong to me," said Trendellsohn.

"But you have them not in your own keeping."

"No, we have not. It is, I believe, the creed of a Christian that he may deal dishonestly with a Jew, though the Jew who shall deal dishonestly with a Christian is to be hanged. It is strange what latitude men will give themselves under the cloak of their religion! But why has Anton spoken to you of this? I did not bid him."

"He sent me with a message to my aunt Sophie."

"He was wrong; he was very foolish; he should have gone himself."

"But, father, I have found out that the papers you want are certainly in my uncle's keeping in the Ross Markt."

"Of course they are, my dear. Anton might have known that without employing you."

So far Nina had performed but a small part of the task which she had before her. She found it easier to talk to the old man about the title- deeds of the house in the Kleinseite than she did to tell him of her own affairs. But the thing was to be done, though the doing of it was difficult; and, after a pause, she persevered. "And I told aunt Sophie," she said, with her eyes turned upon the ground, "of my engagement with Anton."

"You did?"

"Yes; and I told father."

"And what did your father say?"

"Father did not say much. He is poorly and weak."

"Yes, yes; not strong enough to fight against the abomination of a Jew son-in-law. And what did your aunt say? She is strong enough to fight anybody."

"She was very angry."

"I suppose so, I suppose so. Well, she is right. As the world goes in Prague, my child, you will degrade yourself by marrying a Jew."

"I want nothing prouder than to be Anton's wife," said Nina.

"And to speak sooth," said the old man, "the Jew will degrade himself fully as much by marrying you."

"Father, I would not have that. If I thought that my love would injure him, I would leave him."

"He must judge for himself," said Trendellsohn, relenting somewhat.

"He must judge for himself and for me too," said Nina.

"He will be able, at any rate, to keep a house over your head."

"It is not for that," said Nina, thinking of her cousin Ziska's offer. She need not want for a house and money if she were willing to sell herself for such things as them.

"Anton will be rich, Nina, and you are very poor."

"Can I help that, father? Such as I am, I am his. If all Prague were mine I would give it to him."

The old man shook his head. "A Christian thinks that it is too much honor for a Jew to marry a Christian, though he be rich, and she have not a ducat for her dower."

"Father, your words are cruel. Do you believe I would give Anton my hand if I did not love him? I do not know much of his wealth; but, father, I might be the promised wife of a Christian tomorrow, who is, perhaps, as rich as he--if that were anything."

"And who is that other lover, Nina?"

"It matters not. He can be nothing to me--nothing in that way. I love Anton Trendellsohn, and I could not be the wife of any other but him."

"I wish it were otherwise. I tell you so plainly to your face. I wish it were otherwise. Jews and Christians have married in Prague, I know, but good has never come of it. Anton should find a wife among his own people; and you--it would be better for you to take that other offer of which you spoke."

"It is too late, father."

"No, Nina, it is not too late. If Anton would be wise, it is not too late."

"Anton can do as he pleases. It is too late for me. If Anton thinks it well to change his mind, I shall not reproach him. You can tell him so, father--from me."

"He knows my mind already, Nina. I will tell him, however, what you say of your own friends. They have heard of your engagement, and are angry with you, of course."

"Aunt Sophie and her people are angry."

"Of course they will oppose it. They will set their priests at you, and frighten you almost to death. They will drive the life out of your young heart with their curses. You do not know what sorrows are before you."

"I can bear all that. There is only one sorrow that I fear. If Anton is true to me, I will not mind all the rest."

The old man's heart was softened towards her. He could not bring himself to say a word to her of direct encouragement, but he kissed her before she went, telling her that she was a good girl, and bidding her have no care as to the house in the Kleinseite. As long as he lived, and her father, her father should not be disturbed. And as for deeds, he declared, with something of a grim smile on his old visage, that though a Jew had always a hard fight to get his own from a Christian, the hard fighting did generally prevail at last. "We shall get them, Nina, when they have put us to such trouble and expense as their laws may be able to devise. Anton knows that as well as I do."

At the door of the house Nina found the old man's grand-daughter waiting for her. Ruth Jacobi was the girl's name, and she was the orphaned child of a daughter of old Trendellsohn. Father and mother were both dead; and of her father, who had been dead long, Ruth had no memory. But she still wore some remains of the black garments which had been given to her at her mother's funeral; and she still grieved bitterly for her mother, having no woman with her in that gloomy house, and no other child to comfort her. Her grandfather and her uncle were kind to her--kind after their own gloomy fashion; but it was a sad house for a young girl, and Ruth, though she knew nothing of any better abode, found the days to be very long, and the months to be very wearisome.

"What has he been saying to you, Nina?" the girl asked, taking hold of her friend's dress, to prevent her escape into the street. "You need not be in a hurry for a minute. He will not come down."

"I am not afraid of him. Ruth."

"I am, then. But perhaps he is not cross to you."

"Why should he be cross to me?"

"I know why, Nina, but I will not say. Uncle Anton has been out all the day, and was not home to dinner. It is much worse when he is away."

"Is Anton ever cross to you, Ruth?"

"Indeed he is--sometimes. He scolds much more than grandfather. But he is younger, you know."

"Yes; he is younger, certainly."

"Not but what he is very old, too; much too old for you, Nina. When I have a lover I will never have an old man."

"But Anton is not old."

"Not like grandfather, of course. But I should like a lover who would laugh and be gay. Uncle Anton is never gay. My lover shall be only two years older than myself. Uncle Anton must be twenty years older than you, Nina."

"Not more than ten--or twelve at the most."

"He is too old to laugh and dance."

"Not at all, dear; but he thinks of other things."

"I should like a lover to think of the things that I think about. It is all very well being steady when you have got babies of your own; but that should be after ever so long. I should like to keep my lover as a lover for two years. And all that time he should like to dance with me, and to hear music, and to go about just where I would like to go."

"And what then, Ruth?"

"Then? Why, then I suppose I should marry him, and become stupid like the rest. But I should have the two years to look back at and to remember. Do you think, Nina, that you will ever come and live here when you are married?"

"I do not know that I shall ever be married, Ruth."

"But you mean to marry uncle Anton?"

"I cannot say. It may be so."

"But you love him, Nina?"

"Yes, I love him. I love him with all my heart. I love him better than all the world besides. Ruth, you cannot tell how I love him. I would lie down and die if he were to bid me."

"He will never bid you do that."

"You think that he is old, and dull, and silent, and cross. But when he will sit still and not say a word to me for an hour together, I think that I almost love him the best. I only want to be near him, Ruth."

"But you do not like him to be cross."

"Yes, I do. That is, I like him to scold me if he is angry. If he were angry, and did not scold a little, I should think that he was really vexed with me."

Then you must be very much in love, Nina?"

"I am in love--very much."

"And does it make you happy?"

"Happy! Happiness depends on so many things. But it makes me feel that there can only be one real unhappiness; and unless that should come to me, I shall care for nothing. Good-bye, love. Tell your uncle that I was here, and say--say to him when no one else can hear, that I went away with a sad heart because I had not seen him."

It was late in the evening when Anton Trendellsohn came home, but Ruth remembered the message that had been entrusted to her, and managed to find a moment in which to deliver it. But her uncle took it amiss, and scolded her. "You two have been talking nonsense together here half the day, I suppose."

"I spoke to her for five minutes, uncle; that was all."

"Did you do your lessons with Madame Pulsky?"

"Yes, I did, uncle--of course. You know that."

"I know that it is a pity you should not be better looked after."

"Bring Nina home here and she will look after me."

"Go to bed, miss--at once, do you hear?"

Then Ruth went off to her bed, wondering at Nina's choice, and declaring to herself, that if ever she took in hand a lover at all, he should be a lover very different from her uncle, Anton Trendellsohn.

Chapter 5

The more Madame Zamenoy thought of the terrible tidings which had reached her, the more determined did she become to prevent the degradation of the connection with which she was threatened. She declared to her husband and son that all Prague were already talking of the horror, forgetting, perhaps, that any knowledge which Prague had on the subject must have come from herself. She had, indeed, consulted various persons on the subject in the strictest confidence. We have already seen that she had told Lotta Luxa and her son, and she had, of course, complained frequently on the matter to her husband. She had unbosomed herself to one or two trusty female friends who lived near her, and she had applied for advice and assistance to two priests. To Father Jerome she had gone as Nina's confessor, and she had also applied to the reverend pastor who had the charge of her own little peccadilloes. The small amount of assistance which her clerical allies offered to her had surprised her very much. She had, indeed, gone so far as to declare to Lotta that she was shocked by their indifference. Her own confessor had simply told her that the matter was in the hands of Father Jerome, as far as it could be said to belong to the Church at all; and had satisfied his conscience by advising his dear friend to use all the resources which female persecution put at her command. "You will frighten her out of it, Madame Zamenoy, if you go the right way about it," said the priest. Madame Zamenoy was well inclined to go the right way about it, if she only knew how. She would make Nina's life a burden to her if she could only get hold of the girl, and would scruple at no threats as to this world or the next. But she thought that her priest ought to have done more for her in such a crisis than simply giving her such ordinary counsel. Things were not as they used to be, she knew; but there was even yet something of the prestige of power left to the Church, and there were convents with locks and bars, and excommunication might still be made terrible, and public opinion, in the shape of outside persecution, might, as Madame Zamenoy thought, have been brought to bear. Nor did she get much more comfort from Father Jerome. His reliance was placed chiefly on operations to be carried on with the Jew; and, failing them, on the opposition which the Jew would experience among his own people. "They think more of it than we do," said Father Jerome.

"How can that be, Father Jerome?"

"Well, they do. He would lose caste among all his friends by such a marriage, and would, I think, destroy all his influence among them. When he perceives this more fully he will be shy enough about it himself. Besides, what is he to get?"

"He will get nothing."

"He will think better of it. And you might manage something with those deeds. Of course he should have them sooner or later, but they might be surrendered as the price of his giving her up. I should say it might be managed."

All this was not comfortable for Madame Zamenoy; and she fretted and fumed till her husband had no peace in his house, and Ziska almost wished that he might hear no more of the Jew and his betrothal. She could not even commence her system of persecution, as Nina did not go near her, and had already told Lotta Luxa that she must decline to discuss the question of her marriage any further. So, at last, Madame Zamenoy found herself obliged to go over in person to the house in the Kleinseite. Such visits had for many years been very rare with her. Since her sister's death and the days in which the Balatkas had been prosperous, she had preferred that all intercourse between the two families should take place at her own house; and thus, as Josef Balatka himself rarely left his own door, she had not seen him for more than two years. Frequent intercourse, however, had been maintained, and aunt Sophie knew very well how things were going on in the Kleinseite. Lotta had no compunctions as to visiting the house, and Lotta's eyes were very sharp. And Nina had been frequently in the Windberg-gasse, having hitherto believed it to be her duty to attend to her aunt's behests. But Nina was no longer obedient, and Madame Zamenoy was compelled to go herself to her brother-in-law, unless she was disposed to leave the Balatkas absolutely to their fate. Let her do what she would, Nina must be her niece, and therefore she would yet make a struggle.

On this occasion Madame Zamenoy walked on foot, thinking that her carriage and horses might be too conspicuous at the arched gate in the little square. The carriage did not often make its way over the bridge into the Kleinseite, being used chiefly among the suburbs of the New Town, where it was now well known and quickly recognized; and she did not think that this was a good opportunity for breaking into new ground with her equipage. She summoned Lotta to attend her, and after her one o'clock dinner took her umbrella in her hand and went forth. She was a stout woman, probably not more than forty-five years of age, but a little heavy, perhaps from too much indulgence with her carriage. She walked slowly, therefore; and Lotta, who was nimble of foot and quick in all her ways, thanked her stars that it did not suit her mistress to walk often through the city.

"How very long the bridge is, Lotta!" said Madame Zamenoy.

"Not longer, ma'am, than it always has been," said Lotta, pertly.

"Of course it is not longer than it always has been; I know that; but still I say it is very long. Bridges are not so long in other places."

"Not where the rivers are narrower," said Lotta. Madame Zamenoy trudged on, finding that she could get no comfort from her servant, and at last reached Balatka's door. Lotta, who was familiar with the place, entered the house first, and her mistress followed her. Hanging about the broad passage which communicated with all the rooms on the ground-floor, they found Souchey, who told them that his master was in bed, and that Nina was at work by his bedside. He was sent in to announce the grand arrival, and when Madame Zamenoy entered the sitting-room Nina was there to meet her.

"Child," she said, "I have come to see your father."

"Father is in bed, but you can come in," said Nina.

"Of course I can go in," said Madame Zamenoy, "but before I go in let me know this. Has he heard of the disgrace which you purpose to bring upon him?"

Nina drew herself up and made no answer; whereupon Lotta spoke. "The old gentleman knows all about it, ma'am, as well as you do."

"Lotta, let the child speak for herself. Nina, have you had the audacity to tell your father--that which you told me?"

"I have told him everything," said Nina; "will you come into his room?" Then Madame Zamenoy lifted up the hem of her garment and stepped proudly into the old man's chamber.

By this time Balatka knew what was about to befall him, and was making himself ready for the visit. He was well aware that he should be sorely perplexed as to what he should say in the coming interview. He could not speak lightly of such an evil as this marriage with a Jew; nor when his sister-in-law should abuse the Jews could he dare to defend them. But neither could he bring himself to say evil words of Nina, or to hear evil words spoken of her without making some attempt to screen her. It might be best, perhaps, to lie under the bed-clothes and say nothing, if only his sister-in-law would allow him to lie there. "Am I to come in with you, aunt Sophie?" said Nina. "Yes child," said the aunt; "come and hear what I have to say to your father." So Nina followed her aunt, and Lotta and Souchey were left in the sitting-room.

"And how are you, Souchey?" said Lotta, with unusual kindness of tone. "I suppose you are not so busy but you can stay with me a few minutes while she is in there?"

"There is not so much to do that I cannot spare the time," said Souchey.

"Nothing to do, I suppose, and less to get?" said Lotta.

"That's about it, Lotta; but you wouldn't have had me leave them?"

"A man has to look after himself in the world; but you were always easy-minded, Souchey."

"I don't know about being so easy-minded. I know what would make me easy-minded enough."

"You'll have to be servant to a Jew now."

"No; I'll never be that."

"I suppose he gives you something at odd times?"

"Who? Trendellsohn? I never saw the color of his money yet, and do not wish to see it."

"But he comes here--sometimes?"

"Never, Lotta. I haven't seen Anton Trendellsohn within the doors these six months."

"But she goes to him?"

"Yes; she goes to him."

"That's worse--a deal worse."

"I told her how it was when I saw her trotting off so often to the Jews' quarter. 'You see too much of Anton Trendellsohn,' I said to her; but it didn't do any good."

"You should have come to us, and have told us."

"What, Madame there? I could never have brought myself to that; she is so upsetting, Lotta."

"She is upsetting, no doubt; but she don't upset me. Why didn't you tell me, Souchey?"

"Well, I thought that if I said a word to her, perhaps that would be enough. Who could believe that she would throw herself at once into a Jew's arms--such a fellow as Anton Trendellsohn, too, old enough to be her father, and she the bonniest girl in all Prague?"

"Handsome is that handsome does, Souchey."

"I say she's the sweetest girl in all Prague; and more's the pity she should have taken such a fancy as this."

"She mustn't marry him, of course, Souchey."

"Not if it can be helped, Lotta."

"It must be helped. You and I must help it, if no one else can do so."

"That's easy said, Lotta."

"We can do it, if we are minded--that is, if you are minded. Only think what a thing it would be for her to be the wife of a Jew! Think of her soul, Souchey!"

Souchey shuddered. He did not like being told of people's souls, feeling probably that the misfortunes of this world were quite heavy enough for a poor wight like himself, without any addition in anticipation of futurity. "Think of her soul, Souchey," repeated Lotta, who was at all points a good churchwoman.

"It's bad enough any way," said Souchey.

"And there's our Ziska would take her tomorrow in spite of the Jew."

"Would he now?"

"That he would, without anything but what she stands up in. And he'd behave very handsome to anyone that would help him."

"He'd be the first of his name that ever did, then. I have known the time when old Balatka there, poor as he is now, would give a florin when Karil Zamenoy begrudged six kreutzers."

"And what has come of such giving? Josef Balatka is poor, and Karil Zamenoy bids fair to be as rich as any merchant in Prague. But no matter about that. Will you give a helping hand? There is nothing I wouldn't do for you, Souchey, if we could manage this between us."

"Would you now?" And Souchey drew near, as though some closer bargain might be practicable between them.

"I would indeed; but, Souchey, talking won't do it."

"What will do it?"

Lotta paused a moment, looking round the room carefully, till suddenly her eyes fell on a certain article which lay on Nina's work-table. "What am I to do?" said Souchey, anxious to be at work with the prospect of so great a reward.

"Never mind," said Lotta, whose tone of voice was suddenly changed. "Never mind it now at least. And, Souchey, I think you'd better go to your work. We've been gossiping here ever so long."

"Perhaps five minutes; and what does it signify?"

"She'd think it so odd to find us here together in the parlor."

"Not odd at all."

"Just as though we'd been listening to what they'd been saying. Go now, Souchey--there's a good fellow; and I'll come again the day after to- morrow and tell you. Go, I say. There are things that I must think of by myself." And in this way she got Souchey to leave the room.

"Josef," said Madame Zamenoy, as she took her place standing by Balatka's bedside--"Josef, this is very terrible." Nina also was standing close by her father's head, with her hand upon her father's pillow. Balatka groaned, but made no immediate answer.

"It is terrible, horrible, abominable, and damnable," said Madame Zamenoy, bringing out one epithet after the other with renewed energy. Balatka groaned again. What could he say in reply to such an address?

"Aunt Sophie," said Nina, "do not speak to father like that. He is ill."

"Child," said Madame Zamenoy, "I shall speak as I please. I shall speak as my duty bids me speak. Josef, this that I hear is very terrible. It is hardly to be believed that any Christian girl should think of marrying--a Jew."

"What can I do?" said the father. "How can I prevent her?"

"How can you prevent her, Josef? Is she not your daughter? Does she mean to say, standing there, that she will not obey her father? Tell me. Nina, will you or will you not obey your father?"

"That is his affair, aunt Sophie; not yours."

"His affair! It is his affair, and my affair, and all our affairs. Impudent girl!--brazen-faced, impudent, bad girl! Do you not know that you would bring disgrace upon us all?"

"You are thinking about yourself, aunt Sophie; and I must think for myself."

"You do not regard your father, then?"

"Yes, I do regard my father. He knows that I regard him. Father, is it true that I do not regard you?"

"She is a good daughter," said the father.

"A good daughter, and talk of marrying a Jew!" said Madame Zamenoy. "Has she your permission for such a marriage? Tell me that at once, Josef, that I may know. Has she your sanction for--for--for this accursed abomination?" Then there was silence in the room for a few moments. "You can at any rate answer a plain question, Josef," continued Madame Zamenoy. "Has Nina your leave to betroth herself to the Jew, Trendellsohn?"

"No, I have not got his leave," said Nina.

"I am speaking to your father, miss," said the enraged aunt.

"Yes; you are speaking very roughly to father, and he is ill. Therefore I answer for him."

"And has he not forbidden you to think of marrying this Jew?"

"No, he has not," said Nina.

"Josef, answer for yourself like a man," said Madame Zamenoy. "Have you not forbidden this marriage? Do you not forbid it now? Let me at any rate hear you say that you have forbidden it." But Balatka found silence to be his easiest course, and answered not at all. "What am I to think of this?" continued Madame Zamenoy. "It cannot be that you wish your child to be the wife of a Jew!"

"You are to think, aunt Sophie, that father is ill, and that he cannot stand against your violence."

"Violence, you wicked girl! It is you that are violent."

"Will you come out into the parlor, aunt?"

"No, I will not come out into the parlor. I will not stir from this spot till I have told your father all that I think about it. Ill, indeed! What matters illness when it is a question of eternal damnation!" Madame Zamenoy put so much stress upon the latter word that her brother-in-law almost jumped from under the bed-clothes. Nina raised herself, as she was standing, to her full height, and a smile of derision came upon her face. "Oh, yes! I daresay you do not mind it," said Madame Zamenoy. "I daresay you can laugh now at all the pains of hell. Castaways such as you are always blind to their own danger; but your father, I hope, has not fallen so far as to care nothing for his religion, though he seems to have forgotten what is due to his family."

"I have forgotten nothing," said old Balatka.

"Why then do you not forbid her to do this thing?" demanded Madame Zamenoy. But the old man had recognized too well the comparative security of silence to be drawn into argument, and therefore merely hid himself more completely among the clothes. "Am I to get no answer from you, Josef?" said Madame Zamenoy. No answer came, and therefore she was driven to turn again upon Nina.

"Why are you doing this thing, you poor deluded creature? Is it the man's money that tempts you?"

"It is not the man's money. If money could tempt me, I could have it elsewhere, as you know."

"It cannot be love for such a man as that. Do you not know that he and his father between them have robbed your father of everything?"

"I know nothing of the kind."

"They have; and he is now making a fool of you in order that he may get whatever remains."

"Nothing remains. He will get nothing."

"Nor will you. I do not believe that after all he will ever marry you. He will not be such a fool."

"Perhaps not, aunt; and in that case you will have your wish."

"But no one can ever speak to you again after such a condition. Do you think that I or your uncle could have you at our house when all the world shall know that you have been jilted by a Jew?"

"I will not trouble you by going to your house."

"And is that all the satisfaction I am to have?"

"What do you want me to say?"

I want you to say that you will give this man up, and return to your duty as a Christian."

"I will never give him up--never. I would sooner die."

"Very well. Then I shall know how to act. You will not be a bit nearer marrying him; I can promise you that. You are mistaken if you think that in such a matter as this a girl like you can do just as she pleases." Then she turned again upon the poor man in bed. "Josef Balatka, I am ashamed of you. I am indeed--I am ashamed of you."

"Aunt Sophie," said Nina, "now that you are here, you can say what you please to me; but you might as well spare father."

"I will not spare him. I am ashamed of him--thoroughly ashamed of him. What can I think of him when he will lie there and not say a word to save his daughter from the machinations of a filthy Jew?"

"Anton Trendellsohn is not a filthy Jew."

"He is a robber. He has cheated your father out of everything."

"He is no robber. He has cheated no one. I know who has cheated father, if you come to that."

"Whom do you mean, hussey?"

"I shall not answer you; but you need not tell me any more about the Jews cheating us. Christians can cheat as well as Jews, and can rob from their own flesh and blood too. I do not care for your threats, aunt Sophie, nor for your frowns. I did care for them, but you have said that which makes it impossible that I should regard them any further."

"And this is what I get for all my trouble--for all your uncle's generosity!" Again Nina smiled. "But I suppose the Jew gives more than we have given, and therefore is preferred. You poor creature--poor wretched creature!"

During all this time Balatka remained silent; and at last, after very much more scolding, in which Madame Zamenoy urged again and again the terrible threat of eternal punishment, she prepared herself for going. "Lotta Luxa," she said, "--where is Lotta Luxa?" She opened the door, and found Lotta Luxa seated demurely by the window. "Lotta," she said, "I shall go now, and shall never come back to this unfortunate house. You hear what I say; I shall never return here. As she makes her bed, so must she lie on it. It is her own doing, and no one can save her. For my part, I think that the Jew has bewitched her."

"Like enough," said Lotta.

"When once we stray from the Holy Church, there is no knowing what terrible evils may come upon us," said Madame Zamenoy.

"No indeed, ma'am," said Lotta Luxa.

"But I have done all in my power."

"That you have, ma'am."

"I feel quite sure, Lotta, that the Jew will never marry her. Why should a man like that, who loves money better than his soul, marry a girl who has not a kreutzer to bless herself?"

"Why indeed, ma'am! It's my mind that he don't think of marrying her."

"And, Jew as he is, he cares for his religion. He will not bring trouble upon everybody belonging to him by taking a Christian for his wife."

"That he will not, ma'am, you may be sure," said Lotta.

"And where will she be then? Only fancy, Lotta--to have been jilted by a Jew!" Then Madame Zamenoy, without addressing herself directly to Nina, walked out of the room; but as she did so she paused in the doorway, and again spoke to Lotta. "To be jilted by a Jew, Lotta! Think of that."

"I should drown myself," said Lotta Luxa. And then they both were gone.

The idea that the Jew might jilt her disturbed Nina more than all her aunt's anger, or than any threats as to the penalties she might have to encounter in the next world. She felt a certain delight, an inward satisfaction, in giving up everything for her Jew lover--a satisfaction which was the more intense, the more absolute was the rejection and the more crushing the scorn which she encountered on his behalf from her own people. But to encounter this rejection and scorn, and then to be thrown over by the Jew, was more than she could endure. And would it, could it, be so? She sat down to think of it; and as she thought of it terrible fears came upon her. Old Trendellsohn had told her that such a marriage on his son's part would bring him into great trouble; and old Trendellsohn was not harsh with her as her aunt was harsh. The old man, in his own communications with her, had always been kind and forbearing.

And then Anton himself was severe to her. Though he would now and again say some dear, well-to-be-remembered happy word, as when he told her that she was his sun, and that he looked to her for warmth and light, such soft speakings were few with him and far between. And then he never mentioned any time as the probable date of their marriage. If only a time could be fixed, let it be ever so distant, Nina thought that she could still endure all the cutting taunts of her enemies. But what would she do if Anton were to announce to her some day that he found himself, as a Jew, unable to marry with her as a Christian? In such a case she thought that she must drown herself, as Lotta had suggested to her.

As she sat thinking of this, her eyes suddenly fell upon the one key which she herself possessed, and which, with a woman's acuteness of memory, she perceived to have been moved from the spot on which she had left it. It was the key of the little desk which stood in the corner of the parlor, and in which, on the top of all the papers, was deposited the necklace with which she intended to relieve the immediate necessities of their household. She at once remembered that Lotta had been left for a long time in the room, and with anxious, quick suspicion she went to the desk. But her suspicions had wronged Lotta. There, lying on a bundle of letters, was the necklace, in the exact position in which she had left it. She kissed the trinket, which had come to her from her mother, replaced it carefully, and put the key into her pocket.

What should she do next? How should she conduct herself in her present circumstances? Her heart prompted her to go off at once to Anton Trendellsohn and tell him everything; but she greatly feared that Anton would not be glad to see her. She knew that it was not well that a girl should run after her lover; but yet how was she to live without seeing him? What other comfort had she? and from whom else could she look for guidance? She declared to herself at last that she, in her position, would not be stayed by ordinary feelings of maiden reserve. She would tell him everything, even to the threat on which her aunt had so much depended, and would then ask him for his counsel. She would describe to him, if words from her could describe them, all her difficulties, and would promise to be guided by him absolutely in everything. "Everything," she would say to him, "I have given up for you. I am yours entirely, body and soul. Do with me as you will." If he should then tell her that he would not have her, that he did not want the sacrifice, she would go away from him--and drown herself. But she would not go to him today--no, not today; not perhaps tomorrow. It was but a day or two as yet since she had been over at the Trendellsohns' house, and though on that occasion she had not seen Anton, Anton of course would know that she had been there. She did not wish him to think that she was hunting him. She would wait yet two or three days-- till the next Sunday morning perhaps--and then she would go again to the Jews' quarter. On the Christian Sabbath Anton was always at home, as on that day business is suspended in Prague both for Christian and Jew.

Then she went back to her father. He was still lying with his face turned to the wall, and Nina, thinking that he slept, took up her work and sat by his side. But he was awake, and watching. "Is she gone?" he said, before her needle had been plied a dozen times.

"Aunt Sophie? Yes, father, she has gone."

"I hope she will not come again."

"She says that she will never come again."

"What is the use of her coming here? We are lost and are perishing. We are utterly gone. She will not help us, and why should she disturb us with her curses?"

"Father, there may be better days for us yet."

"How can there be better days when you are bringing down the Jew upon us? Better days for yourself, perhaps, if mere eating and drinking will serve you."

"Oh, father!"

"Have you not ruined everything with your Jew lover? Did you not hear how I was treated? What could I say to your aunt when she stood there and reviled us?"

"Father, I was so grateful to you for saying nothing!"

"But I knew that she was right. A Christian should not marry a Jew. She said it was abominable; and so it is."

"Father, father, do not speak like that! I thought that you had forgiven me. You said to aunt Sophie that I was a good daughter. Will you not say the same to me--to me myself?"

"It is not good to love a Jew."

"I do love him, father. How can I help it now? I cannot change my heart."

"I suppose I shall be dead soon," said old Balatka, "and then it will not matter. You will become one of them, and I shall be forgotten."

"Father, have I ever forgotten you?" said Nina, throwing herself upon him on his bed. "Have I not always loved you? Have I not been good to you? Oh, father, we have been true to each other through it all. Do not speak to me like that at last."

Chapter 6

Anton Trendellsohn had learned from his father that Nina had spoken to her aunt about the title-deeds of the houses in the Kleinseite, and that thus, in a roundabout way, a demand had been made for them. "Of course, they will not give them up," he had said to his father. "Why should they, unless the law makes them? They have no idea of honor or honesty to one of us." The elder Jew had then expressed his opinion that Josef Balatka should be required to make the demand as a matter of business, to enforce a legal right; but to this Anton had replied that the old man in the Kleinseite was not in a condition to act efficiently in the matter himself. It was to him that the money had been advanced, but to the Zamenoys that it had in truth been paid; and Anton declared his purpose of going to Karil Zamenoy and himself making his demand. And then there had been a discussion, almost amounting to a quarrel, between the two Trendellsohns as to Nina Balatka. Poor Nina need not have added another to her many causes of suffering by doubting her lover's truth. Anton Trendellsohn, though not given to speak of his love with that demonstrative vehemence to which Nina had trusted in her attempts to make her friends understand that she could not be talked out of her engagement, was nevertheless sufficiently firm in his purpose. He was a man very constant in all his purposes, whom none who knew him would have supposed likely to jeopardize his worldly interests for the love of a Christian girl, but who was very little apt to abandon aught to which he had set his hand because the voices of those around him might be against him. He had thought much of his position as a Jew before he had spoken of love to the penniless Christian maiden who frequented his father's house, pleading for her father in his poverty; but the words when spoken meant much, and Nina need not have feared that he would forget them. He was a man not much given to dalliance, not requiring from day to day the soft sweetness of a woman's presence to keep his love warm; but his love could maintain its own heat, without any softness or dalliance. Had it not been so, such a girl as Nina would hardly have surrendered to him her whole heart as she had done.

"You will fall into trouble about the maiden," the elder Trendellsohn had said.

"True, father; there will be trouble enough. In what that we do is there not trouble?"

"A man in the business of his life must encounter labor and grief and disappointment. He should take to him a wife to give him ease in these things, not one who will be an increase to his sorrows."

"That which is done is done."

"My son, this thing is not done."

"She has my plighted word, father. Is not that enough?"

"Nina is a good girl. I will say for her that she is very good. I have wished that you might have brought to my house as your wife the child of my old friend Baltazar Loth; but if that may not be, I would have taken Nina willingly by the hand--had she been one of us."

"It may be that God will open her eyes."

"Anton, I would not have her eyes opened by anything so weak as her love for a man. But I have said that she was good. She will hear reason; and when she shall know that her marriage among us would bring trouble on us, she will restrain her wishes. Speak to her, Anton, and see if it be not so."

"Not for all the wealth which all our people own in Bohemia! Father, to do so would be to demand, not to ask. If she love me, could she refuse such a request were I to ask it?"

"I will speak a word to Nina, my son, and the request shall come from her."

"And if it does, I will never yield to it. For her sake I would not yield, for I know she loves me. Neither for my own would I yield; for as truly as I worship God, I love her better than all the world beside. She is to me my cup of water when I am hot and athirst, my morsel of bread when I am faint with hunger. Her voice is the only music which I love. The touch of her hand is so fresh that it cools me when I am in fever. The kiss of her lips is so sweet and balmy that it cures when I shake with an ague fit. To think of her when I am out among men fighting for my own, is such a joy, that now, methinks now, that I have had it belonging to me, I could no longer fight were I to lose it. No. father; she shall not be taken from me. I love her, and I will keep her."

Oh that Nina could have heard him! How would all her sorrows have fled from her, and left her happy in her poverty! But Anton Trendellsohn, though he could speak after this manner to his father, could hardly bring himself to talk of his feelings to the woman who would have given her eyes, could she for his sake have spared them, to hear him. Now and again, indeed, he would say a word, and then would frown and become gloomy, as though angry with himself for such outward womanly expression of what he felt. As it was, the words fell upon ears which they delighted not. "Then, my son, you will live to rue the day in which you first saw her," said the elder Jew. "She will be a bone of contention in your way that will separate you from all your friends. You will become neither Jew nor Christian, and will be odious alike to both. And she will be the same."

"Then, father, we will bear our sorrows together."

"Yes; and what happens when sorrows come from such causes? The man learns to hate the woman who has caused them, and ill-uses her, and feels himself to be a Cain upon the earth, condemned by all, but by none so much as by himself. Do you think that you have strength to bear the contempt of all those around you?"

Anton waited a moment or two before he answered, and then spoke very slowly. "If it be necessary to bear so much, I will at least make the effort. It may be that I shall find the strength."

"Nothing then that your father says to you avails aught?"

"Nothing, father, on that matter. You should have spoken sooner."

"Then you must go your own way. As for me, I must look for another son to bear the burden of my years." And so they parted.

Anton Trendellsohn understood well the meaning of the old man's threat. He was quite alive to the fact that his father had expressed his intention to give his wealth and his standing in trade and the business of his house to some younger Jew, who would be more true than his own son to the traditional customs of their tribes. There was Ruth Jacobi, his granddaughter--the only child of the house--who had already reached an age at which she might be betrothed; and there was Samuel Loth, the son of Baltazar Loth, old Trendellsohn's oldest friend. Anton Trendellsohn did not doubt who might be the adopted child to be taken to fill his place. It has been already explained that there was no partnership actually existing between the two Trendellsohns. By degrees the son had slipt into the father's place, and the business by which the house had grown rich had for the last five or six years been managed chiefly by him. But the actual results of the son's industry and the son's thrift were still in the possession of the father. The old man might no doubt go far towards ruining his son if he were so minded.

Dreams of a high ambition had, from very early years, flitted across the mind of the younger Trendellsohn till they had nearly formed themselves into a settled purpose. He had heard of Jews in Vienna, in Paris, and in London, who were as true to their religion as any Jew of Prague, but who did not live immured in a Jews' quarter, like lepers separate and alone in some loathed corner of a city otherwise clean. These men went abroad into the world as men, using the wealth with which their industry had been blessed, openly as the Christians used it. And they lived among Christians as one man should live with his fellow-men--on equal terms, giving and taking, honoring and honored. As yet it was not so with the Jews of Prague, who were still bound to their old narrow streets, to their dark houses, to their mean modes of living, and who, worst of all, were still subject to the isolated ignominy of Judaism. In Prague a Jew was still a Pariah. Anton's father was rich--very rich. Anton hardly knew what was the extent of his father's wealth, but he did know that it was great. In his father's time, however, no change could be made. He did not scruple to speak to the old man of these things; but he spoke of them rather as dreams, or as distant hopes, than as being the basis of any purpose of his own. His father would merely say that the old house, looking out upon the ancient synagogue, must last him his time, and that the changes of which Anton spoke must be postponed--not till he died--but till such time as he should feel it right to give up the things of this world. Anton Trendellsohn, who knew his father well, had resolved that he would wait patiently for everything till his father should have gone to his last home, knowing that nothing but death would close the old man's interest in the work of his life. But he had been content to wait--to wait, to think, to dream, and only in part to hope. He still communed with himself daily as to that House of Trendellsohn which might, perhaps, be heard of in cities greater than Prague, and which might rival in the grandeur of its wealth those mighty commercial names which had drowned the old shame of the Jew in the new glory of their great doings. To be a Jew in London, they had told him, was almost better than to be a Christian, provided that he was rich, and knew the ways of trade--was better for such purposes as were his purposes. Anton Trendellsohn believed that he would be rich, and was sure that he knew the ways of trade; and therefore he nursed his ambition, and meditated what his action should be when the days of his freedom should come to him.

Then Nina Balatka had come across his path. To be a Jew, always a Jew, in all things a Jew, had been ever a part of his great dream. It was as impossible to him as it would be to his father to forswear the religion of his people. To go forth and be great in commerce by deserting his creed would have been nothing to him. His ambition did not desire wealth so much as the possession of wealth in Jewish hands, without those restrictions upon its enjoyment to which Jews under his own eye had ever been subjected. It would have delighted him to think that, by means of his work, there should no longer be a Jews' quarter in Prague, but that all Prague should be ennobled and civilized and made beautiful by the wealth of Jews. Wealth must be his means, and therefore he was greedy; but wealth was not his last or only aim, and therefore his greed did not utterly destroy his heart. Then Nina Balatka had come across his path, and he was compelled to shape his dreams anew. How could a Jew among Jews hold up his head as such who had taken to his bosom a Christian wife?

But again he shaped his dreams aright--so far aright that he could still build the castles of his imagination to his own liking. Nina should be his wife. It might be that she would follow the creed of her husband, and then all would be well. In those far cities to which he would go, it would hardly in such case be known that she had been born a Christian; or else he would show the world around him, both Jews and Christians, how well a Christian and a Jew might live together. To crush the prejudice which had dealt so hardly with his people--to make a Jew equal in all things to a Christian--this was his desire; and how could this better be fulfilled than by his union with a Christian? One thing at least was fixed with him--one thing was fixed, even though it should mar his dreams. He had taken the Christian girl to be part of himself, and nothing should separate them. His father had spoken often to him of the danger which he would incur by marrying a Christian, but had never before uttered any word approaching to a personal threat. Anton had felt himself to be so completely the mainspring of the business in which they were both engaged--was so perfectly aware that he was so regarded by all the commercial men of Prague--that he had hardly regarded the absence of any positive possession in his father's wealth as detrimental to him. He had been willing that it should be his father's while his father lived, knowing that any division would be detrimental to them both. He had never even asked his father for a partnership, taking everything for granted. Even now he could not quite believe that his father was in earnest. It could hardly be possible that the work of his own hands should be taken from him because he had chosen a bride for himself! But this he felt, that should his father persevere in the intention which he had expressed, he would be upheld in it by every Jew of Prague. "Dark, ignorant, and foolish," Anton said to himself, speaking of those among whom he lived; "it is their pride to live in disgrace, while all the honors of the world are open to them if they chose to take them!"

He did not for a moment think of altering his course of action in consequence of what his father had said to him. Indeed, as regarded the business of the house, it would stand still altogether were he to alter it. No successor could take up the work when he should leave it. No other hand could continue the webs which were of his weaving. So he went forth, as the errands of the day called him, soon after his father's last words were spoken, and went through his work as though his own interest in it were in no danger.

On that evening nothing was said on the subject between him and his father, and on the next morning he started immediately after breakfast for the Ross Markt, in order that he might see Karil Zamenoy, as he had said that he would do. The papers, should he get them, would belong to his father, and would at once be put into his father's hands. But the feeling that it might not be for his own personal advantage to place them there did not deter him. His father was an old man, and old men were given to threaten. He at least would go on with his duty.

It was about eleven o'clock in the day when he entered the open door of the office in the Ross Markt, and found Ziska and a young clerk sitting opposite to each other at their desks. Anton took off his hat and bowed to Ziska, whom he knew slightly, and asked the young man if his father were within.

"My father is here," said Ziska, "but I do not know whether he can see you."

"You will ask him, perhaps," said Trendellsohn.

"Well, he is engaged. There is a lady with him."

"Perhaps he will make an appointment with me, and I will call again. If he will name an hour, I will come at his own time."

"Cannot you say to me, Herr Trendellsohn, that which you wish to say to him?"

"Not very well."

"You know that I am in partnership with my father."

"He and you are happy to be so placed together. But if your father can spare me five minutes, I will take it from him as a favor."

Then, with apparent reluctance, Ziska came down from his seat and went into the inner room. There he remained some time, while Trendellsohn was standing, hat in hand, in the outer office. If the changes which he hoped to effect among his brethren could be made, a Jew in Prague should, before long, be asked to sit down as readily as a Christian. But he had not been asked to sit, and he therefore stood holding his hat in his hand during the ten minutes that Ziska was away. At last young Zamenoy returned, and, opening the door, signified to the Jew that his father would see him at once if he would enter. Nothing more had been said about the lady, and there, when Trendellsohn went into the room, he found the lady, who was no other than Madame Zamenoy herself. A little family council had been held, and it had been settled among them that the Jew should be seen and heard.

"So, sir, you are Anton Trendellsohn," began Madame Zamenoy, as soon as Ziska was gone--for Ziska had been told to go--and the door was shut.

"Yes, madame; I am Anton Trendellsohn. I had not expected the honor of seeing you, but I wish to say a few words on business to your husband."

"There he is; you can speak to him."

"Anything that I can do, I shall be very happy," said Karil Zamenoy, who had risen from his chair to prevent the necessity of having to ask the Jew to sit down.

"Herr Zamenoy," began the Jew, "you are, I think, aware that my father has purchased from your friend and brother-in-law, Josef Balatka, certain houses in the Kleinseite, in one of which the old man still lives."

"Upon my word, I know nothing about it," said Zamenoy--"nothing, that is to say, in the way of business;" and the man of business laughed. "Mind I do not at all deny that you did so--you or your father, or the two together. Your people are getting into their hands lots of houses all over the town; but how they do it nobody knows. They are not bought in fair open market."

"This purchase was made by contract, and the price was paid in full before the houses were put into our hands."

"They are not in your hands now, as far as I know."

"Not the one, certainly, in which Balatka lives. Motives of friendship--"

"Friendship!" said Madame Zamenoy, with a sneer.

"And now motives of love," continued Anton, "have induced us to leave the use of that house with Josef Balatka."

"Love!" said Madame Zamenoy, springing from her chair; love indeed! Do not talk to me of love for a Jew."

"My dear, my dear!" said her husband, expostulating.

"How dares he come here to talk of his love? It is filthy--it is worse than filthy--it is profane."

"I came here, madame," continued Anton, "not to talk of my love, but of certain documents or title-deeds respecting those houses, which should be at present in my father's custody. I am told that your husband has them in his safe custody."

"My husband has them not," said Madame Zamenoy.

"Stop, my dear--stop," said the husband.

"Not that he would be bound to give them up to you if he had got them, or that he would do so; but he has them not."

"In whose hands are they then?"

"That is for you to find out, not for us to tell you."

"Why should not all the world be told, so that the proper owner may have his own?"

"It is not always so easy to find out who is the proper owner," said Zamenoy the elder.

"You have seen this contract before, I think, said Trendellsohn, bringing forth a written paper.

"I will not look at it now at any rate. I have nothing to do with it, and I will have nothing to do with it. You have heard Madame Zamenoy declare that the deed which you seek is not here. I cannot say whether it is here or no. I do not say--as you will be pleased to remember. If it were here it would be in safe keeping for my brother-in-law, and only to him could it be given."

"But will you not say whether it is in your hands? You know well that Josef Balatka is ill, and cannot attend to such matters."

"And who has made him ill, and what has made him ill?" said Madame Zamenoy. "Ill! of course he is ill. Is it not enough to make any man ill to be told that his daughter is to marry a Jew?"

"I have not come hither to speak of that," said Trendellsohn.

"But I speak of it; and I tell you this, Anton Trendellsohn--you shall never marry that girl."

"Be it so; but let me at any rate have that which is my own."

"Will you give her up if it is given to you?"

"It is here then?"

"No; it is not here. But will you abandon this mad thought if I tell you where it is?"

"No; certainly not."

"What a fool the man is!" said Madame Zamenoy. "He comes to us for what he calls his property because he wants to marry the girl, and she is deceiving him all the while. Go to Nina Balatka, Trendellsohn, and she will tell you who has the document. She will tell you where it is, if it suits her to do so."

"She has told me, and she knows that it is here."

"She knows nothing of the kind, and she has lied. She has lied in order that she may rob you. Jew as you are, she will be too many for you. She will rob you, with all her seeming simplicity."

"I trust her as I do my own soul," said Trendellsohn.

"Very well; I tell you that she, and she only, knows where these papers are. For aught I know, she has them herself. I believe that she has them. Ziska," said Madame Zamenoy, calling aloud--"Ziska, come hither;" and Ziska entered the room. "Ziska, who has the title-deeds of your uncle's houses in the Kleinseite?" Ziska hesitated a moment without answering. "You know, if anybody does," said his mother; "tell this man, since he is so anxious, who has got them."

"I do not know why I should tell him my cousin's secrets."

"Tell him, I say. It is well that he should know."

"Nina has them, as I believe," said Ziska, still hesitating.

"Nina has them!" said Trendellsohn.

"Yes; Nina Balatka," said Madame Zamenoy. "We tell you, to the best of our knowledge at least. At any rate, they are not here."

"It is impossible that Nina should have them," said Trendellsohn. "How should she have got them?"

"That is nothing to us," said Madame Zamenoy. "The whole thing is nothing to us. You have heard all that we can tell you, and you had better go."

"You have heard more than I would have told you myself," said Ziska, "had I been left to my opinion."

Trendellsohn stood pausing for a moment, and then he turned to the elder Zamenoy. "What do you say, sir? Is it true that these papers are at the house in the Kleinseite?"

"I say nothing," said Karil Zamenoy. "It seems to me that too much has been said already."

"A great deal too much," said the lady. "I do not know why I should have allowed myself to be surprised into giving you any information at all. You wish to do us the heaviest injury that one man can do another, and I do not know why we should speak to you at all. Now you had better go."

"Yes; you had better go," said Ziska, holding the door open, and looking as though he were inclined to threaten. Trendellsohn paused for a moment on the threshold, fixing his eyes full upon those of his rival; but Ziska neither spoke nor made any further gesture, and then the Jew left the house.

"I would have told him nothing," said the elder Zamenoy when they were left alone.

"My dear, you don't understand; indeed you do not," said his wife. "No stone should be left unturned to prevent such a horrid marriage as this. There is nothing I would not say--nothing I would not do."

"But I do not see that you are doing anything."

"Leave this little thing to me, my dear--to me and Ziska. It is impossible that you should do everything yourself. In such a matter as this, believe me that a woman is best."

"But I hate anything that is really dishonest."

"There shall be no dishonesty--none in the world. You don't suppose that I want to get the dirty old tumble-down houses. God forbid! But you would not give up everything to a Jew! Oh, I hate them! I do hate them! Anything is fair against a Jew." If such was Madame Zamenoy's ordinary doctrine, it may well be understood that she would scruple at using no weapon against a Jew who was meditating so great an injury against her as this marriage with her niece. After this little discussion old Zamenoy said no more, and Madame Zamenoy went home to the Windberg-gasse.

Trendellsohn, as he walked homewards, was lost in amazement. He wholly disbelieved the statement that the document he desired was in Nina's hands, but he thought it possible that it might be in the house in the Kleinseite. It was, after all, on the cards that old Balatka was deceiving him. The Jew was by nature suspicious, though he was also generous. He could be noble in his confidence, and at the same time could become at a moment distrustful. He could give without grudging, and yet grudge the benefits which came of his giving. Neither he nor his father had ever positively known in whose custody were the title- deeds which he was so anxious to get into his own hands. Balatka had said that they must be with the Zamenoys, but even Balatka had never spoken as of absolute knowledge. Nina, indeed, had declared positively that they were in the Ross Markt, saying that Ziska had so stated in direct terms; but there might be a mistake in this. At any rate he would interrogate Nina, and if there were need, would not spare the old man any questions that could lead to the truth. Trendellsohn, as he thought of the possibility of such treachery on Balatka's part, felt that, without compunction, he could be very cruel, even to an old man, under such circumstances as those.

Chapter 7

Madame Zamenoy and her son no doubt understood each other's purposes, and there was another person in the house who understood them--Lotta Luxa, namely; but Karil Zamenoy had been kept somewhat in the dark. Touching that piece of parchment as to which so much anxiety had been expressed, he only knew that he had, at his wife's instigation, given it into her hand in order that she might use it in some way for putting an end to the foul betrothal between Nina and the Jew. The elder Zamenoy no doubt understood that Anton Trendellsohn was to be bought off by the document; and he was not unwilling to buy him off so cheaply, knowing as he did that the houses were in truth the Jew's property; but Madame Zamenoy's scheme was deeper than this. She did not believe that the Jew was to be bought off at so cheap a price; but she did believe that it might be possible to create such a feeling in his mind as would make him abandon Nina out of the workings of his own heart. Ziska and his mother were equally anxious to save Nina from the Jew, but not exactly with the same motives. He had received a promise, both from his father and mother, before anything was known of the Jew's love, that Nina should be received as a daughter-in-law, if she would accept his suit; and this promise was still in force. That the girl whom he loved should love a Jew distressed and disgusted Ziska; but it did not deter him from his old purpose. It was shocking, very shocking, that Nina should so disgrace herself; but she was not on that account less pretty or less charming in her cousin's eyes. Madame Zamenoy, could she have had her own will, would have rescued Nina from the Jew-- firstly, because Nina was known all over Prague to be her niece--and, secondly, for the good of Christianity generally; but the girl herself, when rescued, she would willingly have left to starve in the poverty of the old house in the Kleinseite, as a punishment for her sin in having listened to a Jew.

"I would have nothing more to say to her," said the mother to her son.

"Nor I either," said Lotta, who was present. "She has demeaned herself far too much to be a fit wife for Ziska."

"Hold your tongue, Lotta; what business have you to speak about such a matter?" said the young man.

"All the same, Ziska, if I were you, I would give her up," said the mother.

"If you were me, mother, you would not give her up. If every man is to give up the girl he likes because somebody else interferes with him, how is anybody to get married at all? It's the way with them all."

"But a Jew, Ziska!"

"So much the more reason for taking her away from him." Then Ziska went forth on a certain errand, the expediency of which he had discussed with his mother.

"I never thought he'd be so firm about it, ma'am," said Lotta to her mistress.

"If we could get Trendellsohn to turn her off, he would not think much of her afterwards," said the mother. "He wouldn't care to take the Jew's leavings."

"But he seems to be so obstinate," said Lotta. "Indeed I did not think there was so much obstinacy in him."

"Of course he is obstinate while he thinks the other man is to have her," said the mistress; "but all that will be changed when the girl is alone in the world."

It was a Saturday morning, and Ziska had gone out with a certain fixed object. Much had been said between him and his mother since Anton Trendellsohn's visit to the office, and it had been decided that he should now go and see the Jew in his own home. He should see him and speak him fair, and make him understand if possible that the whole question of the property should be settled as he wished it--if he would only give up his insane purpose of marrying a Christian girl. Ziska would endeavor also to fill the Jew's mind with suspicion against Nina. The former scheme was Ziska's own; the second was that in which Ziska's mother put her chief trust. "If once he can be made to think that the girl is deceiving him, he will quarrel with her utterly," Madame Zamenoy had said.

On Saturday there is but little business done in Prague, because Saturday is the Sabbath of the Jews. The shops are of course open in the main streets of the town, but banks and counting-houses are closed, because the Jews will not do business on that day--so great is the preponderance of the wealth of Prague in the hands of that people! It suited Ziska, therefore, to make his visit on a Saturday, both because he had but little himself to do on that day, and because he would be almost sure to find Trendellsohn at home. As he made his way across the bottom of the Kalowrat-strasse and through the centre of the city to the narrow ways of the Jews' quarter, his heart somewhat misgave him as to the result of his visit. He knew very well that a Christian was safe among the Jews from any personal ill-usage; but he knew also that such a one as he would be known personally to many of them as a Christian rival, and probably as a Christian enemy in the same city, and he thought that they would look at him askance. Living in Prague all his life, he had hardly been above once or twice in the narrow streets which he was now threading. Strangers who come to Prague visit the Jews' quarter as a matter of course, and to such strangers the Jews of Prague are invariably courteous. But the Christians of the city seldom walk through the heart of the Jews' locality, or hang about the Jews' synagogue, or are seen among their houses unless they have special business. The Jews' quarter, though it is a banishment to the Jews from the fairer portions of the city, is also a separate and somewhat sacred castle in which they may live after their old fashion undisturbed. As Ziska went on, he became aware that the throng of people was unusually great, and that the day was in some sort more peculiar than the ordinary Jewish Sabbath. That the young men and girls should be dressed in their best clothes was, as a matter of course, incidental to the day; but he could perceive that there was an outward appearance of gala festivity about them which could not take place every week. The tall bright-eyed black-haired girls stood talking in the streets, with something of boldness in their gait and bearing, dressed many of them in white muslin, with bright ribbons and full petticoats, and that small bewitching Hungarian hat which they delight to wear. They stood talking somewhat loudly to each other, or sat at the open windows; while the young men in black frock-coats and black hats, with crimson cravats, clustered by themselves, wishing, but not daring so early in the day, to devote themselves to the girls, who appeared, or attempted to appear, unaware of their presence. Who can say why it is that those encounters, which are so ardently desired by both sides, are so rarely able to get themselves commenced till the enemies have been long in sight of each other? But so it is among Jews and Christians, among rich and poor, out under the open sky, and even in the atmosphere of the ball-room, consecrated though it be to such purposes. Go into any public dancing-room of Vienna, where the girls from the shops and the young men from their desks congregate to waltz and make love, and you shall observe that from ten to twelve they will dance as vigorously as at a later hour, but that they will hardly talk to each other till the mellowness of the small morning hours has come upon them.

Among these groups in the Jewish quarter Ziska made his way, conscious that the girls eyed him and whispered to each other something as to his presence, and conscious also that the young men eyed him also, though they did so without speaking of him as he passed. He knew that Trendellsohn lived close to the synagogue, and to the synagogue he made his way. And as he approached the narrow door of the Jews' church, he saw that a crowd of men stood round it, some in high caps and some in black hats, but all habited in short muslin shirts, which they wore over their coats. Such dresses he had seen before, and he knew that these men were taking part from time to time in some service within the synagogue. He did not dare to ask of one of them which was Trendellsohn's house, but went on till he met an old man alone just at the back of the building, dressed also in a high cap and shirt, which shirt, however, was longer than those he had seen before. Plucking up his courage, he asked of the old man which was the house of Anton Trendellsohn.

"Anton Trendellsohn has no house," said the old man; "but that is his father's house, and there Anton Trendellsohn lives. I am Stephen Trendellsohn, and Anton is my son."

Ziska thanked him, and, crossing the street to the house, found that the door was open, and that two girls were standing just within the passage. The old man had gone, and Ziska, turning, had perceived that he was out of sight before he reached the house.

"I cannot come till my uncle returns," said the younger girl.

"But, Ruth, he will be in the synagogue all day," said the elder, who was that Rebecca Loth of whom the old Jew had spoken to his son.

"Then all day I must remain," said Ruth; "but it may be he will be in by one." Then Ziska addressed them, and asked if Anton Trendellsohn did not live there.

"Yes; he lives there," said Ruth, almost trembling, as she answered the handsome stranger.

"And is he at home?"

"He is in the synagogue," said Ruth. "You will find him there if you will go in."

"But they are at worship there," said Ziska, doubtingly.

"They will be at worship all day, because it is our festival," said Rebecca, with her eyes fixed upon the ground; "but if you are a Christian they will not object to your going in. They like that Christians should see them. They are not ashamed."

Ziska, looking into the girl's face, saw that she was very beautiful; and he saw also at once that she was exactly the opposite of Nina, though they were both of a height. Nina was fair, with grey eyes, and smooth brown hair which seemed to demand no special admiration, though it did in truth add greatly to the sweet delicacy of her face; and she was soft in her gait, and appeared to be yielding and flexible in all the motions of her body. You would think that if you were permitted to embrace her, the outlines of her body would form themselves to yours, as though she would in all things fit herself to him who might be blessed by her love. But Rebecca Loth was dark, with large dark-blue eyes and jet black tresses, which spoke out loud to the beholder of their own loveliness. You could not fail to think of her hair and of her eyes, as though they were things almost separate from herself. And she stood like a queen, who knew herself to be all a queen, strong on her limbs, wanting no support, somewhat hard withal, with a repellant beauty that seemed to disdain while it courted admiration, and utterly rejected the idea of that caressing assistance which men always love to give, and which women often love to receive. At the present moment she was dressed in a frock of white muslin, looped round the skirt, and bright with ruby ribbons. She had on her feet colored boots, which fitted them to a marvel, and on her glossy hair a small new hat, ornamented with the plumage of some strange bird. On her shoulders she wore a colored jacket, open down the front, sparkling with jeweled buttons, over which there hung a chain with a locket. In her ears she carried long heavy earrings of gold. Were it not that Ziska had seen others as gay in their apparel on his way, he would have fancied that she was tricked out for the playing of some special part, and that she should hardly have shown herself in the streets with her gala finery. Such was Rebecca Loth the Jewess, and Ziska almost admitted to himself that she was more beautiful than Nina Balatka.

"And are you also of the family?" Ziska asked.

"No; she is not of the family," said Ruth. "She is my particular friend, Rebecca Loth. She does not live here. She lives with her brother and her mother."

"Ruth, how foolish you are! What does it signify to the gentleman?"

"But he asked, and so I supposed he wanted to know."

"I have to apologize for intruding on you with any questions young ladies," said Ziska; "especially on a day which seems to be solemn."

"That does not matter at all," said Rebecca. "Here is my brother, and he will take you into the synagogue if you wish to see Anton Trendellsohn." Samuel Loth, her brother, then came up and readily offered to take Ziska into the midst of the worshippers. Ziska would have escaped now from the project could he have done so without remark; but he was ashamed to seem afraid to enter the building, as the girls seemed to make so light of his doing so. He therefore followed Rebecca's brother, and in a minute or two was inside the narrow door.

The door was very low and narrow, and seemed to be choked up by men with short white surplices, but nevertheless he found himself inside, jammed among a crowd of Jews; and a sound of many voices, going together in a sing-song wail or dirge, met his ears. His first impulse was to take off his hat, but that was immediately replaced upon his head, he knew not by whom; and then he observed that all within the building were covered. His guide did not follow him, but whispered to some one what it was that the stranger required. He could see that those inside the building were all clothed in muslin shirts of different lengths, and that it was filled with men, all of whom had before them some sort of desk, from which they were reading, or rather wailing out their litany. Though this was the chief synagogue in Prague, and, as being the so-called oldest in Europe, is a building of some consequence in the Jewish world, it was very small. There was no ceiling, and the high-pitched roof, which had once probably been colored, and the walls, which had once certainly been white, were black with the dirt of ages. In the centre there was a cage, as it were, or iron grille, within which five or six old Jews were placed, who seemed to wail louder than the others. Round the walls there was a row of men inside stationary desks, and outside them another row, before each of whom there was a small movable standing desk, on which there was a portion of the law of Moses. There seemed to be no possible way by which Ziska could advance, and he would have been glad to retreat had retreat been possible. But first one Jew and then another moved their desks for him, so that he was forced to advance, and some among them pointed to the spot where Anton Trendellsohn was standing. But as they pointed, and as they moved their desks to make a pathway, they still sang and wailed continuously, never ceasing for an instant in their long, loud, melancholy song of prayer. At the further end there seemed to be some altar, in front of which the High Priest wailed louder than all, louder even than the old men within the cage; and even he, the High Priest, was forced to move his desk to make way for Ziska. But, apparently without displeasure, he moved it with his left hand, while he swayed his right hand backwards and forwards as though regulating the melody of the wail. Beyond the High Priest Ziska saw Anton Trendellsohn, and close to the son he saw the old man whom he had met in the street, and whom he recognized as Anton's father. Old Trendellsohn seemed to take no notice of him, but Anton had watched him from his entrance, and was prepared to speak to him, though he did not discontinue his part in the dirge till the last moment.

"I had a few words to say to you, if it would suit you," said Ziska, in a low voice.

"Are they of import?" Trendellsohn asked. "If so, I will come to you."

Ziska then turned to make his way back, but he saw that this was not to be his road for retreat. Behind him the movable phalanx had again formed itself into close rank, but before him the wailing wearers of the white shirts were preparing for the commotion of his passage by grasping the upright stick of their movable desks in their hands. So he passed on, making the entire round of the synagogue; and when he got outside the crowded door, he found that the younger Trendellsohn had followed him. "We had better go into the house," said Anton; "it will not be well for us to talk here on any matter of business. Will you follow me?"

Then he led the way into the old house, and there at the front door still stood the two girls talking to each other.

"You have come back, uncle," said Ruth.

"Yes; for a few moments, to speak to this gentleman."

"And will you return to the synagogue?"

"Of course I shall return to the synagogue."

"Because Rebecca wishes me to go out with her," said the younger girl, in a plaintive voice.

"You cannot go out now. Your grandfather will want you when he returns."

"But, uncle Anton, he will not come till sunset."

"My mother wished to have Ruth with her this afternoon if it were possible," said Rebecca, hardly looking at Anton as she spoke to him; "but of course if you will not give her leave I must return without her."

"Do you not know, Rebecca," said Anton, "that she is needful to her grandfather?"

"She could be back before sunset."

"I will trust to you, then, that she is brought back." Ruth, as soon as she heard the words, scampered up-stairs to array herself in such finery as she possessed, while Rebecca still stood at the door.

"Will you not come in, Rebecca, while you wait for her?" said Anton.

"Thank you, I will stand here. I am very well here."

"But the child will be ever so long making herself ready. Surely you will come in."

But Rebecca was obstinate, and kept her place at the door. "He has that Christian girl there with him day after day," she said to Ruth as they went away together. "I will never enter the house while she is allowed to come there."

"But Nina is very good," said Ruth.

"I do not care for her goodness."

"Do you not know that she is to be uncle Anton's wife?"

"They have told me so, but she shall be no friend of mine, Ruth. Is it not shameful that he should wish to marry a Christian?"

When the two men had reached the sitting-room in the Jew's house, and Ziska had seated himself, Anton Trendellsohn closed the door, and asked, not quite in anger, but with something of sternness in his voice, why he had been disturbed while engaged in an act of worship.

"They told me that you would not mind my going in to you," said Ziska, deprecating his wrath.

"That depends on your business. What is it that you have to say to me?"

"It is this. When you came to us the other day in the Ross Markt, we were hardly prepared for you. We did not expect you."

"Your mother could hardly have received me better had she expected me for a twelvemonth."

"You cannot be surprised that my mother should be vexed. Besides, you would not be angry with a lady for what she might say."

"I care but little what she says. But words, my friend, are things, and are often things of great moment. All that, however, matters very little. Why have you done us the honor of coming to our house?"

Even Ziska could perceive, though his powers of perception in such matters were perhaps not very great, that the Jew in the Jews' quarter, and the Jew in the Ross Markt, were very different persons. Ziska was now sitting while Anton Trendellsohn was standing over him. Ziska, when he remembered that Anton had not been seated in his father's office-- had not been asked to sit down--would have risen himself, and have stood during the interview, but he did not know how to leave his seat. And when the Jew called him his friend, he felt that the Jew was getting the better of him--was already obtaining the ascendant. "Of course we wish to prevent this marriage," said Ziska, dashing at once at his subject.

"You cannot prevent it. The law allows it. If that is what you have to come to do, you may as well return."

"But listen to me, my friend," said Ziska, taking a leaf out of the Jew's book. "Only listen to me, and then I shall go."

"Speak, then, and I will listen; but be quick."

"You want, of course, to be made right about those houses?"

"My father, to whom they belong, wishes to be made right, as you call it."

"It is all the same thing. Now, look here. The truth is this. Everything shall be settled for you, and the whole thing given up regularly into your hands, if you will only give over about Nina Balatka."

"But I will not give over about Nina Balatka. Am I to be bribed out of my love by an offer of that which is already mine own? But that you are in my father's house, I would be wrathful with you for making me such an offer."

"Why should you seek a Christian wife, with such maidens among you as her whom I saw at the door?"

"Do not mind the maiden whom you saw at the door. She is nothing to you."

"No; she is nothing to me. Of course, the lady is nothing to me. If I were to come here looking for her, you would be angry, and would bid me seek for beauty among my own people. Would you not do so? Answer me now."

"Like enough. Rebecca Loth has many friends who would take her part."

"And why should we not take Nina's part--we who are her friends?"

"Have you taken her part? Have you comforted her when she was in sorrow? Have you wiped her tears when she wept? Have you taken from her the stings of poverty, and striven to make the world to her a pleasant garden? She has no mother of her own. Has yours been a mother to her? Why is it that Nina Balatka has cared to receive the sympathy and the love of a Jew? Ask that girl whom you saw at the door for some corner in her heart, and she will scorn you. She, a Jewess, will scorn you, a Christian. She would so look at you that you would not dare to repeat your prayer. Why is it that Nina has not so scorned me? We are lodged poorly here, while Nina's aunt has a fine house in the New Town. She has a carriage and horses, and the world around her is gay and bright. Why did Nina come to the Jews' quarter for sympathy, seeing that she, too, has friends of her own persuasion? Take Nina's part, indeed! It is too late now for you to take her part. She has chosen for herself, and her resting-place is to be here." Trendellsohn, as he spoke, put his hand upon his breast, within the fold of his waistcoat; but Ziska hardly understood that his doing so had any special meaning. Ziska supposed that the "here" of which the Jew spoke was the old house in which they were at that moment talking to each other.

"I am sure we have meant to be kind to her," said Ziska.

"You see the effect of your kindness. I tell you this only in answer to what you said as to the young woman whom you saw at the door. Have you aught else to say to me? I utterly decline that small matter of traffic which you have proposed to me."

"It was not traffic exactly."

"Very well. What else is there that I can do for you?"

"I hardly know how to go on, as you are so--so hard in all that you say."

"You will not be able to soften me, I fear."

"About the houses--though you say that I am trafficking, I really wish to be honest with you."

"Say what you have to say, then, and be honest."

"I have never seen but one document which conveys the ownership of those houses."

"Let my father, then, have that one document."

"It is in Balatka's house."

"That can hardly be possible," said Trendellsohn.

"As I am a Christian gentleman," said Ziska, "I believe it to be in that house."

"As I am a Jew, sir, fearing God," said the other, "I do not believe it. Who in that house has the charge of it?"

Ziska hesitated before he replied. "Nina, as I think," he said at last. "I suppose Nina has it herself."

"Then she would be a traitor to me."

"What am I to say as to that?" said Ziska, smiling. Trendellsohn came to him and sat down close at his side, looking closely into his face. Ziska would have moved away from the Jew, but the elbow of the sofa did not admit of his receding; and then, while he was thinking that he would escape by rising from his seat, Anton spoke again in a low voice --so low that it was almost a whisper, but the words seemed to fall direct into Ziska's ears, and to hurt him. "What are you to say? You called yourself just now a Christian gentleman. Neither the one name nor the other goes for aught with me. I am neither the one nor the other. But I am a man; and I ask you, as another man, whether it be true that Nina Balatka has that paper in her possession--in her own possession, mind you, I say." Ziska had hesitated before, but his hesitation now was much more palpable. "Why do you not answer me?" continued the Jew. "You have made this accusation against her. Is the accusation true?"

"I think she has it," said Ziska. "Indeed I feel sure of it."

"In her own hands?"

"Oh yes; in her own hands. Of course it must be in her own hands."

"Christian gentleman," said Anton, rising again from his seat, and now standing opposite to Ziska, "I disbelieve you. I think that you are lying to me. Despite your Christianity, and despite your gentility--you are a liar. Now, sir, unless you have anything further to say to me, you may go."

Ziska, when thus addressed, rose of course from his seat. By nature he was not a coward, but he was unready, and knew not what to do or to say on the spur of the moment. "I did not come here to be insulted," he said.

"No; you came to insult me, with two falsehoods in your mouth, either of which proves the other to be a lie. You offer to give me up the deeds on certain conditions, and then tell me that they are with the girl! If she has them, how can you surrender them? I do not know whether so silly a story might prevail between two Christians, but we Jews have been taught among you to be somewhat observant. Sir, it is my belief that the document belonging to my father is in your father's desk in the Ross Markt."

"By heaven, it is in the house in the Kleinseite."

"How could you then have surrendered it?"

"It could have been managed."

It was now the Jew's turn to pause and hesitate. In the general conclusion to which his mind had come, he was not far wrong. He thought that Ziska was endeavoring to deceive him in the spirit of what he said, but that as regarded the letter, the young man was endeavoring to adhere to some fact for the salvation of his conscience as a Christian. If Anton Trendellsohn could but find out in what lay the quibble, the discovery might be very serviceable to him. "It could have been managed--could it?" he said, speaking very slowly. "Between you and her, perhaps."

"Well, yes; between me and Nina--or between some of us," said Ziska.

"And cannot it be managed now?"

"Nina is not one of us now. How can we deal with her?"

"Then I will deal with her myself. I will manage it if it is to be managed. And, sir, if I find that in this matter you have told me the simple truth--not the truth, mind you, as from a gentleman, or the truth as from a Christian, for I suspect both--but the simple truth as from man to man, then I will express my sorrow for the harsh words I have used to you." As he finished speaking, Trendellsohn held the door of the room open in his hand, and Ziska, not being ready with any answer, passed through it and descended the stairs. The Jew followed him and also held open the house door, but did not speak again as Ziska went out. Nor did Ziska say a word, the proper words not being ready to his tongue. The Jew returned at once into the synagogue, having during the interview with Ziska worn the short white surplice in which he had been found; and Ziska returned at once to his own house in the Windberg-gasse.

Chapter 8

Early on the following morning--the morning of the Christian Sunday-- Nina Balatka received a note, a very short note, from her lover the Jew. "Dearest, meet me on the bridge this evening at eight. I will be at your end on the right-hand pathway exactly at eight. Thine, ever and always, A. T." Nina, directly she had read the words, rushed out to the door in order that she might give assurance to the messenger that she would do as she was bidden; but the messenger was gone, and Nina was obliged to reconcile herself to the prospect of silent obedience. The note, however, had made her very happy, and the prospect pleased her well. It was on this very day that she had intended to go to her lover; but it was in all respects much pleasanter to her that her lover should come to her. And then, to walk with him was of all things the most delightful, especially in the gloom of the evening, when no eyes could see her--no eyes but his own. She could hang upon his arm, and in this way she could talk more freely with him than in any other. And then the note had in it more of the sweetness of a love-letter than any written words which she had hitherto received from him. It was very short, no doubt, but he had called her "Dearest," instead of "Dear Nina," as had been his custom, and then he had declared that he was hers ever and always. No words could have been sweeter. She was glad that the note was so short, because there was nothing in it to mar her pleasure. Yes, she would be there at eight. She was quite determined that she would not keep him waiting.

At half-past seven she was on the bridge. There could be no reason, she thought, why she should not walk across it to the other side and then retrace her steps, though in doing so she was forced, by the rule of the road upon the bridge, to pass to the Old Town by the right-hand pathway in going, while he must come to her by the opposite side. But she would walk very quickly and watch very closely. If she did not see him as she crossed and recrossed, she would at any rate be on the spot indicated at the time named. The autumn evenings had become somewhat chilly, and she wrapped her thin cloak close round her, as she felt the night air as she came upon the open bridge. But she was not cold. She told herself that she could not and would not be cold. How could she be cold when she was going to meet her lover? The night was dark, for the moon was now gone and the wind was blowing; but there were a few stars bright in the heaven, and when she looked down through the parapets of the bridge, there was just light enough for her to see the black water flowing fast beneath her. She crossed quickly to the figure of St John, that she might look closely on those passing on the other side, and after a few moments recrossed the road. It was the figure of the saint, St John Nepomucene, who was thrown from this very bridge and drowned, and who has ever since been the protector of good Christians from the fate which he himself had suffered. Then Nina bethought herself whether she was a good Christian, and whether St John of the Bridge would be justified in interposing on her behalf, should she be in want of him. She had strong doubts as to the validity of her own Christianity, now that she loved a Jew; and feared that it was more than probable that St John would do nothing for her, were she in such a strait as that in which he was supposed to interfere. But why now should she think of any such danger? Lotta Luxa had told her to drown herself when she should find herself to have been jilted by her Jew lover; but her Jew lover was true to her; she had his dear words at that moment in her bosom, and in a few moments her hand would be resting on his arm. So she passed on from the statue of St John, with her mind made up that she did not want St John's aid. Some other saint she would want, no doubt, and she prayed a little silent prayer to St Nicholas, that he would allow her to marry the Jew without taking offence at her. Her circumstances had been very hard, as the saint must know, and she had meant to do her best. Might it not be possible, if the saint would help her, that she might convert her husband? But as she thought of this, she shook her head. Anton Trendellsohn was not a man to be changed in his religion by any words which she could use. It would be much more probable, she knew, that the conversion would be the other way. And she thought she would not mind that, if only it could be a real conversion. But if she were induced to say that she was a Jewess, while she still believed in St Nicholas and St John, and in the beautiful face of the dear Virgin--if to please her husband she were to call herself a Jewess while she was at heart a Christian--then her state would be very wretched. She prayed again to St Nicholas to keep her from that state. If she were to become a Jewess, she hoped that St Nicholas would let her go altogether, heart and soul, into Judaism.

When she reached the end of the long bridge she looked anxiously up the street by which she knew that he must come, endeavoring to discover his figure by the glimmering light of an oil-lamp that hung at an angle in the street, or by the brighter glare which came from the gas in a shop-window by which he must pass. She stood thus looking and looking till she thought he would never come. Then she heard the clock in the old watch-tower of the bridge over her head strike three-quarters, and she became aware that, instead of her lover being after his time, she had yet to wait a quarter of an hour for the exact moment which he had appointed. She did not in the least mind waiting. She had been a little uneasy when she thought that he had neglected or forgotten his own appointment. So she turned again and walked back towards the Kleinseite, fixing her eyes, as she had so often done, on the rows of windows which glittered along the great dark mass of the Hradschin Palace. What were they all doing up there, those slow and faded courtiers to an ex-Emperor, that they should want to burn so many candles? Thinking of this she passed the tablet on the bridge, and, according to her custom, put the end of her fingers on it. But as she was raising her hand to her mouth to kiss it she remembered that the saint might not like such service from one who was already half a Jew at heart, and she refrained. She refrained, and then considered whether the bridge might not topple down with her into the stream because of her iniquity. But it did not topple down, and now she was standing beyond any danger from the water at the exact spot which Trendellsohn had named. She stood still lest she might possibly miss him by moving, till she was again cold. But she did not regard that, though she pressed her cloak closely round her limbs. She did not move till she heard the first sound of the bell as it struck eight, and then she gave a little jump as she found that her lover was close upon her.

"So you are here, Nina," he said, putting his hand upon her arm.

"Of course I am here, Anton. I have been looking, and looking, and looking, thinking you never would come; and how did you get here?"

"I am as punctual as the clock, my love."

"Oh yes, you are punctual, I know; but where did you come from?"

"I came down the hill from the Hradschin. I have had business there. It did not occur to your simplicity that I could reach you otherwise than by the direct road from my own home."

"I never thought of your coming from the side of the Hradschin," said Nina, wondering whether any of those lights she had seen could have been there for the use of Anton Trendellsohn. "I am so glad you have come to me. It is so good of you."

"It is good of you to come and meet me, my own one. But you are cold. Let us walk, and you will be warmer."

Nina, who had already put her hand upon her lover's arm, thrust it in a little farther, encouraged by such sweet words; and then he took her little hand in his, and drew her still nearer to him, till she was clinging to him very closely. "Nina, my own one," he said again. He had never before been in so sweet a mood with her. Walk with him? Yes; she would walk with him all night if he would let her. Instead of turning again over the bridge as she had expected, he took her back into the Kleinseite, not bearing round to the right in the direction of her own house, but going up the hill into a large square, round which the pathway is covered by the overhanging houses, as is common for avoidance of heat in Southern cities. Here, under the low colonnade, it was very dark, and the passengers going to and fro were not many. At each angle of the square where the neighboring streets entered it, in the open space, there hung a dull, dim oil-lamp; but other light there was none. Nina, however, did not mind the darkness while Anton Trendellsohn was with her. Even when walking close under the buttresses of St Nicholas--of St Nicholas, who could not but have been offended-- close under the very niche in which stood the statue of the saint--she had no uncomfortable qualms. When Anton was with her she did not much regard the saints. It was when she was alone that those thoughts on her religion came to disturb her mind. "I do so like walking with you," she said. "It is the nicest way of talking in the world."

"I want to ask you a question, Nina," said Anton; "or perhaps two questions." The tight grasping clasp made on his arm by the tips of her fingers relaxed itself a little as she heard his words, and remarked their altered tone. It was not, then, to be all love; and she could perceive that he was going to be serious with her, and, as she feared, perhaps angry. Whenever he spoke to her on any matter of business, his manner was so very serious as to assume in her eyes, when judged by her feelings, an appearance of anger. The Jew immediately felt the little movement of her fingers, and hastened to reassure her. "I am quite sure that your answers will satisfy me."

"I hope so," said Nina. But the pressure of her hand upon his arm was not at once repeated.

"I have seen your cousin Ziska, Nina; indeed, I have seen him twice lately; and I have seen your uncle and your aunt."

"I suppose they did not say anything very pleasant about me."

"They did not say anything very pleasant about anybody or about anything. They were not very anxious to be pleasant; but that I did not mind."

"I hope they did not insult you, Anton?"

"We Jews are used as yet to insolence from Christians, and do not mind it."

They shall never more be anything to me, if they have insulted you."

"It is nothing, Nina. We bear those things, and think that such of you Christians as use that liberty of a vulgar tongue, which is still possible towards a Jew in Prague, are simply poor in heart and ignorant."

"They are poor in heart and ignorant."

"I first went to your uncle's office in the Ross Markt, where I saw him and your aunt and Ziska. And afterwards Ziska came to me, at our own house. He was tame enough then."

"To your own house?"

"Yes; to the Jews' quarter. Was it not a condescension? He came into our synagogue and ferreted me out. You may be sure that he had something very special to say when he did that. But he looked as though he thought that his life were in danger among us."

"But, Anton, what had he to say?"

"I will tell you. He wanted to buy me off."

"Buy you off!"

"Yes; to bribe me to give you up. Aunt Sophie does not relish the idea of having a Jew for her nephew."

"Aunt Sophie!--but I will never call her Aunt Sophie again. Do you mean that they offered you money?"

"They offered me property, my dear, which is the same. But they did it economically, for they only offered me my own. They were kind enough to suggest that if I would merely break my word to you, they would tell me how I could get the title-deeds of the houses, and thus have the power of turning your father out into the street."

"You have the power. He would go at once if you bade him."

"I do not wish him to go. As I have told you often, he is welcome to the use of the house. He shall have it for his life, as far as I am concerned. But I should like to have what is my own."

"And what did you say?" Nina, as she asked the question, was very careful not to tighten her hold upon his arm by the weight of a single ounce.

"What did I say? I said that I had many things that I valued greatly, but that I had one thing that I valued more than gold or houses--more even than my right."

"And what is that?" said Nina, stopping suddenly, so that she might hear clearly every syllable of the words which were to come. "What is that?" She did not even yet add an ounce to the pressure; but her fingers were ready.

"A poor thing," said Anton; "just the heart of a Christian girl."

Then the hand was tightened, or rather the two hands, for they were closed together upon his arm; and his other arm was wound round her waist; and then, in the gloom of the dark colonnade, he pressed her to his bosom, and kissed her lips and her forehead, and then her lips again. "No," he said, "they have not bribed high enough yet to get from me my treasure--my treasure."

"Dearest, am I your treasure?"

"Are you not? What else have I that I make equal to you?" Nina was supremely happy--triumphant in her happiness. She cared nothing for her aunt, nothing for Lotta Luxa and her threats; and very little at the present moment even for St Nicholas or St John of the Bridge. To be told by her lover that she was his own treasure, was sufficient to banish for the time all her miseries and all her fears.

"You are my treasure. I want you to remember that, and to believe it," said the Jew.

"I will believe it," said Nina, trembling with anxious eagerness. Could it be possible that she would ever forget it?

"And now I will ask my questions. Where are those title-deeds?"

"Where are they?" said she, repeating his question.

"Yes; where are they?"

"Why do you ask me? And why do you look like that?"

"I want you to tell me where they are, to the best of your knowledge."

"Uncle Karil has them--or else Ziska."

"You are sure of that?"

"How can I be sure? I am not sure at all. But Ziska said something which made me feel sure of it, as I told you before. And I have supposed always that they must be in the Ross Markt. Where else can they be?"

"Your aunt says that you have got them."

"That I have got them?"

"Yes, you. That is what she intends me to understand." The Jew had stopped at one of the corners, close under the little lamp, and looked intently into Nina's face as he spoke to her.

"And you believe her?" said Nina.

But he went on without noticing her question. "She intends me to believe that you have got them, and are keeping them from me fraudulently! cheating me, in point of fact--that you are cheating me, so that you may have some hold over the property for your own purposes. That is what your aunt wishes me to believe. She is a wise woman, is she not? and very clever. In one breath she tries to bribe me to give you up, and in the next she wants to convince me that you are not worth keeping."

"But, Anton--"

"Nay, Nina, I will not put you to the trouble of protestation. Look at that star. I should as soon suspect the light which God has placed in the heaven of misleading me, as I should suspect you."

"Oh, Anton, dear Anton, I do so love you for saying that! Would it be possible that I should keep anything from you?"

"I think you would keep nothing from me. Were you to do so, you could not be my own love any longer. A man's wife must be true to him in everything, or she is not his wife. I could endure not only no fraud from you, but neither could I endure falsehood."

"I have never been false to you. With God's help I never will be false to you."

"He has given you His help. He has made you true-hearted, and I do not doubt you. Now answer me another question. Is it possible that your father should have the paper?"

Nina paused a moment, and then she replied with eagerness, "Quite impossible. I am sure that he knows nothing of it more than you know." When she had so spoken they walked in silence for a few yards, but Anton did not at once reply to her. "You do not think that father is keeping anything from you, do you," said Nina.

"I do not know," said the Jew. "I am not sure."

"You may be sure. You may be quite sure. Father is at least honest."

"I have always thought so."

"And do you not think so still?"

"Look here, Nina. I do not know that there is a Christian in Prague who would feel it to be beneath him to rob a Jew, and I do not altogether blame them. They believe that we would rob them, and many of us do so. We are very sharp, each on the other, dealing against each other always in hatred, never in love--never even in friendship."

"But, for all that, my father has never wronged you."

"He should not do so, for I am endeavoring to be kind to him. For your sake, Nina, I would treat him as though he were a Jew himself."

"He has never wronged you; I am sure that he has never wronged you."

"Nina, you are more to me than you are to him."

"Yes. I am--I am your own; but yet I will declare that he has never wronged you."

"And I should be more to you than he is."

"You are more--you are everything to me; but, still, I know that he has never wronged you."

Then the Jew paused again, still walking onwards through the dark colonnade with her hand upon his arm. They walked in silence the whole side of the large square. Nina waiting patiently to hear what would come next, and Trendellsohn considering what words he would use. He did suspect her father, and it was needful to his purpose that he should tell her so; and it was needful also, as he thought, that she should be made to understand that in her loyalty and truth to him she must give up her father, or even suspect her father, if his purpose required that she should do so. Though she were still a Christian herself, she must teach herself to look at other Christians, even at those belonging to herself, with Jewish eyes. Unless she could do so she would not be true and loyal to him with that troth and loyalty which he required. Poor Nina! It was the dearest wish of her heart to be true and loyal to him in all things; but it might be possible to put too hard a strain even upon such love as hers. "Nina," the Jew said, "I fear your father. I think that he is deceiving us."

"No, Anton, no! he is not deceiving you. My aunt and uncle and Ziska are deceiving you."

"They are trying to deceive me, no doubt; but as far as I can judge from their own words and looks, they do believe that at this moment the document which I want is in your father's house. As far as I can judge their thoughts from their words, they think that it is there."

"It is not there," said Nina, positively.

"That is what we must find out. Your uncle was silent. He said nothing, or next to nothing."

"He is the best of the three, by far," said Nina.

"Your aunt is a clever woman in spite her blunder about you; and had I dealt with her only I should have thought that she might have expressed herself as she did, and still have had the paper in her own keeping. I could not read her mind as I could read his. Women will lie better than men."

"But men can lie too," said Nina.

"Your cousin Ziska is a fool."

"He is a fox," said Nina.

"He is a fool in comparison with his mother. And I had him in my own house, under my thumb, as it were. Of course he lied. Of course he tried to deceive me. But, Nina, he believes that the document is here-- in your house. Whether it be there or not, Ziska thinks that it is there."

"Ziska is more fox than fool," said Nina.

"Let that be as it may. I tell you the truth of him. He thinks it is here. Now, Nina, you must search for it."

"It is not there, Anton. I tell you of my own knowledge, it is not in the house. Come and search yourself. Come tomorrow. Come tonight, if you will."

"It would be of no use. I could not search as you can do. Tell me, Nina; has your father no place locked up which is not open to you?"

"Yes; he has his old desk; you know it, where it stands in the parlor."

"You never open that?"

"No, never; but there is nothing there--nothing of that nature."

"How can you tell? Or he can keep it about his person?"

"He keeps it nowhere. He has not got it. Dear Anton, put it out of your head. You do not know my cousin Ziska. That he has it in his own hands I am now sure."

"And I, Nina, am sure that it is here in the Kleinseite--or at least am sure that he thinks it to be so. The question now is this: Will you obey me in what directions I may give you concerning it?" Nina could not bring herself to give an unqualified reply to this demand on the spur of the moment. Perhaps it occurred to her that the time for such implicit obedience on her part had hardly yet come--that as yet at least she must not be less true to her father than to her lover. She hesitated, therefore, in answering him. "Do you not understand me, Nina?" he said roughly. "I asked you whether you will do as I would have you do, and you make no reply. We two, Nina, must be one in all things, or else we must be apart--in all things."

"I do not know what it is you wish of me," she said, trembling.

"I wish you to obey me."

"But suppose--"

"I know that you must trust me first before you can obey me."

"I do trust you. You know that I trust you."

"Then you should obey me."

"But not to suspect my own father!"

"I do not ask you to suspect him."

"But you suspect him?"

"Yes; I do. I am older than you, and know more of men and their ways than you can do. I do suspect him. You must promise me that you will search for this deed."

Again she paused, but after a moment or two a thought struck her, and she replied eagerly, "Anton, I will tell you what I will do. I will ask him openly. He and I have always been open to each other."

"If he is concealing it, do you think he will tell you?"

"Yes, he would tell me. But he is not concealing it."

"Will you look?"

"I cannot take his keys from him and open his box."

"You mean that you will not do as I bid you?"

"I cannot do it. Consider of it, Anton. Could you treat your own father in such a way?"

"I would cling to you sooner than to him. I have told him so, and he has threatened to turn me penniless from his house. Still I shall cling to you, because you are my love. I shall do so if you are equally true to me. That is my idea of love. There can be no divided allegiance."

And this also was Nina's idea of love--an idea up to which she had striven to act and live when those around her had threatened her with all that earth and heaven could do to her if she would not abandon the Jew. But she had anticipated no such trial as that which had now come upon her. "Dear Anton," she said, appealing to him weakly in her weakness, "if you did but know how I love you!"

"You must prove your love."

"Am I not ready to prove it? Would I not give up anything, everything, for you?"

"Then you must assist me in this thing, as I am desiring you." As he said this they had reached the corner from whence the street ran in the direction of the bridge, and into this he turned instead of continuing their walk round the square. She said nothing as he did so; but accompanied him, still leaning upon his arm. He walked on quickly and in silence till they came to the turn which led towards Balatka's house, and then he stopped. "It is late," said he, "and you had better go home."

"May I not cross the bridge with you?"

"You had better go home." His voice was very stern, and as she dropped her hand from his arm she felt it to be impossible to leave him in that way. Were she to do so, she would never be allowed to speak to him or to see him again. "Good-night," he said, preparing to turn from her.

"Anton, Anton, do not leave me like that."

"How then shall I leave you? Shall I say that it does not matter whether you obey me or not? It does matter. Between you and me such obedience matters everything. If we are to be together, I must abandon everything for you, and you must comply in everything with me." Then Nina, leaning close upon him, whispered into his ear that she would obey him.

Volume 2

Chapter 9

Nina's misery as she went home was almost complete. She had not, indeed, quarreled with her lover, who had again caressed her as she left him, and assured her of his absolute confidence, but she had undertaken a task against which her very soul revolted. It gave her no comfort to say to herself that she had undertaken to look for that which she knew she would not find, and that therefore her search could do no harm. She had, in truth, consented to become a spy upon her father, and was so to do in furtherance of the views of one who suspected her father of fraud, and who had not scrupled to tell her that her father was dishonest. Now again she thought of St Nicholas, as she heard the dull chime of the clock from the saint's tower, and found herself forced to acknowledge that she was doing very wickedly in loving a Jew. Of course troubles would come upon her. What else could she expect? Had she not endeavored to throw behind her and to trample under foot all that she had learned from her infancy under the guidance of St Nicholas? Of course the saint would desert her. The very sound of the chime told her that he was angry with her. How could she hope again that St John would be good to her? Was it not to be expected that the black-flowing river over which she understood him to preside would become her enemy and would swallow her up--as Lotta Luxa had predicted? Before she returned home, when she was quite sure that Anton Trendellsohn had already passed over, she went down upon the bridge, and far enough along the causeway to find herself over the river, and there, crouching down, she looked at the rapid-running silent black stream beneath her. The waters were very silent and very black, but she could still see or feel that they were running rapidly. And they were cold, too. She herself at the present moment was very cold. She shuddered as she looked down, pressing her face against the stone-work, with her two hands resting on two of the pillars of the parapet. It would be very terrible. She did not think that she much cared for death. The world had been so hard to her, and was growing so much harder, that it would be a good thing to get away from it. If she could become ill and die, with a good kind nun standing by her bedside, and with the cross pressed to her bosom, and with her eyes fixed on the sweet face of the Virgin Mother as it was painted in the little picture in her room--in that way she thought that death might even be grateful. But to be carried away she knew not whither in the cold, silent, black- flowing Moldau! And yet she half believed the prophecy of Lotta. Such a quiet death as that she had pictured to herself could not be given to her! What nun would come to her bedside--to the bed of a girl who had declared to all Prague that she intended to marry a Jew? For weeks past she had feared even to look at the picture of the Virgin.

"I'm afraid you'll think I am very late, father," she said, as soon as she reached home.

Her father muttered something, but not angrily, and she soon busied herself about him, doing some little thing for his comfort, as was her wont. But as she did so she could not but remember that she had undertaken to be a spy upon him, to secrete his key, and to search surreptitiously for that which he was supposed to be keeping fraudulently. As she sat by him empty-handed--for it was Sunday night, and as a Christian she never worked with a needle upon the Sunday--she told herself that she could not do it. Could there be any harm done were she to ask him now, openly, what papers he kept in that desk? But she desired to obey her lover where obedience was possible, and he had expressly forbidden her to ask any such question. She sat, therefore, and said no word that could tend to ease her suffering; and then, when the time came, she went suffering to her bed.

On the next day there seemed to come to her no opportunity for doing that which she had to do. Souchey was in and out of the house all the morning, explaining to her that they had almost come to the end of the flour and of the potatoes which he had bought, that he himself had swallowed on the previous evening the last tip of the great sausage-- for, as he had alleged, it was no use a fellow dying of starvation outright--and that there was hardly enough of chocolate left to make three cups. Nina had brought out her necklace and had asked Souchey to take it to the shop and do the best with it he could; but Souchey had declined the commission, alleging that he would be accused of having stolen it; and Nina had then prepared to go herself, but her father had called her, and he had come out into the sitting-room and had remained there during the afternoon, so that both the sale of the trinket and the search in the desk had been postponed. The latter she might have done at night, but when the night came the deed seemed to be more horrid than it would be even in the day.

She observed also, more accurately than she had ever done before, that he always carried the key of his desk with him. He did not, indeed, put it under his pillow, or conceal it in bed, but he placed it with an old spectacle-case which he always carried, and a little worn pocket-book which Nina knew to be empty, on a low table which stood at his bed- head; and now during the whole of the afternoon he had the key on the table beside him. Nina did not doubt but that she could take the key while he was asleep; for when he was even half asleep--which was perhaps his most customary state--he would not stir when she entered the room. But if she took it at all, she would do so in the day. She could not bring herself to creep into the room in the night, and to steal the key in the dark. As she lay in bed she still thought of it. She had promised her lover that she would do this thing. Should she resolve not to do it, in spite of that promise, she must at any rate tell Anton of her resolution. She must tell him, and then there would be an end of everything. Would it be possible for her to live without her love?

On the following morning it occurred to her that she might perhaps be able to induce her father to speak of the houses, and of those horrid documents of which she had heard so much, without disobeying any of Trendellsohn's behests. There could, she thought, be no harm in her asking her father some question as to the ownership of the houses, and as to the Jew's right to the property. Her father had very often declared in her presence that old Trendellsohn could turn him into the street at any moment. There had been no secrets between her and her father as to their poverty, and there could be no reason why her tongue should now be silenced, so long as she refrained from any positive disobedience to her lover's commands. That he must be obeyed she still recognized as the strongest rule of all--obeyed, that is, till she should go to him and lay down her love at his feet, and give back to him the troth which he had given her.

"Father," she said to the old man about noon that day, "I suppose this house does belong to the Trendellsohns?"

"Of course it does," said he, crossly.

"Belongs to them altogether, I mean?" she said.

"I don't know what you call altogether. It does belong to them, and there's an end of it. What's the good of talking about it?"

"Only if so, they ought to have those deeds they are so anxious about. Everybody ought to have what is his own. Don't you think so, father?"

"I am keeping nothing from them," said he; "you don't suppose that I want to rob them?"

"Of course you do not." Then Nina paused again. She was drawing perilously near to forbidden ground, if she were not standing on it already; and yet she was very anxious that the subject should not be dropped between her and her father.

"I'm sure you do not want to rob anyone, father. But--"

"But what? I suppose young Trendellsohn has been talking to you again about it. I suppose he suspects me; if so, no doubt, you will suspect me too."

"Oh, father! how can you be so cruel?"

"If he thinks the papers are here, it is his own house; let him come and search for them."

"He will not do that, I am sure."

"What is it he wants, then? I can't go out to your uncle and make him give them up."

"They are, then, with uncle?"

"I suppose so; but how am I to know? You see how they treat me. I cannot go to them, and they never come to me--except when that woman comes to scold."

"But they can't belong to uncle."

"Of course they don't."

"Then why should he keep them? What good can they do him? When I spoke to Ziska, Ziska said they should be kept, because Trendellsohn is a Jew; but surely a Jew has a right to his own. We at any rate ought to do what we can for him, Jew as he is, since he lets us live in his house."

The slight touch of irony which Nina had thrown into her voice when she spoke of what was due to her lover even though he was a Jew was not lost upon her father. "Of course you would take his part against a Christian," he said.

"I take no one's part against anyone," said she, "except so far as right is concerned. If we take a Jew's money, I think we should give him the thing which he purchases."

"Who is keeping him from it?" said Balatka, angrily.

"Well--I suppose it is my uncle," replied Nina.

"Why cannot you let me be at peace then?"

Having so said he turned himself round to the wall, and Nina felt herself to be in a worse position than ever. There was nothing now for her but to take the key, or else to tell her lover that she would not obey him. There could be no further hope in diplomacy. She had just resolved that she could not take the key--that in spite of her promise she could not bring herself to treat her father after such fashion as that--when the old man turned suddenly round upon her again, and went back to the subject.

"I have got a letter somewhere from Karil Zamenoy," said he, "telling me that the deed is in his own chest."

"Have you, father?" said she, anxiously, but struggling to repress her anxiety.

"I had it, I know. It was written ever so long ago--before I had settled with the Trendellsohns; but I have seen it often since. Take the key and unlock the desk, and bring me the bundle of papers that are tied with an old tape; or--stop--bring me all the papers." With trembling hand Nina took the key. She was now desired by her father to do exactly that which her lover wished her to have done; or, better still, her father was about to do the thing himself. She would at any rate have positive proof that the paper was not in her father's desk. He had desired her to bring all the papers, so that there would be no doubt left. She took the key very gently, as softly as was possible to her, and went slowly into the other room. When there she unlocked the desk and took out the bundle of letters tied with an old tape which lay at the top ready to her hand. Then she collected together the other papers, which were not many, and without looking at them carried them to her father. She studiously avoided any scrutiny of what there might be, even by so much as a glance of her eye. "This seems to be all there is, father, except one or two old account-books."

He took the bundle, and with feeble hands untied the tape and moved the documents, one by one. Nina felt that she was fully warranted in looking at them now, as her father was in fact showing them to her. In this way she would be able to give evidence in his favor without having had recourse to any ignoble practice. The old man moved every paper in the bundle, and she could see that they were all letters. She had understood that the deed for which Trendellsohn had desired her to search was written on a larger paper than any she now saw, and that she might thus know it at once. There was, certainly, no such deed among the papers which her father slowly turned over, and which he slowly proceeded to tie up again with the old tape. "I am sure I saw it the other day," he said, fingering among the loose papers while Nina looked on with anxious eyes. Then at last he found the letter from Karil Zamenoy, and having read it himself, gave it her to read. It was dated seven or eight years back, at a time when Balatka was only on his way to ruin--not absolutely ruined, as was the case with him now--and contained an offer on Zamenoy's part to give safe custody to certain documents which were named, and among which the deed now sought for stood first.

"And has he got all those other papers?" Nina asked.

"No! he has none of them, unless he has this. There is nothing left but this one that the Jew wants."

"And uncle Karil has never given that back?"

"Never."

"And it should belong to Stephen Trendellsohn?"

"Yes, I suppose it should."

"Who can wonder, then, that they should be anxious and inquire after it, and make a noise about it? Will not the law make uncle Karil give it up?"

"How can the law prove that he has got it? I know nothing about the law. Put them all back again." Then Nina replaced the papers and locked the desk. She had, at any rate, been absolutely and entirely successful in her diplomacy, and would be able to assure Anton Trendellsohn, of her knowledge, that that which he sought was not in her father's keeping.

On the same day she went out to sell her necklace. She waited till it was nearly dark--till the first dusk of evening had come upon the street--and then she crossed the bridge and hurried to a jeweler's shop in the Grosser Ring which she had observed, and at which she knew such trinkets as hers were customarily purchased. The Grosser Ring is an open space--such as we call a square--in the oldest part of the town, and in it stand the Town Hall and the Theinkirche, which may be regarded as the most special church in Prague, as there for many years were taught the doctrines of Huss, the great Reformer of Bohemia. Here, in the Grosser Ring, there was generally a crowd of an evening, as Nina knew, and she thought that she could go in and out of the jeweler's shop without observation. She believed that she might be able to borrow money on her treasure, leaving it as a deposit; and this, if possible, she would do. There were regular pawnbrokers in the town, by whom no questions would be made, who, of course, would lend her money in the ordinary way of their trade; but she believed that such people would advance to her but a very small portion of the value of her necklace; and then, if, as would be too probable, she could not redeem it, the necklace would be gone, and gone without a price!

"Yes, it is my own, altogether my own--my very own." She had to explain all the circumstances to the jeweler, and at last, with a view of quelling any suspicion, she told the jeweler what was her name, and explained how poor were the circumstances of her house. "But you must be the niece of Madame Zamenoy, in the Windberg-gasse," said the jeweler. And then, when Nina with hesitation acknowledged that such was the case, the man asked her why she did not go to her rich aunt, instead of selling a trinket which must be so valuable.

"No!" said Nina, "I cannot do that. If you will lend me something of its value, I shall be so much obliged to you."

"But Madame Zamenoy would surely help you?"

"We would not take it from her. But we will not speak of that, sir. Can I have the money?" Then the jeweler gave her a receipt for the necklace and took her receipt for the sum he lent her. It was more than Nina had expected, and she rejoiced that she had so well completed her business. Nevertheless she wished that the jeweler had known nothing of her aunt. She was hardly out of the shop before she met her cousin Ziska, and she so met him that she could not escape him. She heard his voice, indeed, almost as soon as she recognized him, and had stopped at his summons before she had calculated whether it might not be better to run away. "What, Nina! is that you?" said Ziska, taking her hand before she knew how to refuse it to him.

"Yes; it is I," said Nina.

"What are you doing here?"

"Why should I not be in the Grosser Ring as well as another? It is open to rich and poor."

"So is Rapinsky's shop; but poor people do not generally have much to do there." Rapinsky was the name of the jeweler who had advanced the money to Nina.

"No, not much," said Nina. "What little they have to sell is soon sold."

"And have you been selling anything?"

"Nothing of yours, Ziska."

"But have you been selling anything?"

"Why do you ask me? What business is it of yours?"

"They say that Anton Trendellsohn, the Jew, gives you all that you want," said Ziska.

"Then they say lies," said Nina, her eyes flashing fire upon her Christian lover through the gloom of the evening. "Who says so? You say so. No one else would be mean enough to be so false."

"All Prague says so."

"All Prague! I know what that means. And did all Prague go to the Jews' quarter last Saturday, to tell Anton Trendellsohn that the paper which he wants, and which is his own, was in father's keeping? Was it all Prague told that falsehood also?" There was a scorn in her face as she spoke which distressed Ziska greatly, but which he did not know how to meet or how to answer. He wanted to be brave before her; and he wanted also to show his affection for her, if only he knew how to do so, without making himself humble in her presence.

"Shall I tell you, Nina, why I went to the Jews' quarter on Saturday?"

"No; tell me nothing. I wish to hear nothing from you. I know enough without your telling me."

"I wish to save you if it be possible, because--because I love you."

"And I--I never wish to see you again, because I hate you. I hate you, because you have been cruel. But let me tell you this; poor as we are, I have never taken a farthing of Anton's money. When I am his wife, as I hope to be--as I hope to be--I will take what he gives me as though it came from heaven. From you!--I would sooner die in the street than take a crust of bread from you." Then she darted from him, and succeeded in escaping without hearing the words with which he replied to her angry taunts. She was woman enough to understand that her keenest weapon for wounding him would be an expression of unbounded love and confidence as to the man who was his rival; and therefore, though she was compelled to deny that she had lived on the charity of her lover, she had coupled her denial with an assurance of her faith and affection, which was, no doubt, bitter enough in Ziska's ears. "I do believe that she is witched," he said, as he turned away towards his own house. And then he reflected wisely on the backward tendency of the world in general, and regretted much that there was no longer given to priests in Bohemia the power of treating with salutary ecclesiastical severity patients suffering in the way in which his cousin Nina was afflicted.

Nina had hardly got out of the Grosser Ring into the narrow street which leads from thence towards the bridge, when she encountered her other lover. He was walking slowly down the centre of the street when she passed him, or would have passed him, had not she recognized his figure through the gloom. "Anton," she said, coming up to him and touching his arm as lightly as was possible. "I am so glad to meet you here."

"Nina?"

"Yes; Nina."

"And what have you been doing?"

"I don't know that I want to tell you; only that I like to tell you everything."

"If so, you can tell me this." Nina, however, hesitated. "If you have secrets, I do not want to inquire into them," said the Jew.

"I would rather have no secrets from you, only--"

"Only what?"

"Well; I will tell you. I had a necklace; and we are not very rich, you know, at home; and I wanted to get something for father, and--"

"You have sold it?"

"No; I have not sold it. The man was very civil, indeed quite kind, and he lent me some money."

"But the kind man kept the necklace, I suppose."

"Of course he kept the necklace. You would not have me borrow money from a stranger, and leave him nothing?"

"No; I would not have you do that. But why not borrow from one who is no stranger?"

"I do not want to borrow at all," said Nina, in her lowest tone.

"Are you ashamed to come to me in your trouble?"

"Yes," said Nina. "I should be ashamed to come to you for money. I would not take it from you."

He did not answer her at once, but walked on slowly while she kept close to his side.

"Give me the jeweler's docket," he said at last. Nina hesitated for a moment, and then he repeated his demand in a sterner voice. "Nina, give me the jeweler's docket." Then she put her hand in her pocket and gave it him. She was very averse to doing so, but she was more averse to refusing him aught that he asked of her.

"I have got something to tell you, Anton," she said, as soon as he had put the jeweler's paper into his purse.

"Well--what is it?"

"I have seen every paper and every morsel of everything that is in father's desk, and there is no sign of the deed you want."

"And how did you see them?"

"He showed them to me."

"You told him, then, what I had said to you?"

"No; I told him nothing about it. He gave me the key, and desired me to fetch him all the papers. He wanted to find a letter which uncle Karil wrote him ever so long ago. In that letter uncle Karil acknowledges that he has the deed."

"I do not doubt that in the least."

"And what is it you do doubt, Anton?"

"I do not say I doubt anything."

"Do you doubt me, Anton?"

There was a little pause before he answered her--the slightest moment of hesitation. But had it been but half as much, Nina's ear and Nina's heart would have detected it. "No," said Anton, "I am not saying that I doubt any one."

"If you doubt me, you will kill me. I am at any rate true to you. What is it you want? What is it you think?"

"They tell me that the document is in the house in the Kleinseite."

"Who are they? Who is it that tells you?"

"More than one. Your uncle and aunt said so--and Ziska Zamenoy came to me on purpose to repeat the same."

"And would you believe what Ziska says? I have hardly thought it worth my while to tell you that Ziska--"

"To tell me what of Ziska?"

"That Ziska pretends to--to want that I should be his wife. I would not look at him if there were not another man in Prague. I hate him. He is a liar. Would you believe Ziska?"

"And another has told me."

"Another?" said Nina, considering.

"Yes, another."

"Lotta Luxa, I suppose."

"Never mind. They say indeed that it is you who have the deed."

"And you believe them?"

"No, I do not believe them. But why do they say so?"

"Must I explain that? How can I tell? Anton, do you not believe that the woman who loves you will be true to you?"

Then he paused again--"Nina, sometimes I think that I have been mad to love a Christian."

"What have I been then? But I do love you, Anton--I love you better than all the world. I care nothing for Jew or Christian. When I think of you, I care nothing for heaven or earth. You are everything to me, because I love you. How could I deceive you?"

"Nina, Nina, my own one!" he said.

"And as I love you, so do you love me? Say that you love me also."

"I do," said he--"I love you as I love my own soul."

Then they parted; and Nina, as she went home, tried to make herself happy with the assurance which had been given to her by the last words her lover had spoken; but still there remained with her that suspicion of a doubt which, if it really existed, would be so cruel an injury to her love.

Chapter 10

Some days passed on after the visit to the jeweler's shop--perhaps ten or twelve--before Nina heard from or saw her lover again; and during that time she had no tidings from her relatives in the Windberg-gasse. Life went on very quietly in the old house, and not the less quietly because the proceeds of the necklace saved Nina from any further immediate necessity of searching for money. The cold weather had come, or rather weather that was cold in the morning and cold in the evening, and old Balatka kept his bed altogether. His state was such that no one could say why he should not get up and dress himself, and he himself continued to speak of some future time when he would do so; but there he was, lying in his bed, and Nina told herself that in all probability she would never see him about the house again. For herself, she was becoming painfully anxious that some day should be fixed for her marriage. She knew that she was, herself, ignorant in such matters; and she knew also that there was no woman near her from whom she could seek counsel. Were she to go to some matron of the neighborhood, her neighbor would only rebuke her, because she loved a Jew. She had boldly told her relatives of her love, and by doing so had shut herself out from all assistance from them. From even her father she could get no sympathy; though with him her engagement had become so far a thing sanctioned, that he had ceased to speak of it in words of reproach. But when was it to be? She had more than once made up her mind that she would ask her lover, but her courage had never as yet mounted high enough in his presence to allow her to do so. When he was with her, their conversation always took such a turn that before she left him she was happy enough if she could only draw from him an assurance that he was not forgetting to love her. Of any final time for her marriage he never said a word. In the mean time she and her father might starve! They could not live on the price of a necklace for ever. She had not made up her mind--she never could make up her mind--as to what might be best for her father when she should be married; but she had made up her mind that when that happy time should come, she would simply obey her husband. He would tell her what would be best for her father. But in the mean time there was no word of her marriage; and now she had been ten days in the Kleinseite without once having had so much as a message from her lover. How was it possible that she should continue to live in such a condition as this?

She was sitting one morning very forlorn in the big parlor, looking out upon the birds who were pecking among the dust in the courtyard below, when her eye just caught the drapery of the dress of some woman who had entered the arched gateway. Nina, from her place by the window, could see out through the arch, and no one therefore could come through their gate while she was at her seat without passing under her eye; but on this occasion the birds had distracted her attention, and she had not caught a sight of the woman's face or figure. Could it be her aunt come to torture her again--her and her father? She knew that Souchey was down-stairs, hanging somewhere in idleness about the door, and therefore she did not leave her place. If it were indeed her aunt, her aunt might come up there to seek her. Or it might possibly be Lotta Luxa, who, next to her aunt, was of all women the most disagreeable to Nina. Lotta, indeed, was not so hard to bear as aunt Sophie, because Lotta could be answered sharply, and could be told to go, if matters proceeded to extremities. In such a case Lotta no doubt would not go; but still the power of desiring her to do so was much. Then Nina remembered that Lotta never wore her petticoats so full as was the morsel of drapery which she had seen. And as she thought of this there came a low knock at the door. Nina, without rising, desired the stranger to come in. Then the door was gently opened, and Rebecca Loth the Jewess stood before her. Nina had seen Rebecca, but had never spoken to her. Each girl had heard much of the other from their younger friend Ruth Jacobi. Ruth was very intimate with them both, and Nina had been willing enough to be told of Rebecca, as had Rebecca also to be told of Nina. "Grandfather wants Anton to marry Rebecca," Ruth had said more than once; and thus Nina knew well that Rebecca was her rival. "I think he loves her better than his own eyes," Ruth had said to Rebecca, speaking of her uncle and Nina. Rut Rebecca had heard from a thousand sources of information that he who was to have been her lover had forgotten his own people and his own religion, and had given himself to a Christian girl. Each, therefore, now knew that she looked upon an enemy and a rival; but each was anxious to be very courteous to her enemy.

Nina rose from her chair directly she saw her visitor, and came forward to meet her. "I suppose you hardly know who I am, Fraeulein?" said Rebecca.

"Oh, yes," said Nina, with her pleasantest smile; "you are Rebecca Loth."

"Yes, I am Rebecca Loth, the Jewess."

"I like the Jews," said Nina.

Rebecca was not dressed now as she had been dressed on that gala occasion when we saw her in the Jews' quarter. Then she had been as smart as white muslin and bright ribbons and velvet could make her. Now she was clad almost entirely in black, and over her shoulders she wore a dark shawl, drawn closely round her neck. But she had on her head, now as then, that peculiar Hungarian hat which looks almost like a coronet in front, and gives an aspect to the girl who wears it half defiant and half attractive; and there were there, of course, the long, glossy, black curls, and the dark-blue eyes, and the turn of the face, which was so completely Jewish in its hard, bold, almost repellant beauty. Nina had said that she liked the Jews, but when the words were spoken she remembered that they might be open to misconstruction, and she blushed. The same idea occurred to Rebecca, but she scorned to take advantage of even a successful rival on such a point as that. She would not twit Nina by any hint that this assumed liking for the Jews was simply a special predilection for one Jew in particular. "We are not ungrateful to you for coming among us and knowing us," said Rebecca. Then there was a slight pause, for Nina hardly knew what to say to her visitor. But Rebecca continued to speak. "We hear that in other countries the prejudice against us is dying away, and that Christians stay with Jews in their houses, and Jews with Christians, eating with them, and drinking with them. I fear it will never be so in Prague."

"And why not in Prague? I hope it may. Why should we not do in Prague as they do elsewhere?"

"Ah, the feeling is so firmly settled here. We have our own quarter, and live altogether apart. A Christian here will hardly walk with a Jew, unless it be from counter to counter, or from bank to bank. As for their living together--or even eating in the same room--do you ever see it?"

Nina of course understood the meaning of this. That which the girl said to her was intended to prove to her how impossible it was that she should marry a Jew, and live in Prague with a Jew as his wife; but she, who stood her ground before aunt Sophie, who had never flinched for a moment before all the threats which could be showered upon her from the Christian side, was not going to quail before the opposition of a Jewess, and that Jewess a rival!

"I do not know why we should not live to see it," said Nina.

"It must take long first--very long," said Rebecca. "Even now, Fraeulein, I fear you will think that I am very intrusive in coming to you. I know that a Jewess has no right to push her acquaintance upon a Christian girl." The Jewess spoke very humbly of herself and of her people; but in every word she uttered there was a slight touch of irony which was not lost upon Nina. Nina could not but bethink herself that she was poor--so poor that everything around her, on her, and about her, told of poverty; while Rebecca was very rich, and showed her wealth even in the somber garments which she had chosen for her morning visit. No idea of Nina's poverty had crossed Rebecca's mind, but Nina herself could not but remember it when she felt the sarcasm implied in her visitor's self-humiliation.

"I am glad that you have come to me--very glad indeed, if you have come in friendship." Then she blushed as she continued, "To me, situated as I am, the friendship of a Jewish maiden would be a treasure indeed."

"You intend to speak of--"

"I speak of my engagement with Anton Trendellsohn. I do so with you because I know that you have heard of it. You tell me that Jews and Christians cannot come together in Prague, but I mean to marry a Jew. A Jew is my lover. If you will say that you will be my friend, I will love you indeed. Ruth Jacobi is my friend; but then Ruth is so young."

"Yes, Ruth is very young. She is a child. She knows nothing."

"A child's friendship is better than none."

"Ruth is very young. She cannot understand. I too love Ruth Jacobi. I have known her since she was born. I knew and loved her mother. You do not remember Ruth Trendellsohn. No; your acquaintance with them is only of the other day."

"Ruth's mother has been dead seven years," said Nina.

"And what are seven years? I have known them for four-and-twenty."

"Nay; that cannot be."

"But I have. That is my age, and I was born, so to say, in their arms. Ruth Trendellsohn was ten years older than I--only ten."

"And Anton?"

"Anton was a year older than his sister; but you know Anton's age. Has he never told you his age?"

"I never asked him; but I know it. There are things one knows as a matter of course. I remember his birthday always."

"It has been a short always."

"No, not so short. Two years is not a short time to know a friend."

"But he has not been betrothed to you for two years?"

"No; not betrothed to me."

"Nor has he loved you so long; nor you him?"

"For him, I can only speak of the time when he first told me so."

"And that was but the other day--but the other day, as I count the time." To this Nina made no answer. She could not claim to have known her lover from so early a date as Rebecca Loth had done, who had been, as she said, born in the arms of his family. But what of that? Men do not always love best those women whom they have known the longest. Anton Trendellsohn had known her long enough to find that he loved her best. Why then should this Jewish girl come to her and throw in her teeth the shortness of her intimacy with the man who was to be her husband? If she, Nina, had also been a Jewess, Rebecca Loth would not then have spoken in such a way. As she thought of this she turned her face away from the stranger, and looked out among the sparrows who were still pecking among the dust in the court. She had told Rebecca at the beginning of their interview that she would be delighted to find a friend in a Jewess, but now she felt sorry that the girl had come to her. For Anton's sake she would bear with much from one whom he had known so long. But for that thought she would have answered her visitor with short courtesy. As it was, she sat silent and looked out upon the birds.

"I have come to you now," said Rebecca Loth, "to say a few words to you about Anton Trendellsohn. I hope you will not refuse to listen."

"That will depend on what you say."

"Do you think it will be for his good to marry a Christian?"

"I shall leave him to judge of that," replied Nina, sharply.

"It cannot be that you do not think of it. I am sure you would not willingly do an injury to the man you love."

"I would die for him, if that would serve him."

"You can serve him without dying. If he takes you for his wife, all his people will turn against him. His own father will become his enemy."

"How can that be? His father knows of it, and yet he is not my enemy."

"It is as I tell you. His father will disinherit him. Every Jew in Prague will turn his back upon him. He knows it now. Anton knows it himself, but he cannot be the first to say the word that shall put an end to your engagement."

"Jews have married Christians in Prague before now," said Nina, pleading her own cause with all the strength she had.

"But not such a one as Anton Trendellsohn. An unconsidered man may do that which is not permitted to those who are more in note."

"There is no law against it now."

"That is true. There is no law. But there are habits stronger than law. In your own case, do you not know that all the friends you have in the world will turn their backs upon you? And so it would be with him. You two would be alone--neither as Jews nor as Christians--with none to aid you, with no friend to love you."

"For myself I care nothing," said Nina. "They may say, if they like, that I am no Christian."

"But how will it be with him? Can you ever be happy if you have been the cause of ruin to your husband?"

Nina was again silent for a while, sitting with her face turned altogether away from the Jewess. Then she rose suddenly from her chair, and, facing round almost fiercely upon the other girl, asked a question, which came from the fullness of her heart, "And you--you yourself, what is it that you intend to do? Do you wish to marry him?"

"I do," said Rebecca, bearing Nina's gaze without dropping her own eyes for a moment. "I do. I do wish to be the wife of Anton Trendellsohn."

"Then you shall never have your wish--never. He loves me, and me only. Ask him, and he will tell you so."

"I have asked him, and he has told me so." There was something so serious, so sad, and so determined in the manner of the young Jewess, that it almost cowed Nina--almost drove her to yield before her visitor. "If he has told you so," she said--then she stopped, not wishing to triumph over her rival.

"He has told me so; but I knew it without his telling. We all know it. I have not come here to deceive you, or to create false suspicions. He does love you. He cares nothing for me, and he does love you. But is he therefore to be ruined? Which had he better lose? All that he has in the world, or the girl that has taken his fancy?"

"I would sooner lose the world twice over than lose him."

"Yes; but you are only a woman. Think of his position. There is not a Jew in all Prague respected among us as he is respected. He knows more, can do more, has more of wit and cleverness, than any of us. We look to him to win for the Jews in Prague something of the freedom which Jews have elsewhere--in Paris and in London. If he takes a Christian for his wife, all this will be destroyed."

"But all will be well if he were to marry you!"

Now it was Rebecca's turn to pause; but it was not for long. "I love him dearly," she said; "with a love as warm as yours."

"And therefore I am to be untrue to him," said Nina, again seating herself.

"And were I to become his wife," continued Rebecca, not regarding the interruption, "it would be well with him in a worldly point of view. All our people would be glad, because there has been friendship between the families from of old. His father would be pleased, and he would become rich; and I also am not without some wealth of my own."

"While I am poor," said Nina; "so poor that--look here, I can only mend my rags. There, look at my shoes. I have not another pair to my feet. But if he likes me, poor and ragged, better than he likes you, rich--" She got so far, raising her voice as she spoke; but she could get no farther, for her sobs stopped her voice.

But while she was struggling to speak, the other girl rose and knelt at Nina's feet, putting her long tapering fingers upon Nina's thread-bare arms, so that her forehead was almost close to Nina's lips. "He does," said Rebecca. "It is true--quite true. He loves you, poor as you are, ten times--a hundred times--better than he loves me, who am not poor. You have won it altogether by yourself, with nothing of outside art to back you. You have your triumph. Will not that be enough for a life's contentment?"

"No--no, no," said Nina. "No, it will not be enough." But her voice now was not altogether sorrowful. There was in it something of a wild joy which had come to her heart from the generous admission which the Jewess made. She did triumph as she remembered that she had conquered with no other weapons than those which nature had given her.

"It is more of contentment than I shall ever have," said Rebecca. "Listen to me. If you will say to me that you will release him from his promise, I will swear to you by the God whom we both worship, that I will never become his wife--that he shall never touch me or speak to me in love." She had risen before she made this proposal, and now stood before Nina with one hand raised, with her blue eyes fixed upon Nina's face, and a solemnity in her manner which for a while startled Nina into silence. "You will believe my word, I am sure," said Rebecca.

"Yes, I would believe you," said Nina.

"Shall it be a bargain between us? Say so, and whatever is mine shall be mine and yours too. Though a Jew may not make a Christian his wife, a Jewish girl may love a Christian maiden; and then, Nina, we shall both know that we have done our very best for him whom we both love better than all the world beside."

Nina was again silent, considering the proposition that had been made to her. There was one thing that she did not see; one point of view in which the matter had not been presented to her. The cause for her sacrifice had been made plain to her, but why was the sacrifice of the other also to become necessary? By not yielding she might be able to keep her lover to herself; but if she were to be induced to abandon him --for his sake, so that he might not be ruined by his love for her-- why, in that case, should he not take the other girl for his wife? In such a case Nina told herself that there would be no world left for her. There would be nothing left for her beyond the accomplishment of Lotta Luxa's prophecy. But yet, though she thought of this, though in her misery she half resolved that she would give up Anton, and not exact from Rebecca the oath which the Jewess had tendered, still, in spite of that feeling, the dread of a rival's success helped to make her feel that she could never bring herself to yield.

"Shall it be as I say?" said Rebecca; "and shall we, dear, be friends while we live?"

"No," said Nina, suddenly.

"You cannot bring yourself to do so much for the man you love?"

"No, I cannot. Could you throw yourself from the bridge into the Moldau, and drown yourself?"

"Yes," said Rebecca, "I could. If it would serve him, I think that I could do so."

"What! in the dark, when it is so cold? The people would see you in the daytime."

"But I would live, that I might hear of his doings, and see his success."

"Ah! I could not live without feeling that he loved me."

"But what will you think of his love when it has ruined him? Will it be pleasant then? Were I to do that, then--then I should bethink myself of the cold river and the dark night, and the eyes of the passers-by whom I should be afraid to meet in the daytime. I ask you to be as I am. Who is there that pities me? Think again, Nina. I know you would wish that he should be prosperous."

Nina did think again, and thought long. And she wept, and the Jewess comforted her, and many words were said between them beyond those which have been here set down; but, in the end, Nina could not bring herself to say that she would give him up. For his sake had she not given up her uncle and her aunt, and St John and St Nicholas--and the very Virgin herself, whose picture she had now removed from the wall beside her bed to a dark drawer? How could she give up that which was everything she had in the world--the very life of her bosom? "I will ask him--him himself," she said at last, hoarsely. "I will ask him, and do as he bids me. I cannot do anything unless it is as he bids me."

"In this matter you must act on your own judgment, Nina."

"No, I will not. I have no judgment. He must judge for me in everything. If he says it is better that we should part, then--then-- then I will let him go."

After this Rebecca left the room and the house. Before she went, she kissed the Christian girl; but Nina did not remember that she had been kissed. Her mind was so full, not of thought, but of the suggestion that had been made to her, that it could now take no impression from anything else. She had been recommended to do a thing as her duty--as a paramount duty towards him who was everything to her--the doing of which it would be impossible that she should survive. So she told herself when she was once more alone, and had again seated herself in the chair by the window. She did not for a moment accuse Rebecca of dealing unfairly with her. It never occurred to her as possible that the Jewess had come to her with false views of her own fabrication. Had she so believed, her suspicions would have done great injustice to her rival; but no such idea presented itself to Nina's mind. All that Rebecca had said to her had come to her as though it were gospel. She did believe that Trendellsohn, as a Jew, would injure himself greatly by marrying a Christian. She did believe that the Jews of Prague would treat him somewhat as the Christians would treat herself. For herself such treatment would be nothing, if she were but once married; but she could understand that to him it would be ruinous. And Nina believed also that Rebecca had been entirely disinterested in her mission--that she came thither, not to gain a lover for herself, but to save from injury the man she loved, without reference to her own passion. Nina knew that Rebecca was strong and good, and acknowledged also that she herself was weak and selfish. She thought that she ought to have been persuaded to make the sacrifice, and once or twice she almost resolved that she would follow Rebecca to the Jews' quarter and tell her that it should be made. But she could not do it. Were she to do so, what would be left to her? With him she could bear anything, everything. To starve would hardly be bitter to her, so that his arm could be round her waist, and that her head could be on his shoulder. And, moreover, was she not his to do with as he pleased? After all her promises to him, how could she take upon herself to dispose of herself otherwise than as he might direct?

But then some thought of the missing document came back upon her, and she remembered in her grief that he suspected her--that even now he had some frightful doubt as to her truth to him--her faith, which was, alas, alas! more firm and bright towards him than towards that heavenly Friend whose aid would certainly suffice to bring her through all her troubles, if only she could bring herself to trust as she asked it. But she could trust only in him, and he doubted her! Would it not be better to do as Rebecca said, and make the most of such contentment as might come to her from her triumph over herself? That would be better--ten times better than to be abandoned by him--to be deserted by her Jew lover, because the Jew would not trust her, a Christian! On either side there could be nothing for her but death; but there is a choice even of deaths. If she did the thing herself, she thought that there might be something sweet even in the sadness of her last hour--something of the flavor of sacrifice. But should it be done by him, in that way there lay nothing but the madness of desolation! It was her last resolve, as she still sat at the window counting the sparrows in the yard, that she would tell him everything, and leave it to him to decide. If he would say that it was better for them to part, then he might go; and Rebecca Loth might become his wife, if he so wished it.

Chapter 11

On one of these days old Trendellsohn went to the office of Karil Zamenoy, in the Ross Markt, with the full determination of learning in truth what there might be to be learned as to that deed which would be so necessary to him, or to those who would come after him, when Josef Balatka might die. He accused himself of having been foolishly soft- hearted in his transactions with this Christian, and reminded himself from time to time that no Jew in Prague would have been so treated by any Christian. And what was the return made to him? Among them they had now secreted that of which he should have enforced the rendering before he had parted with his own money; and this they did because they knew that he would be unwilling to take harsh legal proceedings against a bed-ridden old man! In this frame of mind he went to the Ross Markt, and there he was assured over and over again by Ziska Zamenoy--for Karil Zamenoy was not to be seen--that Nina Balatka had the deed in her own keeping. The name of Nina Balatka was becoming very grievous to the old man. Even he, when the matter had first been broached to him, had not recognized all the evils which would come from a marriage between his son and a Christian maiden; but of late his neighbors had been around him, and he had looked into the thing, and his eyes had been opened, and he had declared to himself that he would not take a Christian girl into his house as his daughter-in-law. He could not prevent the marriage. The law would be on his son's side. The law of the Christian kingdom in which he lived allowed such marriages, and Anton, if he executed the contract which would make the marriage valid, would in truth be the girl's husband. But--and Trendellsohn, as he remembered the power which was still in his hands, almost regretted that he held it--if this thing were done, his son must go out from his house, and be his son no longer.

The old man was very proud of his son. Rebecca had said truly that no Jew in Prague was so respected among Jews as Anton Trendellsohn. She might have added, also, that none was more highly esteemed among Christians. To lose such a son would be a loss indeed. "I will share everything with him, and he shall go away out of Bohemia," Trendellsohn had said to himself. "He has earned it, and he shall have it. He has worked for me--for us both--without asking me, his father, to bind myself with any bond. He shall have the wealth which is his own, but he shall not have it here. Ah! if he would but take that other one as his bride, he should have everything, and his father's blessing--and then he would be the first instead of the last among his people." Such was the purpose of Stephen Trendellsohn towards his son; but this, his real purpose, did not hinder him from threatening worse things. To prevent the marriage was his great object; and if threats would prevent it, why should he not use them?

But now he had conceived the idea that Nina was deceiving his son--that Nina was in truth holding back the deed with some view which he could hardly fathom. Ziska Zamenoy had declared, with all the emphasis in his power, that the document was, to the best of his belief, in Nina's hands; and though Ziska's emphasis would not have gone far in convincing the Jew, had the Jew's mind been turned in the other direction, now it had its effect. "And who gave it her?" Trendellsohn had asked. "Ah, there you must excuse me," Ziska had answered; "though, indeed, I could not tell you if I would. But we have nothing to do with the matter. We have no claim upon the houses. It is between you and the Balatkas."

Then the Jew had left the Zamenoys' office, and had gone home, fully believing that the deed was in Nina's hands.

"Yes, it is so--she is deceiving you," he said to his son that evening.

"No father. I think not."

"Very well. You will find, when it is too late, that my words are true. Have you ever known a Christian who thought it wrong to rob a Jew?"

"I do not believe that Nina would rob me."

"Ah! that is the confidence of what you call love. She is honest, you think, because she has a pretty face."

"She is honest, I think, because she loves me."

"Bah! Does love make men honest, or women either? Do we not see every day how these Christians rob each other in their money dealings when they are marrying? What was the girl's name?--old Thibolski's daughter --how they robbed her when they married her, and how her people tried their best to rob the lad she married. Did we not see it all?"

"It was not the girl who did it--not the girl herself."

"Why should a woman be honester than a man? I tell you, Anton, that this girl has the deed."

"Ziska Zamenoy has told you so?"

"Yes, he has told me. But I am not a man to be deceived because such a one as Ziska wishes to deceive me. You, at least, know me better than that. That which I tell you, Ziska himself believes."

"But Ziska may believe wrongly."

"Why should he do so? Whose interest can it be to make this thing seem so, if it be not so? If the girl have the deed, you can get it more readily from her than from the Zamenoys. Believe me, Anton, the deed is with the girl."

"If it be so, I shall never believe again in the truth of a human being," said the son.

"Believe in the truth of your own people," said the father. "Why should you seek to be wiser than them all?"

The father did not convince the son, but the words which he had spoken helped to create a doubt which already had almost an existence of its own. Anton Trendellsohn was prone to suspicions, and now was beginning to suspect Nina, although he strove hard to keep his mind free from such taint. His better nature told him that it was impossible that she should deceive him. He had read the very inside of her heart, and knew that her only delight was in his love. He understood perfectly the weakness and faith and beauty of her feminine nature, and her trusting, leaning softness was to his harder spirit as water to a thirsting man in the desert. When she clung to him, promising to obey him in everything, the touch of her hands, and the sound of her voice, and the beseeching glance of her loving eyes, were food and drink to him. He knew that her presence refreshed him and cooled him--made him young as he was growing old, and filled his mind with sweet thoughts which hardly came to him but when she was with him. He had told himself over and over again that it must be good for him to have such a one for his wife, whether she were Jew or Christian. He knew himself to be a better man when she was with him than at other moments of his life. And then he loved her. He was thinking of her hourly, though his impatience to see her was not as hers to be with him. He loved her. But yet--yet-- what if she should be deceiving him? To be able to deceive others, but never to be deceived himself, was to him, unconsciously, the glory which he desired. To be deceived was to be disgraced. What was all his wit and acknowledged cunning if a girl--a Christian girl--could outwit him? For himself, he could see clearly enough into things to be aware that, as a rule, he could do better by truth than he could by falsehood. He was not prone to deceive others. But in such matters he desired ever to have the power with him to keep, as it were, the upper hand. He would fain read the hearts of others entirely, and know their wishes, and understand their schemes, whereas his own heart and his own desires and his own schemes should only be legible in part. What if, after all, he were unable to read the simple tablets of this girl's mind--tablets which he had regarded as being altogether in his own keeping?

He went forth for a while, walking slowly through the streets, as he thought of this, wandering without an object, but turning over in his mind his father's words. He knew that his father was anxious to prevent his marriage. He knew that every Jew around him--for now the Jews around him had all heard of it--was keenly anxious to prevent so great a disgrace. He knew all that his father had threatened, and he was well aware how complete was his father's power. But he could stand against all that, if only Nina were true to him. He would go away from Prague. What did it matter? Prague was not all the world. There were cities better, nobler, richer than Prague, in which his brethren, the Jews, would not turn their backs upon him because he had married a Christian. It might be that he would have to begin the world again; but for that, too, he would be prepared. Nina had shown that she could bear poverty. Nina's torn boots and threadbare dress, and the utter absence of any request ever made with regard to her own comfort, had not been lost upon him. He knew how noble she was in bearing--how doubly noble she was in never asking. If only there was nothing of deceit at the back to mar it all!

He passed over the bridge, hardly knowing whither he was going, and turned directly down towards Balatka's house. As he did so he observed that certain repairs were needed in an adjoining building which belonged to his father, and determined that a mason should be sent there on the next day. Then he turned in under the archway, not passing through it into the court, and there he stood looking up at the window, in which Nina's small solitary lamp was twinkling. He knew that she was sitting by the light, and that she was working. He knew that she would be raised almost to a seventh heaven of delight if he would only call her to the door and speak to her a dozen words before he returned to his home. But he had no thought of doing it. Was it possible that she should have this document in her keeping?--that was the thought that filled his mind. He had bribed Lotta Luxa, and Lotta had sworn by her Christian gods that the deed was in Nina's hands. If the thing was false, why should they all conspire to tell the same falsehood? And yet he knew that they were false in their natures. Their manner, the words of each of them, betrayed something of falsehood to his well-tuned ear, to his acute eye, to his sharp senses. But with Nina--from Nina herself--everything that came from her spoke of truth. A sweet savour of honesty hung about her breath, and was a blessing to him when he was near enough to her to feel it. And yet he told himself that he was bound to doubt. He stood for some half-hour in the archway, leaning against the stonework at the side, and looking up at the window where Nina was sitting. What was he to do? How should he carry himself in this special period of his life? Great ideas about the destiny of his people were mingled in his mind with suspicions as to Nina, of which he should have been, and probably was, ashamed. He would certainly take her away from Prague. He had already perceived that his marriage with a Christian would be regarded in that stronghold of prejudice in which he lived with so much animosity as to impede, and perhaps destroy, the utility of his career. He would go away, taking Nina with him. And he would be careful that she should never know, by a word or a look, that he had in any way suffered for her sake. And he swore to himself that he would be soft to her, and gentle, loving her with a love more demonstrative than he had hitherto exhibited. He knew that he had been stern, exacting, and sometimes harsh. All that should be mended. He had learned her character, and perceived how absolutely she fed upon his love; and he would take care that the food should always be there, palpably there, for her sustenance. But--but he must try her yet once more before all this could be done for her. She must pass yet once again through the fire; and if then she should come forth as gold, she should be to him the one pure ingot which the earth contained. With how great a love would he not repay her in future days for all that she would have suffered for his sake?

But she must be made to go through the fire again. He would tax her with the possession of the missing deed, and call upon her to cleanse herself from the accusation which was made against her. Once again he would be harsh with her--harsh in appearance only--in order that his subsequent tenderness might be so much more tender! She had already borne much, and she must be made to endure once again. Did not he mean to endure much for her sake? Was he not prepared to recommence the troubles and toil of his life all from the beginning, in order that she might be that life's companion? Surely he had the right to put her through the fire, and prove her as never gold was proved before.

At last the little light was quenched, and Anton Trendellsohn felt that he was alone. The unseen companion of his thoughts was no longer with him, and it was useless for him to remain there standing in the archway. He blew her a kiss from his lips, and blessed her in his heart, and protested to himself that he knew she would come out of the fire pure altogether and proved to be without dross. And then he went his way. In the mean time Nina, chill and wretched, crept to her cold bed, all unconscious of the happiness that had been so near her. "If he thinks I can be false to him, it will be better to die," she said to herself, as she drew the scanty clothing over her shivering shoulders.

As she did so her lover walked home, and having come to a resolution which was intended to be definite as to his love, he allowed his thoughts to run away with him to other subjects. After all, it would be no evil to him to leave Prague. At Prague how little was there of progress either in thought or in things material! At Prague a Jew could earn money, and become rich--might own half the city; and yet at Prague he could only live as an outcast. As regarded the laws of the land, he, as a Jew, might fix his residence anywhere in Prague or around Prague; he might have gardens, and lands, and all the results of money; he might put his wife into a carriage twice as splendid as that which constituted the great social triumph of Madame Zamenoy--but so strong against such a mode of life were the traditional prejudices of both Jews and Christians, that any such fashion of living would be absolutely impossible to him. It would not be good for him that he should remain at Prague. Knowing his father as he did, he could not believe that the old man would be so unjust as to let him go altogether empty-handed. He had toiled, and had been successful; and something of the corn which he had garnered would surely be rendered to him. With this--or, if need be, without it--he and his Christian wife would go forth and see if the world was not wide enough to find them a spot on which they might live without the contempt of those around them.

Though Nina had quenched her lamp and had gone to bed, it was not late when Trendellsohn reached his home, and he knew that he should find his father waiting for him. But his father was not alone.

Rebecca Loth was sitting with the old man, and they had just supped together when Anton entered the room. Ruth Jacobi was also there, waiting till her friend should go, before she also went to her bed.

"How are you, Anton?" said Rebecca, giving her hand to the man she loved. "It is strange to see you in these days."

"The strangeness, Rebecca, comes from no fault of my own. Few men, I fancy, are more constant to their homes than I am."

"You sleep here and eat here, I daresay."

"My business lies mostly out, about the town."

"Have you been about business now, uncle Anton?" said Ruth.

"Do not ask forward questions, Ruth," said the uncle. "Rebecca, I fear, teaches you to forget that you are still a child."

"Do not scold her," said the old man. "She is a good girl."

"It is Anton that forgets that nature is making Ruth a young woman," said Rebecca.

"I do not want to be a young woman a bit before uncle Anton likes it," said Ruth. "I don't mind waiting ever so long for him. When he is married he will not care what I am."

"If that be so, you may be a woman very soon," said Rebecca.

"That is more than you know," said Anton, turning very sharply on her. "What do you know of my marriage, or when it will be?"

"Are you scolding her too?" said the elder Trendellsohn.

"Nay, father; let him do so," said Rebecca. "He has known me long enough to scold me if he thinks that I deserve it. You are gentle to me and spoil me, and it is only well that one among my old friends should be sincere enough to be ungentle."

"I beg your pardon, Rebecca, if I have been uncourteous."

"There can be no pardon where there is no offence."

"If you are ashamed to hear of your marriage," said the father, "you should be ashamed to think of it."

Then there was silence for a few seconds before anyone spoke. The girls did not dare to speak after words so serious from the father to the son. It was known to both of them that Anton could hardly bring himself to bear a rebuke even from his father, and they felt that such a rebuke as this, given in their presence, would be altogether unendurable. Every one in the room understood the exact position in which each stood to the other. That Rebecca would willingly have become Anton's wife, that she had refused various offers of marriage in order that ultimately it might be so, was known to Stephen Trendellsohn, and to Anton himself, and to Ruth Jacobi. There had not been the pretence of any secret among them in the matter. But the subject was one which could hardly be discussed by them openly. "Father," said Anton, after a while, during which the black thunder-cloud which had for an instant settled on his brow had managed to dispel itself without bursting into a visible storm--"father, I am neither ashamed to think of my intended marriage nor to speak of it. There is no question of shame. But it is unpleasant to make such a subject matter of general conversation when it is a source of trouble instead of joy among us. I wish I could have made you happy by my marriage."

"You will make me very wretched."

"Then let us not talk about it. It cannot be altered. You would not have me false to my plighted word?"

Again there was silence for some minutes, and then Rebecca spoke--the words coming from her in the lowest possible accents.

"It can be altered without breach of your plighted word. Ask the young woman what she herself thinks. You will find that she knows that you are both wrong."

"Of course she knows it," said the father.

"I will ask her nothing of the kind," said the son.

"It would be of no use," said Ruth.

After this Rebecca rose to take her leave, saying something of the falseness of her brother Samuel, who had promised to come for her and to take her home. "But he is with Miriam Harter," said Rebecca, "and, of course, he will forget me."

"I will go home with you," said Anton.

"Indeed you shall not. Do you think I cannot walk alone through our own streets in the dark without being afraid?"

"I am well aware that you are afraid of nothing; but nevertheless, if you will allow me, I will accompany you." There was no sufficient cause for her to refuse his company, and the two left the house together.

As they descended the stairs, Rebecca determined that she would have the first word in what might now be said between them. She had suggested that this marriage with the Christian girl might be abandoned without the disgrace upon Anton of having broken his troth, and she had thereby laid herself open to a suspicion of having worked for her own ends--of having done so with unmaidenly eagerness to gratify her own love. Something on the subject must be said--would be said by him if not by her--and therefore she would explain herself at once. She spoke as soon as she found herself by his side in the street. "I regretted what I said up-stairs, Anton, as soon as the words were out of my mouth."

"I do not know that you said anything to regret."

"I told you that if in truth you thought this marriage to be wrong--"

"Which I do not."

"Pardon me, my friend, for a moment. If you had so thought, I said that there was a mode of escape without falsehood or disgrace. In saying so I must have seemed to urge you to break away from Nina Balatka."

"You are all urging me to do that."

"Coming from the others, such advice cannot even seem to have an improper motive." Here she paused, feeling the difficulty of her task-- aware that she could not conclude it without an admission which no woman willingly makes. But she shook away the impediment, bracing herself to the work, and went on steadily with her speech. "Coming from me, such motive may be imputed--nay, it must be imputed."

"No motive is imputed that is not believed by me to be good and healthy and friendly."

"Our friends," continued Rebecca, "have wished that you and I should be husband and wife. That is now impossible."

"It is impossible--because Nina will be my wife."

"It is impossible, whether Nina should become your wife or should not become your wife. I do not say this from any girlish pride. Before I knew that you loved a Christian woman, I would willingly have been--as our friends wished. You see I can trust you enough for candor. When I was young they told me to love you, and I obeyed them. They told me that I was to be your wife, and I taught myself to be happy in believing them. I now know that they were wrong, and I will endeavor to teach myself another happiness."

"Rebecca, if I have been in fault--"

"You have never been in fault. You are by nature too stern to fall into such faults. It has been my misfortune--perhaps rather I should say my difficulty--that till of late you have given me no sign by which I could foresee my lot. I was still young, and I still believed what they told me, even though you did not come to me as lovers come. Now I know it all; and as any such thoughts--or wishes, if you will--as those I used to have can never return to me, I may perhaps be felt by you to be free to use what liberty of counsel old friendship may give me. I know you will not misunderstand me--and that is all. Do not come further with me."

He called to her, but she was gone, escaping from him with quick running feet through the dark night; and he returned to his father's house, thinking of the girl that had left him.

Chapter 12

Again some days passed by without any meeting between Nina and her lover, and things were going very badly with the Balatkas in the old house. The money that had come from the jeweler was not indeed all expended, but Nina looked upon it as her last resource, till marriage should come to relieve her; and the time of her marriage seemed to be as far from her as ever. So the kreutzers were husbanded as only a woman can husband them, and new attempts were made to reduce the little expenses of the little household.

"Souchey, you had better go. You had indeed," said Nina. "We cannot feed you." Now Souchey had himself spoken of leaving them some days since, urged to do so by his Christian indignation at the abominable betrothal of his mistress. "You said the other day that you would do so, and it will be better."

"But I shall not."

"Then you will be starved."

"I am starved already, and it cannot be worse. I dined yesterday on what they threw out to the dogs in the meat-market."

"And where will you dine today?"

"Ah, I shall dine better today. I shall get a meal in the Windberg- gasse."

"What! at my aunt's house?"

"Yes; at your aunt's house. They live well there, even in the kitchen. Lotta will have for me some hot soup, a mess of cabbage, and a sausage. I wish I could bring it away from your aunt's house to the old man and yourself."

"I would sooner fall in the gutter than eat my aunt's meat."

"That is all very fine for you, but I am not going to marry a Jewess. Why should I quarrel with your aunt, or with Lotta Luxa? If you would give up the Jew, Nina, your aunt's house would be open to you; yes--and Ziska's house."

"I will not give up the Jew," said Nina, with flashing eyes.

"I suppose not. But what will you do when he gives you up? What if Ziska then should not be so forward?"

"Of all those who are my enemies, and whom I hate because they are so cruel, I hate Ziska the worst. Go and tell him so, since you are becoming one of them. In doing so much you cannot at any rate do me harm."

Then she took herself off, forgetting in her angry spirit the prudential motives which had induced her to begin the conversation with Souchey. But Souchey, though he was going to Madame Zamenoy's house to get his dinner, and was looking forward with much eagerness to the mess of hot cabbage and the cold sausage, had by no means become "one of them" in the Windberg-gasse. He had had more than one interview of late with Lotta Luxa, and had perceived that something was going on, of which he much desired to be at the bottom. Lotta had some scheme, which she was half willing and half unwilling to reveal to him, by which she hoped to prevent the threatened marriage between Nina and the Jew. Now Souchey was well enough inclined to take a part in such a scheme-- provided it did not in any way make him a party with the Zamenoys in things general against the Balatkas. It was his duty as a Christian-- though he himself was rather slack in the performance of his own religious duties--to put a stop to this horrible marriage if he could do so; but it behoved him to be true to his master and mistress, and especially true to them in opposition to the Zamenoys. He had in some sort been carrying on a losing battle against the Zamenoys all his life, and had some of the feelings of a martyr, telling himself that he had lost a rich wife by doing so. He would go on this occasion and eat his dinner and be very confidential with Lotta; but he would be very discreet, would learn more than he told, and, above all, would not betray his master or mistress.

Soon after he was gone, Anton Trendellsohn came over to the Kleinseite, and, ringing at the bell of the house, received admission from Nina herself. "What! you, Anton?" she said, almost jumping into his arms, and then restraining herself. "Will you come up? It is so long since I have seen you."

"Yes--it is long. I hope the time is soon coming when there shall be no more of such separation."

"Is it? Is it indeed?"

"I trust it is."

"I suppose as a maiden I ought to be coy, and say that I would prefer to wait; but, dearest love, sorrow and trouble have banished all that. You will not love me less because I tell you that I count the minutes till I may be your wife."

"No; I do not love you less on that account. I would have you be true and faithful in all things."

Though the words themselves were assuring, there was something in the tone of his voice which repressed her. "To you I am true and faithful in all things; as faithful as though you were already my husband. What were you saying of a time that is soon coming?"

He did not answer her question, but turned the subject away into another channel. "I have brought something for you," he said--something which I hope you will be glad to have."

"Is it a present? she asked. As yet he had never given her anything that she could call a gift, and it was to her almost a matter of pride that she had taken nothing from her Jew lover, and that she would take nothing till it should be her right to take everything.

"Hardly a present; but you shall look at it as you will. You remember Rapinsky, do you not?" Now Rapinsky was the jeweler in the Grosser Ring, and Nina, though she well remembered the man and the shop, did not at the moment remember the name. "You will not have forgotten this at any rate," said Trendellsohn, bringing the necklace from out of his pocket.

"How did you get it?" said Nina, not putting out her hand to take it, but looking at it as it lay upon the table.

"I thought you would be glad to have it back again."

"I should be glad if--"

"If what?" Will it be less welcome because it comes through my hands?"

"The man lent me money upon it, and you must have paid the money."

"What if I have? I like your pride, Nina; but be not too proud. Of course I have paid the money. I know Rapinsky, who deals with us often. I went to him after you spoke to me, and got it back again. There is your mother's necklace."

"I am sorry for this, Anton."

"Why sorry?"

"We are so poor that I shall be driven to take it elsewhere again. I cannot keep such a thing in the house while father wants. But better he should want than--"

"Than what, Nina?"

"There would be something like cheating in borrowing money on the same thing twice."

"Then put it by, and I will be your lender."

"No; I will not borrow from you. You are the only one in the world that I could never repay. I cannot borrow from you. Keep this thing, and if I am ever your wife, then you shall give it me."

"If you are ever my wife?"

"Is there no room for such an if? I hope there is not, Anton. I wish it were as certain as the sun's rising. But people around us are so cruel! It seems, sometimes, as though the world were against us. And then you, yourself--"

"What of me myself, Nina?"

"I do not think you trust me altogether; and unless you trust me, I know you will not make me your wife."

"That is certain; and yet I do not doubt that you will be my wife."

"But do you trust me? Do you believe in your heart of hearts that I know nothing of that paper for which you are searching?" She paused for a reply, but he did not at once make any. "Tell me," she went on saying, with energy, "are you sure that I am true to you in that matter, as in all others? Though I were starving--and it is nearly so with me already--and though I loved you beyond even all heaven, as I do, I do--I would not become your wife if you doubted me in any tittle. Say that you doubt me, and then it shall be all over." Still he did not speak. "Rebecca Loth will be a fitter wife for you than I can be," said Nina.

"If you are not my wife, I shall never have a wife," said Trendellsohn.

In her ecstasy of delight, as she heard these words, she took up his hand and kissed it; but she dropped it again, as she remembered that she had not yet received the assurance that she needed. "But you do believe me about this horrid paper?"

It was necessary that she should be made to go again through the fire. In deliberate reflection he had made himself aware that such necessity still existed. It might be that she had some inner reserve as to duty towards her father. There was, possibly, some reason which he could not fathom why she should still keep something back from him in this matter. He did not, in truth, think that it was so, but there was the chance. There was the chance, and he could not bear to be deceived. He felt assured that Ziska Zamenoy and Lotta Luxa believed that this deed was in Nina's keeping. Indeed, he was assured that all the household of the Zamenoys so believed. "If there be a God above us, it is there," Lotta had said, crossing herself. He did not think it was there; he thought that Lotta was wrong, and that all the Zamenoys were wrong, by some mistake which he could not fathom; but still there was the chance, and Nina must be made to bear this additional calamity.

"Do you think it impossible," said he, "that you should have it among your own things?"

"What! without knowing that I have it?" she asked.

"It may have come to you with other papers," he said, "and you may not quite have understood its nature."

"There, in that desk, is every paper that I have in the world. You can look if you suspect me. But I shall not easily forgive you for looking." Then she threw down the key of her desk upon the table. He took it up and fingered it, but did not move towards the desk. "The greatest treasure there," she said, "are scraps of your own, which I have been a fool to value, as they have come from a man who does not trust me."

He knew that it would be useless for him to open the desk. If she were secreting anything from him, she was not hiding it there. "Might it not possibly be among your clothes?" he asked.

"I have no clothes," she answered, and then strode off across the wide room towards the door of her father's apartment. But after she had grasped the handle of the door, she turned again upon her lover. "It may, however, be well that you should search my chamber and my bed. If you will come with me, I will show you the door. You will find it to be a sorry place for one who was your affianced bride."

"Who *is* my affianced bride," said Trendellsohn.

"No, sir!--who was, but is so no longer. You will have to ask my pardon, at my feet, before I will let you speak to me again as my lover. Go and search. Look for your deed--and then you shall see that I will tear out my own heart rather than submit to the ill-usage of distrust from one who owes me so much faith as you do."

"Nina" he said.

"Well, sir."

"I do trust you."

"Yes--with a half trust--with one eye closed, while the other is watching me. You think you have so conquered me that I will be good to you, and yet cannot keep yourself from listening to those who whisper that I am bad to you. Sir, I fear they have been right when they told me that a Jew's nature would surely shock me at last."

The dark frowning cloud, which she had so often observed with fear, came upon his brow; but she did not fear him now. "And do you too taunt me with my religion?" he said.

"No, not so--not with your religion, Anton; but with your nature."

"And how can I help my nature?"

"I suppose you cannot help it, and I am wrong to taunt you. I should not have taunted you. I should only have said that I will not endure the suspicion either of a Christian or of a Jew."

He came up to her now, and put out his arm as though he were about to embrace her. "No," she said;

"not again, till you have asked my pardon for distrusting me, and have given me your solemn word that you distrust me no longer."

He paused a moment in doubt, then put his hat on his head and prepared to leave her. She had behaved very well, but still he would not be weak enough to yield to her in everything at once. As to opening her desk, or going up-stairs into her room, that he felt to be quite impossible. Even his nature did not admit of that. But neither did his nature allow him to ask her pardon and to own that he had been wrong. She had said that he must implore her forgiveness at her feet. One word, however, one look, would have sufficed. But that word and that look were, at the present moment, out of his power. "Good-bye, Nina," he said. "It is best that I should leave you now."

"By far the best; and you will take the necklace with you, if you please."

"No; I will leave that. I cannot keep a trinket that was your mother's."

"Take it, then, to the jeweler's, and get back your money. It shall not be left here. I will have nothing from your hands." He was so far cowed by her manner that he took up the necklace and left the house, and Nina was once more alone.

What they had told her of her lover was after all true. That was the first idea that occurred to her as she sat in her chair, stunned by the sorrow that had come upon her. They had dinned into her ears their accusations, not against the man himself, but against the tribe to which he belonged, telling her that a Jew was, of his very nature, suspicious, greedy, and false. She had perceived early in her acquaintance with Anton Trendellsohn that he was clever, ambitious, gifted with the power of thinking as none others whom she knew could think; and that he had words at his command, and was brave, and was endowed with a certain nobility of disposition which prompted him to wish for great results rather than for small advantages. All this had conquered her, and had made her resolve to think that a Jew could be as good as a Christian. But now, when the trial of the man had in truth come, she found that those around her had been right in what they had said. How base must be the nature which could prompt a man to suspect a girl who had been true to him as Nina had been true to her lover!

She would never see him again--never! He had left the room without even answering the question which she had asked him. He would not even say that he trusted her. It was manifest that he did not trust her, and that he believed at this moment that she was endeavoring to rob him in this matter of the deed. He had asked her if she had it in her desk or among her clothes, and her very soul revolted from the suspicion so implied. She would never speak to him again. It was all over. No; she would never willingly speak to him again.

But what would she do? For a few minutes she fell back, as is so natural with mortals in trouble, upon that religion which she had been so willing to outrage by marrying the Jew. She went to a little drawer and took out a string of beads which had lain there unused since she had been made to believe that the Virgin and the saints would not permit her marriage with Anton Trendellsohn. She took out the beads-- but she did not use them. She passed no berries through her fingers to check the number of prayers said, for she found herself unable to say any prayer at all. If he would come back to her, and ask her pardon-- ask it in truth at her feet--she would still forgive him, regardless of the Virgin and the saints. And if he did not come back, what was the fate that Lotta Luxa had predicted for her, and to which she had acknowledged to herself that she would be driven to submit? In either case how could she again come to terms with St John and St Nicholas? And how was she to live? Should she lose her lover, as she now told herself would certainly be her fate, what possibility of life was left to her? From day to day and from week to week she had put off to a future hour any definite consideration of what she and her father should do in their poverty, believing that it might be postponed till her marriage would make all things easy. Her future mode of living had often been discussed between her and her lover, and she had been candid enough in explaining to him that she could not leave her father desolate. He had always replied that his wife's father should want for nothing, and she had been delighted to think that she could with joy accept that from her husband which nothing would induce her to accept from her lover. This thought had sufficed to comfort her, as the evil of absolute destitution was close upon her. Surely the day of her marriage would come soon.

But now it seemed to her to be certain that the day of her marriage would never come. All those expectations must be banished, and she must look elsewhere--if elsewhere there might be any relief. She knew well that if she would separate herself from the Jew, the pocket of her aunt would be opened to relieve the distress of her father--would be opened so far as to save the old man from perishing of want. Aunt Sophie, if duly invoked, would not see her sister's husband die of starvation. Nay, aunt Sophie would doubtless so far stretch her Christian charity as to see that her niece was in some way fed, if that niece would be duly obedient. Further still, aunt Sophie would accept her niece as the very daughter of her house, as the rising mistress of her own establishment, if that niece would only consent to love her son. Ziska was there as a husband in Anton's place, if Ziska might only gain acceptance.

But Nina, as she rose from her chair and walked backwards and forwards through her chamber, telling herself all these things, clenched her fist, and stamped her foot, as she swore to herself that she would dare all that the saints could do to her, that she would face all the terrors of the black dark river, before she would succumb to her cousin Ziska. As she worked herself into wrath, thinking now of the man she loved, and then of the man she did not love, she thought that she could willingly perish--if it were not that her father lay there so old and so helpless. Gradually, as she magnified to herself the terrible distresses of her heart, the agony of her yearning love for a man who, though he loved her, was so unworthy of her perfect faith, she began to think that it would be well to be carried down by the quick, eternal, almighty stream beyond the reach of the sorrow which encompassed her. When her father should leave her she would be all alone--alone in the world, without a friend to regard her, or one living human being on whom she, a girl, might rely for protection, shelter, or even for a morsel of bread. Would St Nicholas cover her from the contumely of the world, or would St John of the Bridges feed her? Did she in her heart of hearts believe that even the Virgin would assist her in such a strait? No; she had no such belief. It might be that such real belief had never been hers. She hardly knew. But she did know that now, in the hour of her deep trouble, she could not say her prayers and tell her beads, and trust valiantly that the goodness of heaven would suffice to her in her need.

In the mean time Souchey had gone off to the Windberg-gasse, and had gladdened himself with the soup, with the hot mess of cabbage and the sausage, supplied by Madame Zamenoy's hospitality. The joys of such a moment are unknown to any but those who, like Souchey, have been driven by circumstances to sit at tables very ill supplied. On the previous day he had fed upon offal thrown away from a butcher's stall, and habit had made such feeding not unfamiliar to him. As he walked from the Kleinseite through the Old Town to Madame Zamenoy's bright-looking house in the New Town, he had comforted himself greatly with thoughts of the coming feast. The representation which his imagination made to him of the banquet sufficed to produce happiness, and he went along hardly envying any man. His propensities at the moment were the propensities of a beast. And yet he was submitting himself to the terrible poverty which made so small a matter now a matter of joy to him, because there was a something of nobility within him which made him true to the master who had been true to him, when they had both been young together. Even now he resolved, as he sharpened his teeth, that through all the soup and all the sausage he would be true to the Balatkas. He would be true even to Nina Balatka--though he recognized it as a paramount duty to do all in his power to save her from the Jew.

He was seated at the table in the kitchen almost as soon as he had entered the house in the Windberg-gasse, and found his plate full before him. Lotta had felt that there was no need of the delicacy of compliment in feeding a man who was so undoubtedly hungry, and she had therefore bade him at once fall to. "A hearty meal is a thing you are not used to," she had said, "and it will do your old bones a deal of good." The address was not complimentary, especially as coming from a lady in regard to whom he entertained tender feelings; but Souchey forgave the something of coarse familiarity which the words displayed, and, seating himself on the stool before the victuals, gave play to the feelings of the moment. "There's no one to measure what's left of the sausage," said Lotta, instigating him to new feats.

"Ain't there now?" said Souchey, responding to the sound of the trumpet. "I always thought she had the devil's own eye in looking after what was used in the kitchen."

"The devil himself winks sometimes," said Lotta, cutting another half- inch off from the unconsumed fragment, and picking the skin from the meat with her own fair fingers. Hitherto Souchey had been regardless of any such niceness in his eating, the skin having gone with the rest; but now he thought that the absence of the outside covering and the touch of Lotta's fingers were grateful to his appetite.

"Souchey," said Lotta, when he had altogether done, and had turned his stool round to the kitchen fire, "where do you think Nina would go if she were to marry--a Jew?" There was an abrupt solemnity in the manner of the question which at first baffled the man, whose breath was heavy with the comfortable repletion which had been bestowed upon him.

"Where would she go to?" he said, repeating Lotta's words.

"Yes, Souchey, where would she go to? Where would be her eternal home? What would become of her soul? Do you know that not a priest in Prague would give her absolution though she were on her dying bed? Oh, holy Mary, it's a terrible thing to think of! It's bad enough for the old man and her to be there day after day without a morsel to eat; and I suppose if it were not for Anton Trendellsohn it would be bad enough with them--"

"Not a gulden, then, has Nina ever taken from the Jew--nor the value of a gulden, as far as I can judge between them."

"What matters that, Souchey? Is she not engaged to him as his wife? Can anything in the world be so dreadful? Don't you know she'll be--damned for ever and ever?" Lotta, as she uttered the terrible words, brought her face close to Souchey's, looking into his eyes with a fierce glare. Souchey shook his head sorrowfully, owning thereby that his knowledge in the matter of religion did not go to the point indicated by Lotta Luxa. "And wouldn't anything, then, be a good deed that would prevent that?"

"It's the priests that should do it among them."

"But the priests are not the men they used to be, Souchey. And it is not exactly their fault neither. There are so many folks about in these days who care nothing who goes to glory and who does not, and they are too many for the priests."

"If the priests can't fight their own battle, I can't fight it for them," said Souchey.

"But for the old family, Souchey, that you have known so long! Look here; you and I between us can prevent it."

"And how is it to be done?"

"Ah! that's the question. If I felt that I was talking to a real Christian that had a care for the poor girl's soul, I would tell you in a moment."

"So I am; only her soul isn't my business."

"Then I cannot tell you this. I can't do it unless you acknowledge that her welfare as a Christian is the business of us all. Fancy, Souchey, your mistress married to a filthy Jew!"

"For the matter of that, he isn't so filthy neither."

"An abominable Jew! But, Souchey, she will never fall out with him. We must contrive that he shall quarrel with her. If she had a thing about her that he did not want her to have, couldn't you contrive that he should know it?"

"What sort of thing? Do you mean another lover, like?"

"No, you gander. If there was anything of that sort I could manage it myself. But if she had a thing locked up--away from him, couldn't you manage to show it to him? He's very generous in rewarding, you know."

"I don't want to have anything to do with it," said Souchey, getting up from his stool and preparing to take his departure. Though he had been so keen after the sausage, he was above taking a bribe in such a matter as this.

"Stop, Souchey, stop. I didn't think that I should ever have to ask anything of you in vain."

Then she put her face very close to his, so that her lips touched his ear, and she laid her hand heavily upon his arm, and she was very confidential. Souchey listened to the whisper till his face grew longer and longer. "'Tis for her soul," said Lotta--"for her poor soul's sake. When you can save her by raising your hand, would you let her be damned for ever?"

But she could exact no promise from Souchey except that he would keep faith with her, and that he would consider deeply the proposal made to him. Then there was a tender farewell between them, and Souchey returned to the Kleinseite.

Chapter 13

For two days after this Nina heard nothing from the Jews' quarter, and in her terrible distress her heart almost became softened towards the man who had so deeply offended her. She began to tell herself, in the weariness of her sorrow, that men were different from women, and, of their nature, more suspicious; that no woman had a right to expect every virtue in her lover, and that no woman had less of such right than she herself, who had so little to give in return for all that Anton proposed to bestow upon her. She began to think that she could forgive him, even for his suspicion, if he would only come to be forgiven. But he came not, and it was only too plain to her that she could not be the first to go to him after what had passed between them. And then there fell another crushing sorrow upon her. Her father was ill--so ill that he was like to die. The doctor came to him--some son of Galen who had known the merchant in his prosperity--and, with kind assurances, told Nina that her father, though he could pay nothing, should have whatever assistance medical attention could give him; but he said, at the same time, that medical attention could give no aid that would be of permanent service. The light had burned down in the socket, and must go out. The doctor took Nina by the hand, and put his own hand upon her soft tresses, and spoke kind words to console her. And then he said that the sick man ought to take a few glasses of wine every day; and as he was going away, turned back again, and promised to send the wine from his own house. Nina thanked him, and plucked up something of her old spirit during his presence, and spoke to him as though she had no other care than that of her father's health; but as soon as the doctor was gone she thought again of her Jew lover. That her father should die was a great grief. But when she should be alone in the old house, with the corpse lying on the bed, would Anton Trendellsohn come to her then?

He did not come to her now, though he knew of her father's illness. She sent Souchey to the Jews' quarter to tell the sad news--not to him, but to old Trendellsohn. "For the sake of the property it is right that he should know," Nina said to herself, excusing to herself on this plea her weakness in sending any message to the house of Anton Trendellsohn till he should have come and asked her pardon. But even after this he came not. She listened to every footstep that entered the courtyard. She could not keep herself from going to the window, and from looking into the square. Surely now, in her deep sorrow, in her solitude, he would come to her. He would come and say one word--that he did trust her, that he would trust her! But no; he came not at all; and the hours of the day and the night followed slowly and surely upon each other, as she sat by her father's bed watching the last quiver of the light in the socket.

But though Trendellsohn did not come himself, there came to her a messenger from the Jew's house--a messenger from the Jew's house, but not a messenger from Anton Trendellsohn. "Here is a girl from the-- Jew," said Souchey, whispering into her ear as she sat at her father's bedside--"one of themselves. Shall I tell her to go away, because he is so ill?" And Souchey pointed to his master's head on the pillow. "She has got a basket, but she can leave that."

Nina, however, was by no means inclined to send the Jewess away, rightly guessing that the stranger was her friend Ruth. "Stop here, Souchey, and I will go to her," Nina said. "Do not leave him till I return. I will not be long." She would not have let a dog go without a word that had come from Anton's house or from Anton's presence. Perhaps he had written to her. If there were but a line to say, "Pardon me; I was wrong," everything might yet be right. But Ruth Jacobi was the bearer of no note from Anton, nor indeed had she come on her present message with her uncle's knowledge. She had put a heavy basket on the table, and now, running forward, took Nina by the hands, and kissed her.

"We have been so sorry, all of us, to hear of your father's illness," said Ruth.

"Father is very ill," said Nina. "He is dying."

"Nay, Nina; it may be that he is not dying. Life and death both are in the hands of God."

"Yes; it is in God's hands of course; but the doctor says that he will die."

"The doctors have no right to speak in that way," said Ruth, "for how can they know God's pleasure? It may be that he will recover."

"Yes; it may be," said Nina. "It is good of you to come to me, Ruth. I am so glad you have come. Have you any--any--message?" If he would only ask to be forgiven through Ruth, or even if he had sent a word that might be taken to show that he wished to be forgiven, it should suffice.

"I have--brought--a few things in a basket," said Ruth, almost apologetically.

Then Nina lifted the basket. "You did not surely carry this through the streets?"

"I had Shadrach, our boy, with me. He carried it. It is not from me, exactly; though I have been so glad to come with it."

"And who sent it?" said Nina, quickly, with her fingers trembling on its lid. If Anton had thought to send anything to her, that anything should suffice.

"It was Rebecca Loth who thought of it, and who asked me to come," said Ruth.

Then Nina drew back her fingers as though they were burned, and walked away from the table with quick angry steps. "Why should Rebecca Loth send anything to me?" she said. "What is there in the basket?"

"She has written a little line. It is at the top. But she has asked me to say--"

"What has she asked you to say? Why should she say anything to me?"

"Nay, Nina; she is very good, and she loves you."

"I do not want her love."

"I am to say to you that she has heard of your distress, and she hopes that a girl like you will let a girl like her do what she can to comfort you."

"She cannot comfort me."

"She bade me say that if she were ill or in sorrow, there is no hand from which she would so gladly take comfort as from yours--for the sake, she said, of a mutual friend."

"I have no--friend," said Nina.

"Oh, Nina, am not I your friend? Do not I love you?"

"I do not know. If you do love me now, you must cease to love me. You are a Jewess, and I am a Christian, and we must live apart. You, at least, must live. I wish you would tell the boy that he may take back the basket."

"There are things in it for your father, Nina; and, Nina, surely you will read Rebecca's note?"

Then Ruth went to the basket, and from the top she took out Rebecca's letter, and gave it to Nina, and Nina read it. It was as follows:

I shall always regard you as very dear to me, because our hearts have been turned in the same way. It may not be perhaps that we shall know each other much at first; but I hope the days may come when we shall be much older than we are now, and that then we may meet and be able to talk of what has passed without pain. I do not know why a Jewess and a Christian woman should not be friends.

I have sent a few things which may perhaps be of comfort to your father. In pity to me do not refuse them. They are such as one woman should send to another. And I have added a little trifle for your own use. At the present moment you are poor as to money, though so rich in the gifts which make men love. On my knees before you I ask you to accept from my hand what I send, and to think of me as one who would serve you in more things if it were possible. Yours, if you will let me, affectionately, REBECCA.

I see when I look at them that the shoes will be too big.

She stood for a while apart from Ruth, with the open note in her hand, thinking whether or no she would accept the gifts which had been sent. The words which Rebecca had written had softened her heart, especially those in which the Jewess had spoken openly to her of her poverty. "At the present moment you are poor as to money," the girl had said, and had said it as though such poverty were, after all, but a small thing in their relative positions one to another. That Nina should be loved, and Rebecca not loved, was a much greater thing. For her father's sake she would take the things sent--and for Rebecca's sake. She would take even the shoes, which she wanted so sorely. She remembered well, as she read the last word, how, when Rebecca had been with her, she herself had pointed to the poor broken slippers which she wore, not meaning to excite such compassion as had now been shown. Yes, she would accept it all--as one woman should take such things from another.

"You will not make Shadrach carry them back?" said Ruth, imploring her.

"But he--has he sent nothing?--not a word?" She would have thought herself to be utterly incapable, before Ruth had come, of showing so much weakness; but her reserve gave way as she admitted in her own heart the kindness of Rebecca, and she became conquered and humbled. She was so terribly in want of his love at this moment! "And has he sent no word of a message to me?"

"I did not tell him that I was coming."

But he knows--he knows that father is so ill."

"Yes; I suppose he has heard that, because Souchey came to the house. But he has been out of temper with us all, and unhappy, for some days past. I know that he is unhappy when he is so harsh with us."

"And what has made him unhappy?

"Nay, I cannot tell you that. I thought perhaps it was because you did not come to him. You used to come and see us at our house."

Dear Ruth! Dearest Ruth, for saying such dear words! She had done more than Rebecca by the sweetness of the suggestion. If it were really the case that he were unhappy because they had parted from each other in anger, no further forgiveness would be necessary.

"But how can I come, Ruth?" she said. "It is he that should come to me."

"You used to come."

"Ah, yes. I came first with messages from father, and then because I loved to hear him talk to me. I do not mind telling you, Ruth, now. And then I came because--because he said I was to be his wife. I thought that if I was to be his wife it could not be wrong that I should go to his father's house. But now that so many people know it--that they talk about it so much--I cannot go to him now."

"But you are not ashamed of being engaged to him--because he is a Jew?"

"No," said Nina, raising herself to her full height; "I am not ashamed of him. I am proud of him. To my thinking there is no man like him. Compare him and Ziska, and Ziska becomes hardly a man at all. I am very proud to think that he has chosen me."

"That is well spoken, and I shall tell him."

"No, you must not tell him, Ruth. Remember that I talk to you as a friend, and not as a child."

"But I will tell him, because then his brow will become smooth, and he will be happy. He likes to think that people know him to be clever; and he will be glad to be told that you understand him."

"I think him greater and better than all men; but, Ruth, you must not tell him what I say--not now, at least--for a reason."

"What reason, Nina?"

"Well; I will tell you, though I would not tell anyone else in the world. When we parted last I was angry with him--very angry with him."

"He had been scolding you, perhaps?"

"I should not mind that--not in the least. He has a right to scold me."

"He has a right to scold me, I suppose; but I mind it very much."

"But he has no right to distrust me, Ruth. I wish he could see my heart and all my mind, and know every thought in my breast, and then he would feel that he could trust me. I would not deceive him by a word or a look for all the world. He does not know how true I am to him, and that kills me."

"I will tell him everything."

"No, Ruth; tell him nothing. If he cannot find it out without being told, telling will do no good. If you thought a person was a thief, would you change your mind because the person told you he was honest? He must find it out for himself if he is ever to know it."

When Ruth was gone, Nina knew that she had been comforted. To have spoken about her lover was in itself much; and to have spoken about him as she had done seemed almost to have brought him once more near to her. Ruth had declared that Anton was sad, and had suggested to Nina that the cause of his sadness was the same as her own. There could not but be comfort in this. If he really wished to see her, would he not come over to the Kleinseite? There could be no reason why he should not visit the girl he intended to marry, and whom he was longing to see. Of course he had business which must occupy his time. He could not give up every moment to thoughts of love, as she could do. She told herself all this, and once more endeavored to be comforted.

And then she unpacked the basket. There were fresh eggs, and a quantity of jelly, and some soup in a jug ready to be made hot, and such delicacies as invalids will eat when their appetites will serve for nothing else. And Nina, as she took these things out, thought only of her father. She took them as coming for him altogether, without any reference to her own use. But at the bottom of the basket there were stockings, and a handkerchief or two, and a petticoat, and a pair of shoes. Should she throw them out among the ashes behind the kitchen, or should she press them to her bosom as treasures to be loved as long as a single thread of them might hang together? She had taken such alms before--from her aunt Sophie--taking them in bitterness of spirit, and wearing them as though they were made of sackcloth, very sore to the skin. The acceptance of such things, even from her aunt, had been gall to her; but, in the old days, no idea of refusing them had come to her. Of course she must submit herself to her aunt's charity, because of her father's poverty. And garments had come to her which were old and worn, bearing unmistakable signs of Lotta's coarse but reparative energies-- raiment against which her feminine niceness would have rebelled, had it been possible for her, in her misfortunes, to indulge her feminine niceness.

But there was a sweet scent of last summer's roses on the things which now lay in her lap, and each article was of the best; and, though each had been worn, they were all such as one girl would lend to another who was her dearest friend--who was to be made welcome to the wardrobe as though it were her own. There was something of the tenderness of love in the very folding, and respect as well as friendship in the care of the packing. Her aunt's left-off clothes had come to her in a big roll, fastened with a corking-pin. But Rebecca, with delicate fingers, had made each article of her tribute to look pretty, as though for the dress of such a one as Nina prettiness and care must always be needed. It was not possible for her to refuse a present sent to her with so many signs of tenderness.

And then she tried on the shoes. Of all the things she needed these were the most necessary. At her first glance she thought that they were new; but she perceived that they had been worn, and she liked them the better on that account. She put her feet into them and found that they were in truth a little too large for her. And this, even this, tended in some sort to gratify her feelings and soothe the asperity of her grief. "It is only a quarter of a size," she said to herself, as she held up her dress that she might look at her feet. And thus she resolved that she would accept her rival's kindness.

On the following morning the priest came--that Father Jerome whom she had known as a child, and from whom she had been unable to obtain ghostly comfort since she had come in contact with the Jew. Her aunt and her father, Souchey and Lotta Luxa, had all threatened her with Father Jerome; and when it had become manifest to her that it would be necessary that the priest should visit her father in his extremity, she had at first thought that it would be well for her to hide herself. But the cowardice of this had appeared to her to be mean, and she had resolved that she would meet her old friend at her father's bedside. After all, what would his bitterest words be to her after such words as she had endured from her lover?

Father Jerome came, and she received him in the parlor. She received him with downcast eyes and a demeanor of humility, though she was resolved to flare up against him if he should attack her too cruelly. But the man was as mild to her and as kind as ever he had been in her childhood, when he would kiss her, and call her his little nun, and tell her that if she would be a good girl she should always have a white dress and roses at the festival of St Nicholas. He put his hand on her head and blessed her, and did not seem to have any abhorrence of her because she was going to marry a Jew. And yet he knew it.

He asked a few words as to her father, who was indeed better on this morning than he had been for the last few days, and then he passed on into the sick man's room. And there, after a few faintest words of confession from the sick man, Nina knelt by her father's bedside, while the priest prayed for them both, and forgave the sinner his sins, and prepared him for his further journey with such preparation as the extreme unction of his Church would afford.

When the prayer and the ceremony were over, and the viaticum had been duly administered, the priest returned into the parlor, and Nina followed him. "He is stronger than I had expected to find him," said Father Jerome.

"He has rallied a little, Father, because you were coming. You may be sure that he is very ill."

"I know that he is very ill, but I think that he may still last some days. Should it be so, I will come again." After that Nina thought that the priest would have gone; but he paused for a few moments as though hesitating, and then spoke again, putting down his hat, which he had taken up. "But what is all this that I hear about you, Nina?"

"All what?" said Nina, blushing.

"They tell me that you have engaged yourself to marry Anton Trendellsohn, the Jew."

She stood before him confessing her guilt by her silence. "Is it true, Nina?" he asked.

"It is true."

"I am very sorry for that--very sorry. Could you not bring yourself to love some Christian youth, rather than a Jew? Would it not be better, do you think, to do so--for your soul's sake?"

"It is too late now, Father."

"Too late! No; it can never be too late to repent of evil."

"But why should it be evil, Father Jerome? It is permitted; is it not?"

"The law permits it, certainly."

"And when I am a Jew's wife, may I not go to mass?"

"Yes; you may go to mass. Who can hinder you?"

"And if I pray devoutly, will not the saints hear me?"

"It is not for me to limit their mercy. I think that they will hear all prayers that are addressed to them with faith and humility."

"And you, Father, will you not give me absolution if I am a Jew's wife?"

"I would ten times sooner give it you as the wife of a Christian, Nina. My absolution would be nothing to you, Nina, if the while you had a deep sin upon your conscience." Then the priest went, being unwilling to endure further questioning, and Nina seated herself in a glow of triumph. And this was the worst that she would have to endure from the Church after all her aunt's threatenings--after Lotta's bitter words, and the reproaches of all around her! Father Jerome--even Father Jerome himself, who was known to be the strictest priest on that side of the river in opposing the iniquities of his flock--did not take upon himself to say that her case as a Christian would be hopeless, were she to marry the Jew! After that she went to the drawer in her bedroom, and restored the picture of the Virgin to its place.

Chapter 14

Father Jerome had been very mild with Nina, but his mildness did not produce any corresponding feelings of gentleness in the breasts of Nina's relatives in the Windberg-gasse. Indeed, it had the contrary effect of instigating Madame Zamenoy and Lotta Luxa to new exertions. Nina, in her triumph, could not restrain herself from telling Souchey that Father Jerome did not by any means think so badly of her as did the others; and Souchey, partly in defense of Nina, and partly in quest of further sound information on the knotty religious difficulty involved, repeated it all to Lotta. Among them they succeeded in cutting Souchey's ground from under him as far as any defense of Nina was concerned, and they succeeded also in solving his religious doubts. Poor Souchey was at last convinced that the best service he could tender to his mistress was to save her from marrying the Jew, let the means by which this was to be done be, almost, what they might.

As the result of this teaching, Souchey went late one afternoon to the Jews' quarter. He did not go thither direct from the house in the Kleinseite, but from Madame Zamenoy's abode, where he had again dined previously in Lotta's presence. Madame Zamenoy herself had condescended to enlighten his mind on the subject of Nina's peril, and had gone so far as to invite him to hear a few words on the subject from a priest on that side of the water. Souchey had only heard Nina's report of what Father Jerome had said, but he was listening with his own ears while the other priest declared his opinion that things would go very badly with any Christian girl who might marry a Jew. This sufficed for him; and then--having been so far enlightened by Madame Zamenoy herself--he accepted a little commission, which took him to the Jew's house. Lotta had had much difficulty in arranging this; for Souchey was not open to a bribe in the matter, and on that account was able to press his legitimate suit very closely. Before he would start on his errand to the Jew, Lotta was almost obliged to promise that she would yield.

It was late in the afternoon when he got to Trendellsohn's house. He had never been there before, though he well knew the exact spot on which it stood, and had often looked up at the windows, regarding the place with unpleasant suspicions; for he knew that Trendellsohn was now the owner of the property that had once been his master's, and, of course, as a good Christian, he believed that the Jew had obtained Balatka's money by robbery and fraud. He hesitated a moment before he presented himself at the door, having some fear at his heart. He knew that he was doing right, but these Jews in their own quarter were uncanny, and might be dangerous! To Anton Trendellsohn, over in the Kleinseite, Souchey could be independent, and perhaps on occasions a little insolent; but of Anton Trendellsohn in his own domains he almost acknowledged to himself that he was afraid. Lotta had told him that, if Anton were not at home, his commission could be done as well with the old man; and as he at last made his way round the synagogue to the house door, he determined that he would ask for the elder Jew. That which he had to say, he thought, might be said easier to the father than to the son.

The door of the house stood open, and Souchey, who, in his confusion, missed the bell, entered the passage. The little oil-lamp still hung there, giving a mysterious glimmer of light, which he did not at all enjoy. He walked on very slowly, trying to get courage to call, when, of a sudden, he perceived that there was a figure of a man standing close to him in the gloom. He gave a little start, barely suppressing a scream, and then perceived that the man was Anton Trendellsohn himself. Anton, hearing steps in the passage, had come out from the room on the ground-floor, and had seen Souchey before Souchey had seen him.

"You have come from Josef Balatka's," said the Jew. "How is the old man?"

Souchey took off his cap and bowed, and muttered something as to his having come upon an errand. "And my master is something better today," he said, "thanks be to God for all His mercies!"

"Amen," said the Jew.

"But it will only last a day or two; no more than that," said Souchey. "He has had the doctor and the priest, and they both say that it is all over with him for this world."

"And Nina--you have brought some message probably from her?"

"No--no indeed; that is, not exactly; not today, Herr Trendellsohn. The truth is, I had wished to speak a word or two to you about the maiden; but perhaps you are engaged--perhaps another time would be better."

"I am not engaged, and no other time could be better."

They were still out in the passage, and Souchey hesitated. That which he had to say it would behove him to whisper into the closest privacy of the Jew's ear--into the ear of the old Jew or of the young. "It is something very particular," said Souchey.

"Very particular--is it?" said the Jew.

"Very particular indeed." said Souchey. Then Anton Trendellsohn led the way back into the dark room on the ground-floor from whence he had come, and invited Souchey to follow him. The shutters were up, and the place was seldom used. There was a counter running through it, and a cross-counter, such as are very common when seen by the light of day in shops; but the place seemed to be mysterious to Souchey; and always afterwards, when he thought of this interview, he remembered that his tale had been told in the gloom of a chamber that had never been arranged for honest Christian purposes.

"And now, what is it you have to tell me?" said the Jew.

After some fashion Souchey told his tale, and the Jew listened to him without a word of interruption. More than once Souchey had paused, hoping that the Jew would say something; but not a sound had fallen from Trendellsohn till Souchey's tale was done.

"And it is so--is it?" said the Jew when Souchey ceased to speak. There was nothing in his voice which seemed to indicate either sorrow or joy, or even surprise.

"Yes, it is so," said Souchey.

"And how much am I to pay you for the information?" the Jew asked.

"You are to pay me nothing," said Souchey.

"What! you betray your mistress gratis?"

"I do not betray her," said Souchey. I love her and the old man too. I have been with them through fair weather and through foul. I have not betrayed her."

"Then why have you come to me with this story?"

112

The whole truth was almost on Souchey's tongue. He had almost said that his sole object was to save his mistress from the disgrace of marrying a Jew. But he checked himself, then paused a moment, and then left the room and the house abruptly. He had done his commission, and the fewer words which he might have with the Jew after that the better.

On the following morning Nina was seated by her father's bedside, when her quick ear caught through the open door the sound of a footstep in the hall below. She looked for a moment at the old man, and saw that if not sleeping he appeared to sleep. She leaned over him for a moment, gave one gentle touch with her hand to the bed-clothes, then crept out into the parlor, and closed behind her the door of the bed-room. When in the middle of the outer chamber she listened again, and there was clearly a step on the stairs. She listened again, and she knew that the step was the step of her lover. He had come to her at last, then. Now, at this moment, she lost all remembrance of her need of forgiving him. Forgiving him! What could there be to be forgiven to one who could make her so happy as she felt herself to be at this moment? She opened the door of the room just as he had raised his hand to knock, and threw herself into his arms. "Anton, dearest, you have come at last. But I am not going to scold. I am so glad that you have come, my own one!"

While she was yet speaking, he brought her back into the room, supporting her with his arm round her waist; and when the door was closed he stood over her still holding her up, and looking down into her face, which was turned up to his. "Why do you not speak to me, Anton?" she said. But she smiled as she spoke, and there was nothing of fear in the tone of her voice, for his look was kind, and there was love in his eyes.

He stooped down over her, and fastened his lips upon her forehead. She pressed herself closer against his shoulder, and shutting her eyes, as she gave herself up to the rapture of his embrace, told herself that now all should be well with them.

"Dear Nina," he said.

"Dearest, dearest Anton," she replied.

And then he asked after her father; and the two sat together for a while, with their knees almost touching, talking in whispers as to the condition of the old man. And they were still so sitting, and still so talking, when Nina rose from her chair, and put up her forefinger with a slight motion for silence, and a pretty look of mutual interest--as though Anton were already one of the same family; and, touching his hair lightly with her hand as she passed him, that he might feel how delighted she was to be able so to touch him, she went back to the door of the bedroom on tiptoe, and, lifting the latch without a sound, put in her head and listened. But the sick man had not stirred. His face was still turned from her, as though he slept, and then, again closing the door, she came back to her lover.

"He is quite quiet," she said, whispering.

"Does he suffer?"

"I think not; he never complains. When he is awake he will sit with my hand within his own, and now and again there is a little pressure."

"And he says nothing?"

"Very little; hardly a word now and then. When he does speak, it is of his food."

"He can eat, then?"

"A morsel of jelly, or a little soup. But, Anton, I must tell you--I tell you everything, you know--where do you think the things that he takes have come from? But perhaps you know."

"Indeed I do not."

"They were sent to me by Rebecca Loth."

"By Rebecca!"

"Yes; by your friend Rebecca. She must be a good girl."

"She is a good girl, Nina."

"And you shall know everything; see--she sent me these," and Nina showed her shoes; "and the very stockings I have on; I am not ashamed that you should know."

"Your want, then, has been so great as that?"

"Father has been very poor. How should he not be poor when nothing is earned? And she came here, and she saw it."

"She sent you these things?"

"Yes, Ruth came with them; there was a great basket with nourishing food for father. It was very kind of her. But, Anton, Rebecca says that I ought not to marry you, because of our religion. She says all the Jews in Prague will become your enemies."

"We will not stay in Prague; we will go elsewhere. There are other cities besides Prague."

"Where nobody will know us?"

"Where we will not be ashamed to be known."

"I told Rebecca that I would give you back all your promises, if you wished me to do so."

"I do not wish it. I will not give you back your promises, Nina."

The enraptured girl again clung to him. "My own one," she said, "my darling, my husband; when you speak to me like that, there is no girl in Bohemia so happy as I am. Hush! I thought it was father. But no; there is no sound. I do not mind what anyone says to me, as long as you are kind."

She was now sitting on his knee, and his arm was round her waist, and she was resting her head against his brow; he had asked for no pardon, but all the past was entirely forgiven; why should she even think of it again? Some such thought was passing through her mind, when he spoke a word, and it seemed as though a dagger had gone into her heart. "About that paper, Nina?" Accursed document, that it should be brought again between them to dash the cup of joy from her lips at such a moment as this! She disengaged herself from his embrace, almost with a leap. "Well! what about the paper?" she said.

Simply this, that I would wish to know where it is."

"And you think I have it?"

"No; I do not think so; I am perplexed about it, hardly knowing what to believe; but I do not think you have it; I think that you know nothing of it."

"Then why do you mention it again, reminding me of the cruel words which you spoke before?"

"Because it is necessary for both our sakes. I will tell you plainly just what I have heard: your servant

Souchey has been with me, and he says that you have it."

"Souchey!"

"Yes; Souchey. It seemed strange enough to me, for I had always thought him to be your friend."

"Souchey has told you that I have got it?"

"He says that it is in that desk," and the Jew pointed to the old depository of all the treasures which Nina possessed.

"He is a liar."

"I think he is so, though I cannot tell why he should have so lied; but I think he is a liar; I do not believe that it is there; but in such a matter it is well that the fact should be put beyond all dispute. You will not object to my looking into the desk?" He had come there with a fixed resolve that he would demand to search among her papers. It was very unpleasant to him, and he knew that his doing so would be painful to her; but he told himself that it would be best for them both that he should persevere.

"Will you open it, or shall I?" he said; and as he spoke, she looked into his face, and saw that all tenderness and love were banished from it, and that the hard suspicious greed of the Jew was there instead.

"I will not unlock it," she said; "there is the key, and you can do as you please." Then she flung the key upon the table, and stood with her back up against the wall, at some ten paces distant from the spot where the desk stood. He took up the key, and placed it remorselessly in the lock, and opened the desk, and brought all the papers forth on to the table which stood in the middle of the room.

"Are all my letters to be read?" she asked.

"Nothing is to be read," he said.

"Not that I should mind it; or at least I should have cared but little ten minutes since. There are words there may make you think I have been a fool, but a fool only too faithful to you."

He made no answer to this, but moved the papers one by one carefully till he came to a folded document larger than the others. Why dwell upon it? Of course it was the deed for which he was searching. Nina, when from her station by the wall she saw that there was something in her lover's hands of which she had no knowledge--something which had been in her own desk without her privity--came forward a step or two, looking with all her eyes. But she did not speak till he had spoken; nor did he speak at once. He slowly unfolded the document, and perused the heading of it; then he refolded it, and placed it on the table, and stood there with his hand upon it.

"This," said he, "is the paper for which I am looking. Souchey, at any rate, is not a liar."

"How came it there?" said Nina, almost screaming in her agony.

"That I know not; but Souchey is not a liar; nor were your aunt and her servant liars in telling me that I should find it in your hands."

"Anton," she said, "as the Lord made me, I knew not of it;" and she fell on her knees before his feet.

He looked down upon her, scanning every feature of her face and every gesture of her body with hard inquiring eyes. He did not stoop to raise her, nor, at the moment, did he say a word to comfort her. "And you think that I stole it and put it there?" she said. She did not quail before his eyes, but seemed, though kneeling before him, to look up at him as though she would defy him. When first she had sunk upon the ground, she had been weak, and wanted pardon though she was ignorant of all offence; but his hardness, as he stood with his eyes fixed upon her, had hardened her, and all her intellect, though not her heart, was in revolt against him. "You think that I have robbed you?"

"I do not know what to think," he said.

Then she rose slowly to her feet, and, collecting the papers which he had strewed upon the table, put them back slowly into the desk, and locked it.

"You have done with this now," she said, holding the key in her hand.

"Yes; I do not want the key again."

"And you have done with me also?"

He paused a moment or two to collect his thoughts, and then he answered her. "Nina, I would wish to think about this before I speak of it more fully. What step I may next take I cannot say without considering it much. I would not wish to pain you if I could help it."

"Tell me at once what it is that you believe of me?"

"I cannot tell you at once. Rebecca Loth is friendly to you, and I will send her to you tomorrow."

"I will not see Rebecca Loth," said Nina. "Hush! there is father's voice. Anton, I have nothing more to say to you--nothing--nothing." Then she left him, and went into her father's room.

For some minutes she was busy by her father's bed, and went about her work with a determined alacrity, as though she would wipe out of her mind altogether, for the moment, any thought about her love and the Jew and the document that had been found in her desk; and for a while she was successful, with a consciousness, indeed, that she was under the pressure of a terrible calamity which must destroy her, but still with an outward presence of mind that supported her in her work. And her father spoke to her, saying more to her than he had done for days past, thanking her for her care, patting her hand with his, caressing her, and bidding her still be of good cheer, as God would certainly be good to one who had been so excellent a daughter. "But I wish, Nina, he were not a Jew," he said suddenly.

"Dear father, we will not talk of that now."

"And he is a stern man, Nina."

But on this subject she would speak no further, and therefore she left the bedside for a moment, and offered him a cup, from which he drank. When he had tasted it he forgot the matter that had been in his mind, and said no further word as to Nina's engagement.

As soon as she had taken the cup from her father's hand, she returned to the parlor. It might be that Anton was still there. She had left him in the room, and had shut her ears against the sound of his steps, as though she were resolved that she would care nothing ever again for his coming or going. He was gone, however, and the room was empty, and she sat down in solitude, with her back against the wall, and began to realize her position. He had told her that others accused her, but that he had not suspected her. He had not suspected her, but he had thought it necessary to search, and had found in her possession that which had made her guilty in his eyes!

She would never see him again--never willingly. It was not only that he would never forgive her, but that she could never now be brought to forgive him. He had stabbed her while her words of love were warmest in his ear. His foul suspicions had been present to his mind even while she was caressing him. He had never known what it was to give himself up really to his love for one moment. While she was seated on his knee, with her head pressed against his, his intellect had been busy with the key and the desk, as though he were a policeman looking for a thief, rather than a lover happy in the endearments of his mistress. Her vivid mind pictured all this to her, filling her full with every incident of the insult she had endured. No. There must be an end of it now. If she could see her aunt that moment, or Lotta, or even Ziska, she would tell them that it should be so. She would say nothing to Anton--no, not a word again, though both might live for an eternity; but she would write a line to Rebecca Loth, and tell the Jewess that the Jew was now free to marry whom he would among his own people. And some of the words that she thought would be fitting for such a letter occurred to her as she sat there. "I know now that a Jew and a Christian ought not to love each other as we loved. Their hearts are different." That was her present purpose, but, as will be seen, she changed it afterwards.

But ever and again as she strengthened her resolution, her thoughts would run from her, carrying her back to the sweet rapture of some moment in which the man had been gracious to her; and even while she was struggling to teach herself to hate him, she would lean her head on one side, as though by doing so she might once more touch his brow with hers; and unconsciously she would put out her fingers, as though they might find their way into his hand. And then she would draw them back with a shudder, as though recoiling from the touch of an adder.

Hours had passed over her before she began to think whence had come the paper which Trendellsohn had found in her desk; and then, when the idea of some fraud presented itself to her, that part of the subject did not seem to her to be of great moment. It mattered but little who had betrayed her. It might be Rebecca, or Souchey, or Ruth, or Lotta, or all of them together. His love, his knowledge of her whom he loved, should have carried him aloft out of the reach of any such poor trick as that! What mattered it now who had stolen her key, and gone like a thief to her desk, and laid this plot for her destruction? That he should have been capable of being deceived by such a plot against her was enough for her. She did not even speak to Souchey on the subject. In the course of the afternoon he came across her as she moved about the house, looking ashamed, not daring to meet her eyes, hardly able to mutter a word to her. But she said not a syllable to him about her desk. She could not bring herself to plead the cause between her and her lover before her father's servant.

The greater part of the day she passed by her father's bedside, but whenever she could escape from the room, she seated herself in the chair against the wall, endeavoring to make up her mind as to the future. But there was much more of passion than of thought within her breast. Never, never, never would she forgive him! Never again would she sit on his knee caressing him. Never again would she even speak to him. Nothing would she take from his hand, or from the hands of his friends! Nor would she ever stoop to take aught from her aunt, or from Ziska. They had triumphed over her. She knew not how. They had triumphed over her, but the triumph should be very bitter to them-- very bitter, if there was any touch of humanity left among them.

Later in the day there came to be something of motion in the house. Her father was worse in health, was going fast, and the doctor was again there. And in these moments Souchey was with her, busy in the dying man's room; and there were gentle kind words spoken between him and Nina--as would be natural between such persons at such a time. He knew that he had been a traitor, and the thought of his treachery was heavy at his heart; but he perceived that no immediate punishment was to come upon him, and it was some solace to him that he could be sedulous and gentle and tender. And Nina, though she knew that the man had given his aid in destroying her, bore with him not only without a hard word, but almost without a severe thought. What did it matter what such a one as Souchey could do?

In the middle watches of that night the old man died, and Nina was alone in the world. Souchey, indeed, was with her in the house, and took from her all painful charge of the bed at which now her care could no longer be of use. And early in the morning, while it was yet dark, Lotta came down, and spoke words to her, of which she remembered nothing. And then she knew that her aunt Sophie was there, and that some offers were made to her at which she only shook her head. "Of course you will come up to us," aunt Sophie said. And she made many more suggestions, in answer to all of which Nina only shook her head. Then her aunt and Nina, with Lotta's aid, fixed upon some plan--Nina hardly knew what--as to the morrow. She did not care to know what it was that they fixed. They were going to leave her alone for this day, and the day would be very long. She told herself that it would be long enough for her.

The day was very long. When her aunt had left her she saw no one but Souchey and an old woman who was busy in the bedroom which was now closed. She had stood at the foot of the bed with her aunt, but after that she did not return to the chamber. It was not only her father who, for her, was now lying dead. She had loved her father well, but with a love infinitely greater she had loved another; and that other one was now dead to her also. What was there left to her in the world? The charity of her aunt, and Lotta's triumph, and Ziska's love? No indeed! She would bear neither the charity, nor the triumph, nor the love. One other visitor came to the house that day. It was Rebecca Loth. But Nina refused to see Rebecca. "Tell her," she said to Souchey, "that I cannot see a stranger while my father is lying dead." How often did the idea occur to her, throughout the terrible length of that day, that "he" might come to her? But he came not. "So much the better," she said to herself. "Were he to come, I would not see him."

Late in the evening, when the little lamp in the room had been already burning for some hour or two, she called Souchey to her. "Take this note," she said, "to Anton Trendellsohn."

"What! tonight?" said Souchey, trembling.

"Yes, tonight. It is right that he should know that the house is now his own, to do what he will with it."

Then Souchey took the note, which was as follows:

My father is dead, and the house will be empty tomorrow. You may come and take your property without fear that you will be troubled by NINA BALATKA.

Chapter 15

When Souchey left the room with the note, Nina went to the door and listened. She heard him turn the lock below, and heard his step out in the courtyard, and listened till she knew that he was crossing the square. Then she ran quickly up to her own room, put on her hat and her old worn cloak--the cloak which aunt Sophie had given her--and returned once more into the parlor. She looked round the room with anxious eyes, and seeing her desk, she took the key from her pocket and put it into the lock. Then there came a thought into her mind as to the papers; but she resolved that the thought need not arrest her, and she left the key in the lock with the papers untouched. Then she went to the door of her father's room, and stood there for a moment with her hand upon the latch. She tried it ever so gently, but she found that the door was bolted. The bolt, she knew, was on her side, and she could withdraw it; but she did not do so; seeming to take the impediment as though it were a sufficient bar against her entrance. Then she ran down the stairs rapidly, opened the front door, and found herself out in the night air.

It was a cold windy night--not so late, indeed, as to have made her feel that it was night, had she not come from the gloom of the dark parlor, and the glimmer of her one small lamp. It was now something beyond the middle of October, and at present it might be eight o'clock. She knew that there would be moonlight, and she looked up at the sky; but the clouds were all dark, though she could see that they were moving along with the gusts of wind. It was very cold, and she drew her cloak closer about her as she stepped out into the archway.

Up above her, almost close to her in the gloom of the night, there was the long colonnade of the palace, with the lights glimmering in the windows as they always glimmered. She allowed herself for a moment to think who might be there in those rooms--as she had so often thought before. It was possible that Anton might be there. He had been there once before at this time in the evening, as he himself had told her. Wherever he might be, was he thinking of her? But if he thought of her, he was thinking of her as one who had deceived him, who had tried to rob him. Ah! the day would soon come in which he would learn that he had wronged her. When that day should come, would his heart be bitter within him? "He will certainly be unhappy for a time," she said; "but he is hard and will recover, and she will console him. It will be better so. A Christian and a Jew should never love each other."

As she stood the clouds were lifted for a moment from the face of the risen moon, and she could see by the pale clear light the whole facade of the palace as it ran along the steep hillside above her. She could count the arches, as she had so often counted them by the same light. They seemed to be close over her head, and she stood there thinking of them, till the clouds had again skurried across the moon's face, and she could only see the accustomed glimmer in the windows. As her eye fell upon the well-known black buildings around her, she found that it was very dark. It was well for her that it should be so dark. She never wanted to see the light again.

There was a footstep on the other side of the square, and she paused till it had passed away beyond the reach of her ears. Then she came out from under the archway, and hurried across the square to the street which led to the bridge. It was a dark gloomy lane, narrow, and composed of high buildings without entrances, the sides of barracks and old palaces. From the windows above her head on the left, she heard the voices of soldiers. A song was being sung, and she could hear the words. How cruel it was that other people should have so much of light- hearted joy in the world, but that for her everything should have been so terribly sad! The wind, as it met her, seemed to penetrate to her bones. She was very cold! But it was useless to regard that. There was no place on the face of the earth that would ever be warm for her.

As she passed along the causeway leading to the bridge, a sound with which she was very familiar met her ears. They were singing vespers under the shadow of one of the great statues which are placed one over each arch of the bridge. There was a lay friar standing by a little table, on which there was a white cloth and a lighted lamp and a small crucifix; and above the crucifix, supported against the stone-work of the bridge, there was a picture of the Virgin with her Child, and there was a tawdry wreath of paper flowers, so that by the light of the lamp you could see that a little altar had been prepared. And on the table there was a plate containing kreutzers, into which the faithful who passed and took a part in the evening psalm of praise, might put an offering for the honor of the Virgin, and for the benefit of the poor friar and his brethren in their poor cloisters at home. Nina knew all about it well. Scores of times had she stood on the same spot upon the bridge, and sung the vesper hymn, ere she passed on to the Kleinseite.

And now she paused and sang it once again. Around the table upon the pavement there stood perhaps thirty or forty persons, most of them children, and the remainder girls perhaps of Nina's age. And the friar stood close by the table, leaning idly against the bridge, with his eye wandering from the little plate with the kreutzers to the passers-by who might possibly contribute. And ever and anon he with drawling voice would commence some sentence of the hymn, and then the girls and children would take it up, well knowing the accustomed words; and their voices as they sang would sound sweetly across the waters, the loud gurgling of which, as they ran beneath the arch, would be heard during the pauses.

And Nina stopped and sang. When she was a child she had sung there very often, and the friar of those days would put his hand upon her head and bless her, as she brought her small piece of tribute to his plate. Of late, since she had been at variance with the Church by reason of the Jew, she had always passed by rapidly, as though feeling that she had no longer any right to take a part in such a ceremony. But now she had done with the Jew, and surely she might sing the vesper song. So she stopped and sang, remembering not the less as she sang, that that which she was about to do, if really done, would make all such singing unavailing for her.

But then, perhaps, even yet it might not be done. Lotta's first prediction, that the Jew would desert her, had certainly come true; and Lotta's second prediction, that there would be nothing left for her but to drown herself, seemed to her to be true also. She had left the house in which her father's dead body was still lying, with this purpose. Doubly deserted as she now was by lover and father, she could live no longer. It might, however, be possible that that saint who was so powerful over the waters might yet do something for her--might yet interpose on her behalf, knowing, as he did, of course, that all idea of marriage between her, a Christian, and her Jew lover had been abandoned. At any rate she stood and sang the hymn, and when there came the accustomed lull at the end of the verse, she felt in her pocket for a coin, and, taking a piece of ten kreutzers, she stepped quickly up to the plate and put it in. A day or two ago ten kreutzers was an important portion of the little sum which she still had left in hand, but now ten kreutzers could do nothing for her. It was at any rate better that the friar should have it than that her money should go with her down into the blackness of the river. Nevertheless she did not give the friar all. She saw one girl whispering to another as she stepped up to the table, and she heard her own name. "That is Nina Balatka." And then there was an answer which she did not hear, but which she was sure referred to the Jew. The girls looked at her with angry eyes, and she longed to stop and explain to them that she was no longer betrothed to the Jew. Then, perhaps, they would be gentle with her, and she might yet hear a kind word spoken to her before she went. But she did not speak to them. No; she would never speak to man or woman again. What was the use of speaking now? No sympathy that she could receive would go deep enough to give relief to such wounds as hers.

As she dropped her piece of money into the plate her eyes met those of the friar, and she recognized at once a man whom she had known years ago, at the same spot and engaged in the same work. He was old and haggard, and thin, and grey, and very dirty; but there came a smile over his face as he also recognized her. He could not speak to her, for he had to take up a verse in the hymn, and drawl out the words which were to set the crowd singing, and Nina had retired back again before he was silent. But she knew that he had known her, and she almost felt that she had found a friend who would be kind to her. On the morrow, when inquiry would be made--and aunt Sophie would certainly be loud in her inquiries--this friar would be able to give some testimony respecting her.

She passed on altogether across the bridge, in order that she might reach the spot she desired without observation--and perhaps also with some halting idea that she might thus postpone the evil moment. The figure of St John Nepomucene rested on the other balustrade of the bridge, and she was minded to stand for a while under its shadow. Now, at Prague it is the custom that they who pass over the bridge shall always take the right-hand path as they go; and she, therefore, in coming from the Kleinseite, had taken that opposite to the statue of the saint. She had thought of this, and had told herself that she would cross the roadway in the middle of the bridge; but at that moment the moon was shining brightly: and then, too, the night was long. Why need she be in a hurry?

At the further end of the bridge she stood a while in the shade of the watch-tower, and looked anxiously around her. When last she had been over in the Old Town, within a short distance of the spot where she now stood, she had chanced to meet her lover. What if she should see him now? She was sure that she would not speak to him. And yet she looked very anxiously up the dark street, through the glimmer of the dull lamps. First there came one man, and then another, and a third; and she thought, as her eyes fell upon them, that the figure of each was the figure of Anton Trendellsohn. But as they emerged from the darker shadow into the light that was near, she saw that it was not so, and she told herself that she was glad. If Anton were to come and find her there, it might be that he would disturb her purpose. But yet she looked again before she left the shadow of the tower. Now there was no one passing in the street. There was no figure there to make her think that her lover was coming either to save her or to disturb her.

Taking the pathway on the other side, she turned her face again towards the Kleinseite, and very slowly crept along under the balustrade of the bridge. This bridge over the Moldau is remarkable in many ways, but it is specially remarkable for the largeness of its proportions. It is very long, taking its spring from the shore a long way before the actual margin of the river; it is of a fine breadth: the side-walks to it are high and massive; and the groups of statues with which it is ornamented, though not in themselves of much value as works of art, have a dignity by means of their immense size which they lend to the causeway, making the whole thing noble, grand, and impressive. And below, the Moldau runs with a fine, silent, dark volume of water--a very sea of waters when the rains have fallen and the little rivers have been full, though in times of drought great patches of ugly dry land are to be seen in its half-empty bed. At the present moment there were no such patches; and the waters ran by, silent, black, in great volumes, and with unchecked rapid course. It was only by pausing specially to listen to them that the passer-by could hear them as they glided smoothly round the piers of the bridge. Nina did pause and did hear them. They would have been almost less terrible to her, had the sound been rougher and louder.

On she went, very slowly. The moon, she thought, had disappeared altogether before she reached the cross inlaid in the stone on the bridge-side, on which she was accustomed to lay her fingers, in order that she might share somewhat of the saint's power over the river. At that moment, as she came up to it, the night was very dark. She had calculated that by this time the light of the moon would have waned, so that she might climb to the spot which she had marked for herself without observation. She paused, hesitating whether she would put her hand upon the cross. It could not at least do her any harm. It might be that the saint would be angry with her, accusing her of hypocrisy; but what would be the saint's anger for so small a thing amidst the multitudes of charges that would be brought against her? For that which she was going to do now there could be no absolution given. And perhaps the saint might perceive that the deed on her part was not altogether hypocritical--that there was something in it of a true prayer. He might see this, and intervene to save her from the waters. So she put the palm of her little hand full upon the cross, and then kissed it heartily, and after that raised it up again till it rested on the foot of the saint. As she stood there she heard the departing voices of the girls and children singing the last verse of the vesper hymn, as they followed the friar off the causeway of the bridge into the Kleinseite.

She was determined that she would persevere. She had endured that which made it impossible that she should recede, and had sworn to herself a thousand times that she would never endure that which would have to be endured if she remained longer in this cruel world. There would be no roof to cover her now but the roof in the Windberg-gasse, beneath which there was to her a hell upon earth. No; she would face the anger of all the saints rather than eat the bitter bread which her aunt would provide for her. And she would face the anger of all the saints rather than fall short in her revenge upon her lover. She had given herself to him altogether--for him she had been half-starved, when, but for him, she might have lived as a favored daughter in her aunt's house--for him she had made it impossible to herself to regard any other man with a spark of affection--for his sake she had hated her cousin Ziska-- her cousin who was handsome, and young, and rich, and had loved her-- feeling that the very idea that she could accept love from anyone but Anton had been an insult to her. She had trusted Anton as though his word had been gospel to her. She had obeyed him in everything, allowing him to scold her as though she were already subject to his rule; and, to speak the truth, she had enjoyed such treatment, obtaining from it a certain assurance that she was already his own. She had loved him entirely, had trusted him altogether, had been prepared to bear all that the world could fling upon her for his sake, wanting nothing in return but that he should know that she was true to him.

This he had not known, nor had he been able to understand such truth. It had not been possible to him to know it. The inborn suspicion of his nature had broken out in opposition to his love, forcing her to acknowledge to herself that she had been wrong in loving a Jew. He had been unable not to suspect her of some vile scheme by which she might possibly cheat him of his property, if at the last moment she should not become his wife. She told herself that she understood it all now-- that she could see into his mind, dark and gloomy as were its recesses. She had wasted all her heart upon a man who had never even believed in her; and would she not be revenged upon him? Yes, she would be revenged, and she would cure the malady of her own love by the only possible remedy within her reach.

The statue of St John Nepomucene is a single figure, standing in melancholy weeping posture on the balustrade of the bridge, without any of that ponderous strength of wide-spread stone which belongs to the other groups. This St John is always pictured to us as a thin, melancholy, half-starved saint, who has had all the life washed out of him by his long immersion. There are saints to whom a trusting religious heart can turn, relying on their apparent physical capabilities. St Mark, for instance, is always a tower of strength, and St Christopher is very stout, and St Peter carries with him an ancient manliness which makes one marvel at his cowardice when he denied his Master. St Lawrence, too, with his gridiron, and St Bartholomew with his flaying-knife and his own skin hanging over his own arm, look as though they liked their martyrdom, and were proud of it, and could be useful on an occasion. But this St John of the Bridges has no pride in his appearance, and no strength in his look. He is a mild, meek saint, teaching one rather by his attitude how to bear with the malice of the waters, than offering any protection against their violence. But now, at this moment, his aid was the only aid to which Nina could look with any hope. She had heard of his rescuing many persons from death amidst the current of the Moldau. Indeed she thought that she could remember having been told that the river had no power to drown those who could turn their minds to him when they were struggling in the water. Whether this applied only to those who were in sight of his statue on the bridge of Prague, or whether it was good in all rivers of the world, she did not know. Then she tried to think whether she had ever heard of any case in which the saint had saved one who had--who had done the thing which she was now about to do. She was almost sure that she had never heard of such a case as that. But, then, was there not something special in her own case? Was not her suffering so great, her condition so piteous, that the saint would be driven to compassion in spite of the greatness of her sin? Would he not know that she was punishing the Jew by the only punishment with which she could reach him? She looked up into the saint's wan face, and fancied that no eyes were ever so piteous, no brow ever so laden with the deep suffering of compassion. But would this punishment reach the heart of Anton Trendellsohn? Would he care for it? When he should hear that she had--destroyed her own life because she could not endure the cruelty of his suspicion, would the tidings make him unhappy? When last they had been together he had told her, with all that energy which he knew so well how to put into his words, that her love was necessary to his happiness. "I will never release you from your promises," he had said, when she offered to give him back his troth because of the ill-will of his people. And she still believed him. Yes, he did love her. There was something of consolation to her in the assurance that the strings of his heart would be wrung when he should hear of this. If his bosom were capable of agony, he would be agonized.

It was very dark at this moment, and now was the time for her to climb upon the stone-work and hide herself behind the drapery of the saint's statue. More than once, as she had crossed the bridge, she had observed the spot, and had told herself that if such a deed were to be done, that would be the place for doing it. She had always been conscious, since the idea had entered her mind, that she would lack the power to step boldly up on to the parapet and go over at once, as the bathers do when they tumble headlong into the stream that has no dangers for them. She had known that she must crouch, and pause, and think of it, and look at it, and nerve herself with the memory of her wrongs. Then, at some moment in which her heart was wrung to the utmost, she would gradually slacken her hold, and the dark, black, silent river should take her. She climbed up into the niche, and found that the river was very far from her, though death was so near to her and the fall would be so easy. When she became aware that there was nothing between her and the great void space below her, nothing to guard her, nothing left to her in all the world to protect her, she retreated, and descended again to the pavement. And never in her life had she moved with more care, lest, inadvertently, a foot or a hand might slip, and she might tumble to her doom against her will.

When she was again on the pathway she remembered her note to Anton-- that note which was already in his hands. What would he think of her if she were only to threaten the deed, and then not perform it? And would she allow him to go unpunished? Should he triumph, as he would do if she were now to return to the house which she had told him she had left? She clasped her hands together tightly, and pressed them first to her bosom and then to her brow, and then again she returned to the niche from which the fall into the river must be made. Yes, it was very easy. The plunge might be taken at any moment. Eternity was before her, and of life there remained to her but the few moments in which she might cling there and think of what was coming. Surely she need not begrudge herself a minute or two more of life.

She was very cold, so cold that she pressed herself against the stone in order that she might save herself from the wind that whistled round her. But the water would be colder still than the wind, and when once there she could never again be warm. The chill of the night, and the blackness of the gulf before her, and the smooth rapid gurgle of the dark moving mass of waters beneath, were together more horrid to her imagination than even death itself. Thrice she released herself from her backward pressure against the stone, in order that she might fall forward and have done with it, but as often she found herself returning involuntarily to the protection which still remained to her. It seemed as though she could not fall. Though she would have thought that another must have gone directly to destruction if placed where she was crouching--though she would have trembled with agony to see anyone perched in such danger--she appeared to be firm fixed. She must jump forth boldly, or the river would not take her. Ah! what if it were so-- that the saint who stood over her, and whose cross she had so lately kissed, would not let her perish from beneath his feet? In these moments her mind wandered in a maze of religious doubts and fears, and she entertained, unconsciously, enough of doctrinal skepticism to found a school of freethinkers. Could it be that God would punish her with everlasting torments because in her agony she was driven to this as her only mode of relief? Would there be no measuring of her sins against her sorrows, and no account taken of the simplicity of her life? She looked up towards heaven, not praying in words, but with a prayer in her heart. For her there could be no absolution, no final blessing. The act of her going would be an act of terrible sin. But God would know all, and would surely take some measure of her case. He could save her if He would, despite every priest in Prague.

More than one passenger had walked by while she was crouching in her niche beneath the statue-- had passed by and had not seen her. Indeed, the night at present was so dark, that one standing still and looking for her would hardly be able to define her figure. And yet, dark as it was, she could see something of the movement of the waters beneath her, some shimmer produced by the gliding movement of the stream. Ah! she would go now and have done with it. Every moment that she remained was but an added agony.

Then, at that moment, she heard a voice on the bridge near her, and she crouched close again, in order that the passenger might pass by without noticing her. She did not wish that anyone should hear the splash of her plunge, or be called on to make ineffectual efforts to save her. So she would wait again. The voice drew nearer to her, and suddenly she became aware that it was Souchey's voice. It was Souchey, and he was not alone. It must be Anton who had come out with him to seek her, and to save her. But no. He should have no such relief as that from his coming sorrow. So she clung fast, waiting till they should pass, but still leaning a little towards the causeway, so that, if it were possible, she might see the figures as they passed. She heard the voice of Souchey quite plain, and then she perceived that Souchey's companion was a woman. Something of the gentleness of a woman's voice reached her ear, but she could distinguish no word that was spoken. The steps were now very close to her, and with terrible anxiety she peeped out to see who might be Souchey's companion. She saw the figure, and she knew at once by the hat that it was Rebecca Loth. They were walking fast, and were close to her now. They would be gone in an instant.

On a sudden, at the very moment that Souchey and Rebecca were in the act of passing beneath the feet of the saint, the clouds swept by from off the disc of the waning moon, and the three faces were looking at each other in the clear pale light of the night. Souchey started back and screamed. Rebecca leaped forward and put the grasp of her hand tight upon the skirt of Nina's dress, first one hand and then the other, and, pressing forward with her body against the parapet, she got a hold also of Nina's foot. She perceived instantly what was the girl's purpose, but, by God's blessing on her efforts, there should be no cold form found in the river that night; or, if one, then there should be two. Nina kept her hold against the figure, appalled, dumbfounded, awe- stricken, but still with some inner consciousness of salvation that comforted her. Whether her life was due to the saint or to the Jewess she knew not, but she acknowledged to herself silently that death was beyond her reach, and she was grateful.

"Nina," said Rebecca. Nina still crouched against the stone, with her eyes fixed on the other girl's face; but she was unable to speak. The clouds had again obscured the moon, and the air was again black, but the two now could see each other in the darkness, or feel that they did so. "Nina, Nina--why are you here?"

"I do not know," said Nina, shivering.

"For the love of God take care of her," said Souchey, "or she will be over into the river."

"She cannot fall now," said Rebecca. "Nina, will you not come down to me? You are very cold. Come down, and I will warm you."

"I am very cold," said Nina. Then gradually she slid down into Rebecca's arms, and was placed sitting on a little step immediately below the figure of St John. Rebecca knelt by her side, and Nina's head fell upon the shoulder of the Jewess. Then she burst into the violence of hysterics, but after a moment or two a flood of tears relieved her.

"Why have you come to me?" she said. "Why have you not left me alone?"

"Dear Nina, your sorrows have been too heavy for you to bear."

"Yes; they have been very heavy."

"We will comfort you, and they shall be softened."

"I do not want comfort. I only want to--to--to go."

While Rebecca was chafing Nina's hands and feet, and tying a handkerchief from off her own shoulders round Nina's neck, Souchey stood over them, not knowing what to propose. "Perhaps we had better carry her back to the old house," he said.

"I will not be carried back," said Nina.

"No, dear; the house is desolate and cold. You shall not go there. You shall come to our house, and we will do for you the best we can there, and you shall be comfortable. There is no one there but mother, and she is kind and gracious. She will understand that your father has died, and that you are alone."

Nina, as she heard this, pressed her head and shoulders close against Rebecca's body. As it was not to be allowed to her to escape from all her troubles, as she had thought to do, she would prefer the neighborhood of the Jews to that of any Christians. There was no Christian now who would say a kind word to her. Rebecca spoke to her very kindly, and was soft and gentle with her. She could not go where she would be alone. Even if left to do so, all physical power would fail her. She knew that she was weak as a child is weak, and that she must submit to be governed. She thought it would be better to be governed by Rebecca Loth at the present moment than by anyone else whom she knew. Rebecca had spoken of her mother, and Nina was conscious of a faint wish that there had been no such person in her friend's house; but this was a minor trouble, and one which she could afford to disregard amidst all her sorrows. How much more terrible would have been her fate had she been carried away to aunt Sophie's house! "Does he know?" she said, whispering the question into Rebecca's ear.

"Yes, he knows. It was he who sent me." Why did he not come himself? That question flashed across Nina's mind, and it was present also to Rebecca. She knew that it was the question which Nina, within her heart, would silently ask. "I was there when the note came," said Rebecca, "and he thought that a woman could do more than a man. I am so glad he sent me--so very glad. Shall we go, dear?"

Then Nina rose from her seat, and stood up, and began to move slowly. Her limbs were stiff with cold, and at first she could hardly walk; but she did not feel that she would be unable to make the journey. Souchey came to her side, but she rejected his arm petulantly. "Do not let him come," she said to Rebecca. "I will do whatever you tell me; I will indeed." Then the Jewess said a word or two to the old man, and he retreated from Nina's side, but stood looking at her till she was out of sight. Then he returned home to the cold desolate house in the Kleinseite, where his only companion was the lifeless body of his old master. But Souchey, as he left his young mistress, made no complaint of her treatment of him. He knew that he had betrayed her, and brought her close upon the step of death's door. He could understand it all now. Indeed he had understood it all since the first word that Anton Trendellsohn had spoken after reading Nina's note.

"She will destroy herself," Anton had said.

"What! Nina, my mistress?" said Souchey. Then, while Anton had called Rebecca to him, Souchey had seen it all. "Master," he said, when the Jew returned to him, "it was Lotta Luxa who put the paper in the desk. Nina knew nothing of its being there." Then the Jew's heart sank coldly within him, and his conscience became hot within his bosom. He lost nothing of his presence of mind, but simply hurried Rebecca upon her errand. "I shall see you again tonight," he said to the girl.

"You must come then to our house," said Rebecca. "It may be that I shall not be able to leave it."

Rebecca, as she led Nina back across the bridge, at first said nothing further. She pressed the other girl's arm within her own, and there was much of tenderness and regard in the pressure. She was silent, thinking, perhaps, that any speech might be painful to her companion. But Nina could not restrain herself from a question, "What will they say of me?"

"No one, dear, shall say anything."

"But he knows."

"I know not what he knows, but his knowledge, whatever it be, is only food for his love. You may be sure of his love, Nina--quite sure, quite sure. You may take my word for that. If that has been your doubt, you have doubted wrongly."

Not all the healing medicines of Mercury, not wine from the flasks of the gods, could have given Nina life and strength as did those words from her rival's lips. All her memory of his offences against her had again gone in her thought of her own sin. Would he forgive her and still love her? Yes; she was a weak woman--very weak; but she had that one strength which is sufficient to atone for all feminine weakness-- she could really love; or rather, having loved, she could not cease to love. Anger had no effect on her love, or was as water thrown on blazing coal, which makes it burn more fiercely. Ill usage could not crush her love. Reason, either from herself or others, was unavailing against it. Religion had no power over it. Her love had become her religion to Nina. It took the place of all things both in heaven and earth. Mild as she was by nature, it made her a tigress to those who opposed it. It was all the world to her. She had tried to die, because her love had been wounded; and now she was ready to live again because she was told that her lover--the lover who had used her so cruelly-- still loved her. She pressed Rebecca's arm close into her side. "I shall be better soon," she said. Rebecca did not doubt that Nina would soon be better, but of her own improvement she was by no means so certain.

They walked on through the narrow crooked streets into the Jews' quarter, and soon stood at the door of Rebecca's house. The latch was loose, and they entered, and they found a lamp ready for them on the stairs. "Had you not better come to my bed for tonight?" said Rebecca.

"Only that I should be in your way, I should be so glad."

"You shall not be in my way. Come, then. But first you must eat and drink." Though Nina declared that she could not eat a morsel, and wanted no drink but water, Rebecca tended upon her, bringing the food and wine that were in truth so much needed. "And now, dear, I will help you to bed. You are yet cold, and there you will be warm."

"But when shall I see him?"

"Nay, how can I tell? But, Nina, I will not keep him from you. He shall come to you here when he chooses--if you choose it also."

"I do choose it--I do choose it," said Nina, sobbing in her weakness-- conscious of her weakness.

While Rebecca was yet assisting Nina--the Jewess kneeling as the Christian sat on the bedside--there came a low rap at the door, and Rebecca was summoned away. "I shall be but a moment," she said, and she ran down to the front door.

"Is she here?" said Anton, hoarsely.

"Yes, she is here."

"The Lord be thanked! And can I not see her?"

"You cannot see her now, Anton. She is very weary, and all but in bed."

"Tomorrow I may come?"

"Yes, tomorrow."

"And, tell me, how did you find her? Where did you find her?"

"Tomorrow Anton, you shall be told--whatever there is to tell For tonight, is it not enough for you to know that she is with me? She will share my bed, and I will be as a sister to her."

Then Anton spoke a word of warm blessing to his friend, and went his way home.

Chapter 16

Early in the following year, while the ground was yet bound with frost, and the great plains of Bohemia were still covered with snow, a Jew and his wife took their leave of Prague, and started for one of the great cities of the west. They carried with them but little of the outward signs of wealth, and but few of those appurtenances of comfort which generally fall to the lot of brides among the rich; the man, however, was well to do in the world, and was one who was not likely to bring his wife to want. It need hardly be said that Anton Trendellsohn was the man, and that Nina Balatka was his wife.

On the eve of their departure, Nina and her friend the Jewess had said farewell to each other. "You will write to me from Frankfort?" said Rebecca.

"Indeed I will," said Nina; "and you, you will write to me often, very often?"

As often as you will wish it."

"I shall wish it always," said Nina; and you can write; you are clever. You know how to make your words say what there is in your heart."

"But you have been able to make your face more eloquent than any words."

"Rebecca, dear Rebecca! Why was it that he did not love such a one as you rather than me? You are more beautiful."

"But he at least has not thought so."

"And you are so clever and so good; and you could have given him help which I never can give him."

"He does not want help. He wants to have by his side a sweet soft nature that can refresh him by its contrast to his own. He has done right to love you, and to make you his wife; only, I could wish that you were as we are in religion." To this Nina made no answer. She could not promise that she would change her religion, but she thought that she would endeavor to do so. She would do so if the saints would let her. "I am glad you are going away, Nina," continued Rebecca. "It will be better for him and better for you."

"Yes, it will be better."

"And it will be better for me also." Then Nina threw herself on Rebecca's neck and wept. She could say nothing in words in answer to that last assertion. If Rebecca really loved the man who was now the husband of another, of course it would be better that they should be apart. But Nina, who knew herself to be weak, could not understand that Rebecca, who was so strong, should have loved as she had loved.

"If you have daughters," said Rebecca, "and if he will let you name one of them after me, I shall be glad." Nina swore that if God gave her such a treasure as a daughter, that child should be named after the friend who had been so good to her.

There were also a few words of parting between Anton Trendellsohn and the girl who had been brought up to believe that she was to be his wife; but though there was friendship in them, there was not much of tenderness. "I hope you will prosper where you are going," said Rebecca, as she gave the man her hand.

"I do not fear but that I shall prosper, Rebecca."

"No; you will become rich, and perhaps great--as great, that is, as we Jews can make ourselves."

"I hope you will live to hear that the Jews are not crushed elsewhere as they are here in Prague."

"But, Anton, you will not cease to love the old city where your fathers and friends have lived so long?"

"I will never cease to love those, at least, whom I leave behind me. Farewell, Rebecca;" and he attempted to draw her to him as though he would kiss her. But she withdrew from him, very quietly, with no mark of anger, with no ostentation of refusal. "Farewell," she said. "Perhaps we shall see each other after many years."

Trendellsohn, as he sat beside his young wife in the post-carriage which took them out of the city, was silent till he had come nearly to the outskirts of the town; and then he spoke. "Nina," he said, "I am leaving behind me, and for ever, much that I love well."

"And it is for my sake," she said. "I feel it daily, hourly. It makes me almost wish that you had not loved me."

"But I take with me that which I love infinitely better than all that Prague contains. I will not, therefore, allow myself a regret. Though I should never see the old city again, I will always look upon my going as a good thing done." Nina could only answer him by caressing his hand, and by making internal oaths that her very best should be done in every moment of her life to make him contented with the lot he had chosen.

There remains very little of the tale to be told--nothing, indeed, of Nina's tale--and very little to be explained. Nina slept in peace at Rebecca's house that night on which she had been rescued from death upon the bridge--or, more probably, lay awake anxiously thinking what might yet be her fate. She had been very near to death--so near that she shuddered, even beneath the warmth of the bed-clothes, and with the protection of her friend so close to her, as she thought of those long dreadful minutes she had passed crouching over the river at the feet of the statue. She had been very near to death, and for a while could hardly realize the fact of her safety. She knew that she was glad to have been saved; but what might come next was, at that moment, all vague, uncertain, and utterly beyond her own control She hardly ventured to hope more than that Anton Trendellsohn would not give her up to Madame Zamenoy. If he did, she must seek the river again, or some other mode of escape from that worst of fates. But Rebecca had assured her of Anton's love, and in Rebecca's words she had a certain, though a dreamy, faith. The night was long, but she wished it to be longer. To be there and to feel that she was warm and safe was almost happiness for her after the misery she had endured.

On the next day, and for a day or two afterwards, she was feverish and she did not rise, but Rebecca's mother came to her, and Ruth--and at last Anton himself. She never could quite remember how those few days were passed, or what was said, or how it came to be arranged that she was to stay for a while in Rebecca's house; that she was to stay there for a long while--till such time as she should become a wife, and leave it for a house of her own. She never afterwards had any clear conception, though she very often thought of it all, how it came to be a settled thing among the Jews around her, that she was to be Anton's wife, and that Anton was to take her away from Prague. But she knew that her lover's father had come to her, and that he had been kind, and that there had been no reproach cast upon her for the wickedness she had attempted. Nor was it till she found herself going to mass all alone on the third

Sunday that she remembered that she was still a Christian, and that her lover was still a Jew. "It will not seem so strange to you when you are away in another place," Rebecca said to her afterwards. "It will be good for both of you that you should be away from Prague."

Nor did Nina hear much of the attempts which the Zamenoys made to rescue her from the hands of the Jews. Anton once asked her very gravely whether she was quite certain that she did not wish to see her aunt. "Indeed, I am," said Nina, becoming pale at the idea of the suggested meeting. "Why should I see her? She has always been cruel to me." Then Anton explained to her that Madame Zamenoy had made a formal demand to see her niece, and had even lodged with the police a statement that Nina was being kept in durance in the Jews' quarter; but the accusation was too manifestly false to receive attention even when made against a Jew, and Nina had reached an age which allowed her to choose her own friends without interposition from the law. "Only," said Anton, "it is necessary that you should know your own mind."

"I do know it," said Nina, eagerly.

And she saw Madame Zamenoy no more, nor her uncle Karil, nor her cousin Ziska. Though she lived in the same city with them for three months after the night on which she had been taken to Rebecca's house, she never again was brought into contact with her relations. Lotta she once saw, when walking in the street with Ruth; and Lotta too saw her, and endeavored to address her; but Nina fled, to the great delight of Ruth, who ran with her; and Lotta Luxa was left behind at the street corner.

I do not know that Nina ever had a more clearly-defined idea of the trick that Lotta had played upon her, than was conveyed to her by the sight of the deed as it was taken from her desk, and the knowledge that Souchey had put her lover upon the track. She soon learned that she was acquitted altogether by Anton, and she did not care for learning more. Of course there had been a trick. Of course there had been deceit. Of course her aunt and Lotta Luxa and Ziska, who was the worst of them all, had had their hands in it! But what did it signify? They had failed, and she had been successful. Why need she inquire farther?

But Souchey, who repented himself thoroughly of his treachery, spoke his mind freely to Lotta Luxa. "No," said he, "not if you had ten times as many florins, and were twice as clever, for you nearly drove me to be the murderer of my mistress."